"I'm sorry, Cara, I can't do it."

Her gaze shot to his. Wide-eyed. Filled with fear.

"I'm not going to hold you hostage," Simon quickly assured her. "You're free to go. But if you do leave, I have to call the authorities. To alert them to the fact that I am aware of a domestic-violence situation. As a doctor, I'm under legal obligation to do so."

Not technically. He wasn't licensed to practice medicine in Nevada—his helping her was legal only under the Good Samaritan law. And because initially it had been an emergency situation and she'd refused outside medical care.

Her gaze hadn't wavered. The panic was there, almost blindingly so, reminding him of a deer in headlights.

"I mean you no harm," he told her. "To the contrary. Nor am I particularly welcoming of the company. I'm here alone by choice. My reasons for that choice have not changed."

She blinked.

"But I can't let you just walk out of here."

Dear Reader,

Welcome to a very, very special story in my Where Secrets are Safe series. If you've never been to The Lemonade Stand—please, come in. Visitors to the Stand are transitory, so you'll fit right in with the rest of the current batch of residents, who are also new here. If you've been here before, buckle your seat belts, because you're in for a double treat.

This story is very different from anything I've done before. It's two full romances—taking place simultaneously in two states—that, unknown to the heroes and heroines, are intertwined. You, the reader, will see the way these people, from opposite sides of a very sad story, give their hearts and souls to try to find sense in a world that makes no sense.

Sometimes it's hard to know what to believe. Sometimes our thoughts are born through our own perspectives that might not always be completely accurate. Sometimes we act on those thoughts with the best of intentions, and end up places we never meant to be.

Sometimes all we can do is listen to our hearts—like we did as children. Sometimes it takes a child to show us the way...

I love to hear from my readers. Please find me at www.tarataylorquinn.com, Facebook.com/tarataylorquinn and on Twitter, @tarataylorquinn. Or join my open Friendship board on Pinterest, Pinterest.com/tarataylorquinn/friendship!

All the best,

Tara

TARA TAYLOR QUINN

A Family for Christmas

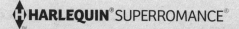

HARLEQUIN®SUPERROMANCE®

Recycling programs
for this product may
not exist in your area.

For my daughter, Rachel (Marie) Stoddard,
and her daughter, Morgan Marie.
I love you both more than life.

ISBN-13: 978-0-373-64050-8

A Family for Christmas

Copyright © 2017 by Tara Taylor Quinn

For questions and comments about the quality of this book,
please contact us at CustomerService@Harlequin.com.

Printed in U.S.A.

Having written over eighty novels, **Tara Taylor Quinn** is a *USA TODAY* bestselling author with more than seven million copies sold. She is known for delivering intense, emotional fiction. Tara is a past president of Romance Writers of America. She has won a Readers' Choice Award and is a five-time finalist for an RWA RITA® Award, a finalist for a Reviewers' Choice Award and a Booksellers' Best Award. She has also appeared on TV across the country, including *CBS Sunday Morning*. She supports the National Domestic Violence Hotline. If you or someone you know might be a victim of domestic violence in the United States, please contact 1-800-799-7233.

Books by Tara Taylor Quinn

HARLEQUIN SUPERROMANCE

Where Secrets are Safe

Wife by Design
Once a Family
Husband by Choice
Child by Chance
Mother by Fate
The Good Father
Love by Association
His First Choice
The Promise He Made Her
Her Secret Life
The Fireman's Son
For Joy's Sake

Shelter Valley Stories

Sophie's Secret
Full Contact

HARLEQUIN HEARTWARMING

Family Secrets

For Love or Money
Her Soldier's Baby
The Cowboy's Twins

MIRA BOOKS

The Friendship Pact
In Plain Sight

Visit the Author Profile page at Harlequin.com for more titles.

Cast of Characters

Wife by Design (Book 1)

Lynn Duncan—Resident nurse at TLS. She has a three-year-old daughter, Kara.

Grant Bishop—Landscape developer hired by TLS.

Maddie Estes—Permanent TLS resident. Childcare provider.

Darin Bishop—Resident at TLS. Works for his brother, Grant. Has a mental disability.

Once a Family (Book 2)

Sedona (Campbell) Malone—Lawyer who volunteers at TLS.

Tanner Malone—Vintner. Brother to **Tatum** and **Talia Malone**.

Tatum Malone—Fifteen-year-old resident at TLS.

Husband by Choice (Book 3)

Meredith (Meri) Bennet—Speech therapist. Mother to two-year-old son, Caleb.

Max Bennet—Pediatrician.

Chantel Harris—Police officer. Friend to Max and his deceased first wife.

Child by Chance (Book 4)

Talia Malone—TLS volunteer. Public-school scrapbook therapist. Student of fashion design.

Sherman Paulson—Political campaign manager. Widower. Single father of adopted ten-year-old son, Kent.

Mother by Fate (Book 5)

Sara Havens—Full-time TLS counselor.

Michael Edwin—Bounty hunter. Widower. Single father to six-year-old daughter, Mari.

The Good Father (Book 6)

Ella Ackerman—Charge nurse at Santa Raquel Children's Hospital. Member of the high-risk team. Divorced.

Brett Ackerman—TLS Founder. National accreditation business owner. Divorced.

Love by Association (Book 7)

Chantel Harris—Santa Raquel detective. Member of the high-risk team.

Colin Fairbanks—Lawyer. Member of Santa Raquel's most elite society. Principal of high-end law firm. Brother to **Julie Fairbanks**.

His First Choice (Book 8)

Lacey Hamilton—Social worker. Member of the high-risk team. Child star. Identical twin to daytime-soap-opera star **Kacey Hamilton**.

Jeremiah (Jem) Bridges—Private contractor with his own business. Divorced. Has custody of four-year-old son, Levi.

The Promise He Made Her (Book 9)

Bloom Larson—Psychiatrist in Santa Raquel. Domestic violence therapist. Divorced.

Samuel Larson—Santa Raquel high-ranking detective. Widower.

Her Secret Life (Book 10)

Kacey Hamilton—Daytime-soap-opera star. Identical twin to **Lacey Hamilton**. Volunteer at TLS.

Michael Valentine—Cybersecurity expert. TLS volunteer. Shooting victim.

The Fireman's Son (Book 11)

Faye Walker—Paramedic. Divorced. Sole custody of eight-year-old son, Elliott, who is in counseling at TLS.

Reese Bristow—Santa Raquel fire chief.

For Joy's Sake (Book 12)

Julie Fairbanks—Philanthropist and children's author. Sister to **Colin Fairbanks**.

Hunter Rafferty—Owns Elite Professional event-planning business, specializing in charity fund-raisers. TLS is one of his clients.

A Family for Christmas (Book 13)

Lila McDaniels—Managing director of The Lemonade Stand (TLS). She has an apartment at the Stand.

Edward Mantle—Primary-care physician. Grandfather to seven-year-old **Joy Amos**. Father to **Cara Amos**.

Cara Amos—On the run from abusive ex. **Joy**'s mother.

Simon Walsh—Pediatric thoracic surgeon. Partially blind.

CHAPTER ONE

Prospector, Nevada

"DAMN." TAKING HIS stinging toe with him, Dr. Simon Walsh carefully and deliberately lifted his right foot and took another step forward. Landed it successfully. Then picked up the left. Success. And the right. Stepping slowly. Adding roots camouflaged by dirt and other ground cover to his list of possible dangers.

After four days of traipsing around several times a day in the forest that served as the borders for his self-imposed captivity, he'd amassed a list that could have been overwhelming if he cared to believe that it would be a permanent part of his life.

He wasn't giving it that much credence.

His left eye stared belligerently at the black patch he'd placed upon it, while his right strained to make out a shape in the cloud cover that had become its vision.

Cloud was better than nothing, which was what he'd had when he'd made it to the emergency room four weeks prior. He had six months to a year before he'd know what good his injured right optic nerve would be, if any. More than four hours of pressure due to swelling would usually be the kiss of death. His had sustained at least five hours. But death meant no sight at all. He had clouds.

And...*whack*! Taking an involuntary step back, Simon lifted a hand to his forehead to inspect for any damage. He was either sweating or bleeding. Didn't feel much of a gash. Not enough to require stitches, at any rate.

His outstretched hands—one holding a stick like a blind man's cane—had missed a branch hanging above shoulder level. And his damned eye...nothing but clouds.

His pits were wet. Long sleeves and jeans in seventy-degree weather tended to do that to a guy exerting himself. It had been forty when he'd gotten up that morning. And in the woods he wasn't ready to trust bare limbs to his right eye.

"Whoever thought this was a good idea?" He asked the question aloud. Talking to himself. When you were a hermit, living alone in a godforsaken wasteland, you tended to do that, he'd learned.

And didn't bother to answer himself. Something else he'd learned...your conversational skills changed when there was only one of you.

It had been his idea to cover his one good eye four times a day to force the weaker one to work.

Everyone knew that muscles had to be exercised to stay strong.

Not that an optic nerve was a muscle, of course. But he couldn't let his brain go soft. He had to keep things working so that if the nerve managed to kick into gear, the rest of him would be ready and able to support it.

His forehead stung.

Lifting the patch off his good eye long enough to get a peek at his fingers, he saw blood. But he'd seen more than that on patients four days postsurgery. He snapped the piece of black cloth back into place.

He wasn't stopping now.

Feeling like a damned freak, he continued staring at white fog, stepping gingerly and making his way. It wasn't like he had anything else to do with his day.

Or his life.

A one-eyed surgeon wasn't going to…cut it.

So much for an attempt at humor. He kicked at the ground. Just to show that he could. That he wasn't afraid to express himself. He threw away his stick. Took two steps. And lifted the patch long enough to find and retrieve the walking aid.

"If they could see me now."

Once one of LA's top children's thoracic surgeons, now unshaven, wearing jeans he'd stained with jelly that morning when he'd made his right eye get him through breakfast, wandering around in a wooded valley in the northern Nevada mountains.

Until a month ago, his idea of camping out had been a room at a moderately priced chain hotel—as opposed to his more likely choice of a suite in an upscale resort. That had been before he'd needed to prove self-sufficiency.

As his spirits continued to sink, he pushed forward. Reminded himself that he was a lucky bastard. That he sure as hell had no right to feel sorry for himself.

He had a good eye. He could see. Watch TV. Read. Hell, he could even drive.

He was alive.

He just couldn't be a surgeon.

And he couldn't ever laugh with little Opus again. Thoughts of his adopted daughter brought him shame at his own selfishness. If ever there'd been a child who'd taken it on the chin and come up with a grin, it had been that feisty little six-year-old.

What did it mean when a guy started thinking in rhymed clichés?

In his case, it meant he wasn't ready to think about Opus, not even after a year.

Jabbing his stick hard into the ground, Simon stood in place. Staring. Willing his eye to see something. Anything. To make out enough of a shape in the shadows to discern what it was. Just as he'd been doing pretty much every waking moment of the month he'd been holed up in his newly purchased cabin.

He'd found the place on the internet. It came furnished, with its own well and electricity provided by solar panels, wind and a generator for backup. Completely off the grid. There was only one way in—a mile-long private road. His nearest neighbor was five miles or more away. The seller was a lawyer handling an estate bequeathed to charity. No one to care. He'd paid cash on the spot. Left his cell phone at home.

He had too many well-meaning friends and peers who thought they knew better for him than he knew for himself. He had a burner phone, though. He wasn't foolish. Careless. Or irresponsible.

He wanted to be left completely alone.

At least until he knew his options. Maybe longer. Maybe he wasn't ever going back…

Simon's stick hit something on the ground in front of him. Something solid…and yet not hard like a rock. Playing a game with himself, he stared in the general direction of the object, tapping around it to fill in the blanks. It was long. More than five feet. When he pushed it, it had some give, but didn't really move. A fallen tree perhaps? What kind of tree?

He continued to follow the mass. Didn't find obvious branches. Apparently a grown man, a surgeon, no less, could be entertained by a fallen tree.

"Now, isn't that one for the books?"

What books he wasn't sure. He was tempted to take off his patch—to take the easy way out and see what was blocking his path. Or just step over it. But he wasn't letting his right eye off that easy. If he'd given up on his young patients as easily as he seemed to want to give up these days, there would be far fewer homes filled with laughter in the Los Angeles valley.

Give him a chest cavity and he could delineate every nerve, vein and muscle. But trees? In Nevada? He knew next to nothing about them. So he thought about fruit. Oranges grew in Nevada. But they'd still be at the little green ball stage this early in the fall. And there were no orange trees in his new yard. Not like a tree with oranges actually growing on it would be fallen over on the ground. More likely it was some kind of cactus.

How far was he from the cabin?

He'd been out about an hour. Didn't think he'd turned enough to be headed back. But at his pace, even walking straight, he wouldn't have gone that far.

He came to one end of whatever was blocking the path.

"Ha!" he exclaimed, as though solving some great conundrum. In his current world, this was one. A fact that might bother him later, when darkness set in and he looked back over his day. At the moment, he was occupied.

Challenging his brain.

He took a small step forward. His walking tool gave suddenly. Stumbling, Simon let go of the stick. The log had to be rotted, which meant any number of things could be living in it. Stepping back, he straightened, instinctively yanking off the eye patch. The first thing he saw was his cabin fifty yards away.

"Damn." He was right back where he'd started. And then he looked down.

"Holy shit." He hadn't been identifying a log.

He'd prodded a body. A body! Feminine. A hooded, long-sleeved sweater covered the top half of her.

He noticed the jeans, the sweater. The feminine curve of hips. But only briefly. Cursorily. His trained good eye had already seen the moving rib cage, indicating life, as he dropped down to the woman lying on her stomach. Her dark hair was long, tangled. Dirty.

And she hadn't said a word.

Of their own accord, his fingers reached for her pulse, registering a steady, strong beat. Yet she made no sound. No reaction to being touched.

She was sweating, though. In a thick sweater, exposed to the sun, so sweat by itself wasn't alarming.

"What the hell…"

He needed to see her face, some age identifier, to look at her eyes, her pupils, her lips, but he didn't dare move her. Not until he knew that her neck was okay...

Already feeling for breaks, he gave an inward shudder as he pictured his idiot self, prodding this poor person with his walking stick.

What had he been thinking?

Finding no obvious breaks, he leaned down, putting an arm around her shoulders. "I'm going to roll you over now," he said. "I'm a doctor and I'm here to help you."

She appeared comatose, but many could hear while in that state.

Lying beside her, he used himself to support her entire body, and turned with her. Then, sliding aside, he sat up. She had major maxillofacial trauma. Severe facial edema. Her face was badly bruised, so swollen he couldn't make out her normal features, with open lacerations on the right cheek and chin. Medical terms came to him, but as a doctor of children who had to remember he was speaking to children even in tense or emergency situations, he'd begun translating in his thoughts as well as his words. Her lips were oddly healthy looking, considering the rest of her face, with no cuts or signs of bleeding. He lifted her lids enough to note pupil activity. Gums had good color. No immediate sign of oxygen deprivation.

Breathing was shallow. Skin warm, but not hot.

Lifting up her sweater, he made a cursory check of her torso, finding nothing unusual.

He couldn't be sure about internal injuries. What he was sure about was getting her inside. Assessing more thoroughly. Doing what he could in the moment.

And then, as loath as he was to expose himself to anyone, anywhere—he was going to have to call for an ambulance to come get her.

Either that or pray that she regained consciousness and could tell him who to call on her behalf.

CHAPTER TWO

HIS ARMS WERE GENTLE. Lying inert, as much by instinct and habit as anything else, Cara remained limp as she awoke to feel him lifting her. He settled her against his body.

Her head shrieked with pain. *Please God, let him be in a good mood.*

Shawn was kind to her, caring, when he wasn't tense.

He'd changed his shirt. The day before he'd had on the denim one over his T-shirt, but this one was softer. Must be the blue flannel she'd bought him for his birthday...

The fact that he was carrying her so carefully boded well. Her head fell sideways, settling against his chest and she almost drifted out again.

But the smell. It was unfamiliar.

Shawn didn't wear aftershave. Or cologne. But they'd been on the run. Maybe he'd stolen a bar of soap from someplace?

He smelled like more than just different toiletries. Nothing that she recognized. Why such a small detail was keeping her conscious, she didn't know. She kept trying to place the scent.

She liked it.

A lot.

It reminded her of something. She had no idea what. But it felt…safe.

He felt safe.

So maybe he was in a good mood. Maybe she'd be okay for a while. At least long enough to sleep off the headache so she could figure out what she was going to do…

"OKAY, MY DEAR, let's get you more comfortable so I can get a look at you." Simon spoke aloud more out of habit than because he expected a response.

The reaction of the woman in his arms was an instantaneous stiffening. She didn't fight him as he carried her through the cabin's main room to the one bedroom. Didn't say a word. She could still be unconscious, but she was coming back to him.

So he kept talking.

"I'm just going to lay you down on the bed," he said, leaning over to keep her against him until the bed took her weight. Slowly, watching as her face came into view, searching for signs of consciousness, he stood up. Cursing the right eye that hindered the normal speed of his initial assessment.

She was older than his usual patients, to be sure, but not old. "You look to be about thirty," he told her. Maybe late twenties. It was hard to tell with the state of her face. In the light from the ceiling fixture he saw something else.

Two things registered at once.

Her eyes had moved beneath her closed lids. Which meant she was conscious.

And the bruises on her face weren't all recent.

"You've been hurt before," he said softly, his mind racing with possibilities. The obvious first one...a spouse hitting her? If they lived off the grid, as he was doing, it could have been happening for years without anyone being the wiser.

It could also mean that the son of a bitch could turn up at his cabin at any time. Looking for his "goods."

"Recently, too," he added, looking for other explanations for the varying degrees of discoloration on her. He could come up with nothing but deliberate torture of some kind. Some of the bruises and lacerations were more than a week old. Maybe even two or three. Some only a day or so.

He'd need to get them cleaned up...

He caught another eyelid movement. Not a twitch. More like an attempt to remain still. And he thought of how this might seem to her. A man carrying her, telling her he was laying her on the bed...

"My name's Dr. Simon Walsh," he said, wishing he'd paid more attention when peers at work had mentioned abused patients. They rarely ended up with heart injuries so hadn't been in his area of expertise. And with *his* peers, the patients had been children. "I'm a thoracic surgeon. On...vacation," he added when he realized the absurdity of his current life within the explanation he felt obliged to give. "I just bought this cabin, came up here a month ago."

He added the latter in case, as he suspected, she was from the area. Probably living somewhere in the mountainous regions of northern Nevada.

A lot of the residents he'd seen in the nearest burg, Prospector—less than a town, but more than nothing—had been Native American. He was living on the border of their reservation.

His current patient was clearly Caucasian.

"I need to see how badly you're hurt," he said next. He wanted to remove her outerwear. To make certain that her limbs weren't misshapen—indicating breaks—or swollen—indicating any number of other things. He needed to see if there were worse lacerations. He needed to call someone.

But first, he grabbed the bag he never traveled without. Pulled out a blood pressure cuff and, pushing up the sleeve of her sweater, wrapped it around her arm and pumped. If her vitals told him this was an emergency, he wouldn't have time to wait for help.

Simon was concentrating so completely on the simple blood-pressure reading—his first medical action since he was attacked and something he hadn't done himself in years—that he was startled to glance at her face and see her watching him.

She was cognizant. Her gaze was clear. Assessing. She glanced at the cuff, as if asking, *Who travels to a cabin on vacation with a blood-pressure cuff?*

"My bag's on the floor," he told her. And then said again, "I'm a doctor. Dr. Simon Walsh," in case she hadn't been fully aware during his earlier introduction.

"A thoracic surgeon, you said." Her voice was soft, a bit rough, her mouth barely moving. Almost as though her throat was sore—and her jaw broken. He looked at the sweater zipped up around her neck, wondering if he'd find marks on her throat, too.

Had someone tried to kill her?

Repeatedly? Based on the bruises.

Or was she into something he probably didn't want to know about?

What if *she* was the bad guy?

He took off the cuff and pulled a stethoscope out of his bag.

"What's your name?"

"Cara."

Pretty sure that a *Cara what?* would garner him nothing, he nodded. "How old are you?"

"Twenty-eight."

Eight years younger than he was.

"I'd like to listen to your heart, if that's okay with you?"

She nodded slightly, timidly. Not like someone who was contemplating some nefarious deed or getaway.

Not that he'd really know. He spent his life with children. Sick children.

Children he'd been forced to leave behind because he could no longer help them…

Leaving her zipper up, he slid the stethoscope chestpiece under the T-shirt he found under her sweater. Her heartbeat was a little fast—nothing to be concerned about, considering the circumstances. Steady. Clear. Even when she took deep breaths as he instructed.

"Can I feel your abdomen? Check for internal injuries?"

She gave the barely discernable nod a second time. But added slowly, "He doesn't ever hit me there."

Simon's fingers didn't miss a beat. His heart did. His first guess had been accurate. She'd been beaten.

By a man.

Her husband?

An accomplice?

Someone trying to rob her?

A kidnapper?

"What about your extremities? Where do you hurt?"

She shook her head. Started to sit up. "I need to

go," she said. "My arms and legs are fine. Some bruises, maybe. I fell. But I can walk."

With gentle hands used to coddling children, Simon urged her back down. Felt around both sides of her jaw bone. There were no obvious fractures.

"I can't just let you walk away from here," he told her. "The Hippocratic Oath and all." He could recite the entire thing.

"It's no longer binding," she told him. Talking brought obvious discomfort, based on her small movements and the expression on her face, but didn't seem to hinder her significantly.

Because she was used to the pain?

He studied her. "You were unconscious when I found you. You should have a CAT scan. And an MRI."

She closed her eyes. Waited a couple of seconds and opened them again.

"I'm an able adult. If you called an ambulance, I would simply leave before it got here." She started to sit up again. "I actually think I've outstayed my welcome as it is. I'll just go ahead and…"

She winced as she rose up, and Simon lowered her back to the bed once again, pulling a second pillow behind her head.

"You've obviously suffered severe trauma to your head. You could have a brain bleed." Her speech told him she was educated—and perhaps not suffering from serious brain damage.

"My vision's not blurred. I'm not slurring my words."

Her Hippocratic Oath comment came back to him. She was right, of course, about how it was no longer binding. Not everyone knew that. "You a doctor?" he asked. Could explain why she was living on or near an Indian reservation.

"No."

"You work in the medical field?"

"No."

The woman had no problem withholding information.

Her pupils weren't enlarged. They were identical in size. And when he shone his light in her eyes, they both responded normally.

"How bad is your headache?" He wasn't giving her a chance to tell him she didn't have one.

"On a scale of one to ten, I'd give it a six."

Medical professionals commonly asked patients to rate their pain on the one to ten scale. But a scale of one to ten was used so much it was almost cliché, too.

"Who hit you?"

"I'd rather not say."

He wanted to push. Didn't want her to leave. Legally, he couldn't make her stay. He could only call for emergency service and hope that she didn't get far enough that they couldn't find her. But she could refuse to go with them even if he did that.

And what if she did manage to escape? And then died out in the wilderness?

"You need to get checked out at a hospital."

"You think the doctors there are better than you?"

They could see with both eyes. He didn't speak aloud. For what he was doing there with her…one eye was plenty.

"They have the equipment to do the proper tests," he told her. He had to advise her. It was his job. His life's work.

"I'm not going to any hospital."

She also didn't try to sit up again.

"So…I'll make a deal with you," he told her, talking on the fly. "You agree to let me get you cleaned up, get a good look at you, do what I can here…you agree to let me take your vitals regularly and to watch you for any sign of more serious injury…and I won't make any calls. For now."

"Okay," she said. Closing her eyes again and opening them. "For now."

She was watching him but looked like the effort to do so was costing her.

He couldn't help but wonder what she was really thinking. But he was pretty sure it had to do with leaving as soon as she could.

"You can trust me," he told her. And then,

reaching down into his bag, he pulled out his ID, showing it to her.

She read. "Los Angeles Children's?"

He nodded and was left with the impression that she knew of the place. Los Angeles was a good ten-hour drive from Prospector, with only enough stops to pee and gas up. Did she know someone from there? Or someone who'd been treated there?

"Do you have any other questions?" He couldn't guarantee he'd answer them, but if he could prove that he wouldn't hurt her, he'd do his best.

"No."

He had questions. And wondered if she'd declined his invitation to ask him anything so that he wouldn't feel free to do the same.

"Who hit you?"

She turned her head.

"You said he doesn't ever hit you in the abdomen."

"Nor on the mouth."

"Your bruises show signs of previous abuse."

"He gets tense and…"

"Who is he?" Simon was pretty sure he knew. But he had to make sure. Had to know what he was letting himself in for.

What he might have to protect them both against.

He had a hunting rifle with him. A basic .22 in case of unwanted varmints.

"My husband."

His heart dropped. Confirmation…and yet… wow. She was so young. With such soulful, intelligent eyes.

And a face swollen almost out of recognition.

"Is he coming after you?" He had to know.

"I don't think so." For the first time, she looked away when she answered him.

"I need to know the truth."

Glancing back at him, she said, "That is the truth. I think he thinks I'm as good as dead, if not gone already. I slurred my words. Started walking crooked. Talking crazy. Told him he had two faces."

Symptoms of a brain bleed. "You need to get to a hospital."

"I lied and faked it all. I just wanted him to quit hitting me."

He had a feeling it hadn't been nearly as easy to fool the bastard as she made it sound.

"Won't he get suspicious when he finds you gone?"

"He drove me up here, hauled me out into the woods and left me there. That was sometime yesterday. I think."

Holy hell! What kind of a beast did that to his own wife?

Studying her face, seeing small lines in her stretched skin, indicating previously healed lacerations, he knew he'd already answered his own silent question. Only a beast would do something like that.

He'd left her to die. And…

Their gazes met. For the first time, he saw stark fear in hers. It was almost as though he'd heard her words before she said them aloud. "He can't know I'm still alive. If you alert anyone, he might find out…"

Simon wasn't in the market for company. At all. Of any kind.

But he wasn't turning her away.

He might be half-blind. A failure. He was not cruel.

"If you stay here, I won't alert anyone. If you go, I will."

"How long do plan to keep me prisoner?" The unflappable voice was back.

Maybe he should have seen the question coming. Figured a woman who was used to beatings might think that way. He was used to trying to put himself in young minds when it came to his patients.

"As a doctor, I can't just let you walk out of here in this condition. You die and it's on me. Believe me, I'm not up for any more of that kind of guilt right now. I want you to stay here for as long as it takes to get you healthy. I need to start you on antibiotics, too," he told her, hurrying there at the end.

He'd said too much. *I'm not up for any more of that kind of guilt right now.*

Clearly, he was out of practice when it came to acting like a rational member of society, or even holding a normal conversation.

Hence his extended trip to the woods. And… maybe…a little bit because of it.

She was studying him. He waited for some takedown regarding his guilt comment. But when she finally spoke, all she said was, "Fair enough, Dr. Walsh. I don't leave, you don't call. Just until I'm recovered enough to disappear on my own."

Simon nodded, not sure if he'd come out from the conversation—the day—unscathed. He'd load his gun—just in case her story didn't hold up. Or whoever had beaten her came looking.

He'd tend to his patient, and then he'd send her on her way. Without alerting anyone to her presence.

From there, she was on her own.

And so would he be.

Just as he'd planned.

CHAPTER THREE

CARA SWALLOWED THE water held to her lips. Whenever the doctor was in the room, she mustered up the wherewithal to speak as though nothing was wrong. Years of practice protecting Shawn—but mostly she had been protecting...

No, she couldn't go there—had honed her ability to continue on through the pain. As though it didn't exist.

Sometimes she wondered if pain was just a figment of the imagination. Thought a lot about the power of mind over matter.

She could deal with living in a body that hurt with every move she made.

It was the emotional stuff that she wasn't so sure about. Wasn't even sure she wanted to try anymore.

What was the point?

Except that...she wasn't dead. Shawn had left her for dead. As she'd traipsed through the Nevada wilderness, hungry, hurting, nearly freezing to death at night until she'd found a ditch to huddle in, finding not even a path on which to walk, she'd accepted that she was going to die.

Had come to peace with doing so.

So why wasn't she dead? Why was she lying on a nice mattress under a soft comforter, wearing a makeshift hospital gown?

The doctor had cut the sleeves off a man's shirt and instructed her to put it on backward, buttoned only halfway up. He'd said nothing about her undies, and though she'd have liked a change, she'd left them on.

She'd shuddered a time or two as he ran his practiced hands over her body, feeling for breaks, discussing his findings. Her ankle was a little swollen—her doing. As was the bruise on her knee and the bit of swelling on her right wrist. The cuts on her arms and face—all of which he'd carefully cleaned, covered with some kind of ointment and then bandaged where applicable—were compliments of Shawn. The arm abrasions had come when she'd held them up to protect her face.

He'd tended to the bruises and cuts on her legs, too. Left there by the steel-toed tips of the boots her husband wore when he wasn't surfing. Since moving to the West Coast he'd begun to fancy himself as some kind of cowboy surfer dude.

In the beginning, she'd thought he looked damned cute in his tight jeans and Western shirts unbuttoned to the navel. But somewhere along the way, everything about Shawn had ceased being a turn-on.

According to him he was the one who'd brought

joy back to her life, which had been something she hadn't felt since before her mother got sick and life had become a series of doctors. With her father's contacts, there'd been a never-ending stream of them. Over and over he'd put her mother through examinations and treatments. All he'd really done was deliver them boatloads of dashed hopes. And…

No, she knew better than to open a door that she'd spent years nailing shut.

Funny, here she was, ready to go herself, and she'd been rescued by a doctor, of all people.

What did that mean?

"Get some rest…" Dr. Walsh had finished tending to her and was pulling the sheet and comforter up to her chin. She'd practically choked getting down the antibiotic and painkiller he'd given her.

A huge believer in accountability and in Karma, Cara decided against thinking for the next few hours. Just long enough to sleep.

Sleep brought clarity, which she needed to figure out what her still being alive meant.

It had been so long since she'd really slept. Without senses on alert. Without fear.

She had nothing else to fear now.

And she really just wanted to sleep.

For as long as he'd let her.

HE WOKE HER in the late afternoon. Checked her vitals. Shone the light in her eyes again. Gave her more to drink. Cara complied with words of thanks. Hoping to slip back into the forgetfulness of sleep.

"You need to eat."

Her burning throat was barely handling the liquid, not that she wanted him to know that. "I'm not hungry."

"I wouldn't expect you to have an appetite," the doctor's kind voice came back at her. "But you've gone over twenty-four hours, at least, without sustenance, and I have no way of starting an IV here. So…you eat…or I make a call."

"You call, I die." Without forethought she played on the guilt he'd exposed earlier. Men sometimes gave you tells.

Still, her words were thick. She was groggy. She couldn't believe she still had fight in her. Probably just habit. It would dissipate.

Dr. Simon Walsh was trying to save her life.

She had no life to live. No intention of walking back into the world again. Ever.

Odd that, having made that determination, Karma had seen fit to deliver her up to a doctor. There was that fact staring her in the face again. Even after sleep. Did fate have a shadow side?

Or a twisted sense of humor?

Of course, she didn't really believe that this doctor, if he was one, which, based on his care, she was pretty sure he was, was really on vacation. He'd said he'd been there a month already. Doctors—especially surgeons—didn't take off that kind of time. And he obviously wasn't planning on leaving in the next little bit, since he'd had no problem with keeping her there with him for as "long as it took."

He couldn't handle a death on his conscience. Pretty obvious he already had one there.

Ha! What if Karma had delivered her up to a doctor who was also a murderer? That one fit better. More like Fate and Karma were working together.

Which was always how she'd thought life worked. Until she'd learned that it didn't. That no matter how good you were, how kind, how many good deeds you did or how hard you tried, love didn't win in the end.

"I've got canned soup—pretty much any kind you'd want. I'd suggest starting with chicken noodle."

She didn't want any soup. Nourishment would only prolong things. But she didn't want to be delivered back to Shawn, either. She'd much rather Walsh killed her. Inject her with something and be done with it.

Now, that would be good Karma. So maybe her good deeds wouldn't go unpunished…

Lord knew, a needle and drifting off to sleep

would be better than being locked up in a jail cell. Which was what she deserved.

If she could only wrap her mind around that truth.

"'Kay." She'd eat his soup.

So he could get on with things. Even if, for now, it was just to go away and let her get back to sleep.

It was dark outside when he woke her again. Ironically, this time Cara felt hungry. Probably because of the whole bowl of soup he'd spooned into her mouth before. She'd had to keep her eyes closed while she swallowed, lest he see the tears that the resulting pain brought to her eyes. She couldn't risk him figuring he'd have to call someone to do something about it.

It would go away in a few days. It always did. Her throat muscles just needed enough time to heal from Shawn's strangling grasp. He never went far enough to do actual damage. Only enough to instill fear. And pain.

Which was why, once she'd known there was no reason to stay with him any longer, she'd had the idea to fake alarming symptoms. He'd been so careful to make certain she never really needed medical attention. Which told her he was afraid of her needing medical attention. She knew him well. Had pegged it right.

Up until the part where she'd been found out in

the middle of nowhere by a surgeon on extended vacation with someone's soul on his conscience…

He put water to her lips. She drank, her throat muscles throbbing with pain at every swallow. Took another pain pill. The antibiotic, he'd said, was only twice a day.

"You need to use the restroom?"

She shook her head. Not badly enough to get up. Or have him carry her there then wait around while she did her business.

Though why she should care made no sense, either.

Still, she'd go when she could get there by herself. She'd once held it for thirty-six hours when Shawn had been on a particularly brutal bender and she'd had Joy safely hidden in the dog house that Shawn had later torn down. Joy, poor little thing, had had to wear torn pieces of Cara's clothes as diapers until her father had sobered up.

Then he'd bought them both new wardrobes. And reminded her, with tenderness, that as a respected business owner, he would be believed when he told people the fight had been her fault. If she said anything. Reminded her, too, the hell he'd rescued her from. How he'd supported her. How he still provided for her and Joy—everything either of them could ever want. He'd been wonderful for over a year after that time…

"Can I get you anything else?"

The doctor had taken her vitals. Shone the light

in her eyes again. Must have been satisfied. She supposed that was fine. If he knew she was on her deathbed, he'd make his damned call.

"No, thank you." Her parents had been sticklers for manners. She had to be polite. Even at the end.

Denying her hunger felt right.

It was dark out and the doctor was wearing sweats. Another flannel shirt. She wondered if it was the middle of the night. Wondered where he was sleeping.

Wondered if he'd set some kind of timer to check on her. Figured by the spike in his short hair and the stubble on his chin that he must have.

What a nice thing to have done.

Santa Raquel, California

THE PHONE WAS RINGING. Lila McDaniels, managing director of The Lemonade Stand, a unique women's shelter on the coast of California, sat straight up in bed. Being awoken in the middle of the night wasn't an oddity in her line of work. It also didn't often happen to her at home, in her condo. Her sacred space.

It was her cell phone. Only a few people had the number. Heart pounding, she grabbed it before she could get her glasses on to see who was calling.

"Hello." Her tone was all business. It was all she knew how to be.

"Lila? I need your help."

Edward. Her heart gave a little leap of a different kind—yet just as unsettling—when she recognized his voice. She'd known him over a month. Had spent a lot of time helping him with his granddaughter. It was not outlandish that she'd know his voice.

"What's wrong?" she asked, already out of bed and pulling on a pair of brown pants. With her career—tending to the needs of abused and at-risk women and children—she was always ready to go.

"Joy's crying and I can't get her stop. She keeps asking for her mother. Wants to know where Julie is. Asking me if Hunter's home. Obviously she wasn't ready to stay with me. I've tried rocking her. Talking to her. Gave her some warm milk. Turned on the TV. Nothing's working. Can I bring her back? Please?"

She'd worried that it might be too soon for Edward's new-to-him seven-year-old granddaughter to spend the night in his hotel suite—a night away from The Lemonade Stand where she'd been living since she'd seen her father beat up her aunt and then cart her mother away.

But he'd been granted temporary custody and would be given full custody in the event that his daughter's body was found. Sara, Joy's counselor, had felt that the sooner the little girl found security within her new family unit, the better. Especially since her father's arrest.

Shawn Amos had been the last one seen with

his wife. Beating her. Hauling her away from their house by her hair. The same day he'd beaten his sister to death. The man was in jail on charges of first-degree murder. His wife, Joy's mother, Cara, was missing—and the man claimed to have no idea where she was. Police were actively searching for her, but many assumed the worst. That they were seeking a dead body, not a live one.

Especially after days had passed since Shawn Amos's arrest and Cara hadn't turned up. If she were able, she'd certainly have sought help. By all accounts, she'd lived for Joy. Nothing would stop her from getting back to her daughter. If she was able.

"I can hear the tension in your voice," Lila said, having pulled the phone away only long enough to slide the beige turtleneck over her head and step into low-heeled brown shoes as she grabbed her jacket.

"I don't know what to do," Edward, a general practitioner from Florida, said. "I love this child more than I thought possible. I'm blowing it already…"

"If I can hear the tension in your voice, so can she," Lila said, keys in hand. "Ask her if she wants to come back to The Lemonade Stand. Talk to her like she's one of your young patients. I'll hold."

She could hear Edward call Joy's name. Hear his impersonal yet kind tone as he did as Lila requested.

Lila heard no response. But no crying, either.

"She nodded." Edward came back on the line.

"Don't bother changing her out of her pajamas," Lila said. "Wrap her in a blanket and carry her down to the lobby. Call for your car first. Talk to her. Doesn't matter what about. Your voice will be reassurance. Your body warmth gives her a sense of security. Make sure she's buckled up. Drive carefully and I'll see you there."

She didn't have to go in. She could call Lynn Bishop, the full-time nurse who lived on the premises. Lynn would get Sara in. Lila could handle the rest in the morning. Any other time, with any other resident under these circumstances—no lives at risk—she would have done so.

But she didn't. For the first time since she'd come to The Lemonade Stand she'd let something get personal.

Edward needed her.

And damn her for needing to be there for him.

CHAPTER FOUR

Prospector, Nevada

CARA SLEPT FOR two days. Two days in which Simon knew moments of peace, of pleasure, and moments when he sank into pure hell. Tending to a patient again—yeah, of course there'd be moments of pleasure. He was a doctor. Doctoring was all he'd ever wanted to do. From the time he was in junior high he'd known his course.

Peace…now, that had surprised him a bit. Sitting in that cabin in the evening, with the light down low and a book in his lap…and upon first waking in the morning, knowing that someone was in the next room, having to keep a schedule, having something to do at a particular time…had brought peace. He should have known. Should have been able to figure out that he needed structure. Human Nature 101.

And sinking into hell—well, that had pretty much been the rest of the time that he wasn't climbing his way back out of it.

His patient, on the morning of her third day with him, woke him when she moved quietly through the body of the cabin to the restroom she'd visited a few times in the previous two days, with him right behind her in case she felt weak. On those occasions, he'd left her at the door. She'd called out to him when she was ready for him to come get her.

When he'd seen her underwear hanging wet and obviously cleaned on the far towel bar the previous morning, he'd taken it out to dry in the sunshine after he'd seen her back to bed. Everything had been right where she left it when she'd made her next trip, and had disappeared from the bar right after.

She'd consumed three cans of soup. Half a cracker. And a couple of glasses of orange juice. Along with more than a quart of water. The previous evening he'd removed the makeshift butterfly bandages he'd put on her face and was encouraged by the pink skin surrounding her worst abrasions. Her skin had been cool to the touch since day one. She was healing nicely with no sign of infection.

Pretending to remain asleep on the pullout as he listened to her cross the floor, move down the short hall and close the bathroom door behind her, Simon considered what the day would bring. She was able to get up, move about without any slowness of step or obvious signs of dizziness. It was time for her to resume minimal activity. Another full day in bed was not going to be good for her.

A woman up and about his cabin, needing another day or two of rest, but no longer requiring the direct supervision of a physician, was not good for him.

As a patient, she'd either been asleep, answering his questions or following his orders. He'd kept his questions strictly professional. And his orders—a couple more bites, deep breath, please—even more so.

He needed her gone so he could get back to the business of getting back to his life. Getting back out in the woods. Challenging himself more than closing one eye indoors would do. He hadn't worn the eye patch since he'd found her.

She had no idea she was dealing with a one-eyed man, and he had every intention of having that state of affairs remain just as it was. But with that, his right eye could grow weaker, letting the left eye do all of its work. Not wanting to leave her alone in the cabin—not completely sure she wouldn't bolt on him—he'd had to settle for closing his left eye and watching the old television set that worked only with the DVD player attached. He'd kept the sound low, so as not to disturb his patient, and was pretty sure that the time he'd thought he'd seen a shadow move across the screen had not been a brain trick brought on by the fact that a female voice in the movie had just said *come here*. He was pretty sure he'd seen that shadow.

And was antsy to get outside in the daylight and test himself.

Just as antsy as he was to have the woman out of his house.

Wanting to no longer have a patient to care for…well, with his usual self-honesty, he had to admit that he wasn't eager for that part of this little time warp to end.

Simon was sitting up, in the sweats and flannel shirt he kept by the couch to put on when he had to tend to his patient during the night, with the bed already folded away by the time Cara came back through the front room. He'd been keeping the place toastier at night, in deference to his patient, but even if he hadn't been, he was a sleep-in-the-buff guy.

She'd dressed herself. That first day, he'd washed her clothes. Left them on top of the wooden trunk at the end of the bed. Her long dark hair was in a ponytail. He didn't know where she'd found the rubber band. The first morning she'd woken in his cabin, he'd offered her a spare comb and toothbrush. She'd brushed but had been too weak, or in pain, to shower. She'd obviously taken care of that this morning.

"You found your clothes." What did you say to a woman you barely knew when she was standing in the middle of your remote hideaway cabin before you'd even been to the bathroom in the morning?

"Yes." Her body faced the bedroom, but she

stood halfway between it and the bathroom, looking at him. Sort of. Her gaze wandered toward the floor.

She appeared to have no curiosity about her surroundings. But then, she'd had two days' worth of trips back and forth to the bathroom to check it out. He hadn't noticed her looking around then, either.

"Uh, thank you. For washing them." She glanced at him, held his gaze and then wavered again.

He couldn't figure her out. The more she recovered, the more docile she seemed to become. Why would a woman have more fight in her when she was physically weak than when her strength had started to return?

"You're welcome," her said after a moment of studying her. "I'm fixing oatmeal and toast for breakfast. You should eat at the table this morning." Because she couldn't spend another full day in bed.

His thoughts were repeating themselves. She had to be up and about. He didn't want her about. She was too weak to hike out of there on her own. And neither of them relished the idea of visitors. All things they had to talk about.

She didn't seem to have anything to say. With a nod, she turned away, entered her room and the cabin grew silent. She hadn't closed the door. He could go look in and see what she was doing.

He made oatmeal, instead.

CARA WASN'T AFRAID. If she'd ever in a million years imagined herself in her current position, she'd have figured herself for terrified, but she wasn't. Her heart was calm. Resigned. At peace. Karma had been fulfilled, and life and death would be what they were.

Fate had led her to this path. Her way was clear. She was completely, utterly alone now.

No one to miss her, either, which made it all easier. Except Mary. But Mary would be much happier now. Shawn loved his sister. Looked out for her. The two had formed a blessed bond during their difficult upbringing. Shawn never spoke harshly to Mary, never lifted a hand to her except when she was interceding on Cara's behalf. Without Cara there...

Shawn. A vision of her husband's smiling sun-drenched face, windblown hair, came to mind. She'd met him on the beach in Florida. His confidence and joy in living had captivated her...

No. These last minutes, last hours, last day or two at the most, were hers. They were days to find her essence. To cling to it. To slide away with her heart firmly attached to its goal and get to those waiting for her on the other side.

If she got there—where they were. Surely she was paying her price here. Bowing her head, she prayed to all that was, to angels and stars and heavens, begging to let her earthly life be the penance. The thought of being anywhere in eternity but with those she'd loved with all her heart who'd gone before her...

Clang! It sounded like a pan had dropped on the old linoleum floor in the kitchen. Picturing the scarred red pattern in her mind, she imagined the doctor picking up whatever he'd dropped. And paused to wonder whether those unsteady fingers had cause him to lose a life.

Staring ahead, she straightened. She couldn't control the future. Or what would happen to her when she passed. She could only have faith. Keep her mind on what must be. She'd escaped Shawn. That had been answer enough for her. She was meant to die out here.

Shawn had thrown her driver's license on the ground near her body—so authorities would be able to identify her, she knew. When she'd started her trek in the woods, she'd slid it inside the cup of her bra. Now it lay in the back pocket of her jeans. She was ready to be identified.

But first, she had to get away from the man hell bent on keeping her alive to salvage his own soul.

Sitting quietly, almost numbly, on the side of the bed, she waited to go eat oatmeal.

SIMON HAD VERY carefully set his place at the end of the wooden table that sat four. Placing her bowl and spoon directly on his left, the brown sugar and plate of buttered toast in front of them, left his uncooperative right eye with little responsibility. He'd called her to the table, set to pouring milk into a pitcher, heard the scrape of her chair and turned to see her sitting in his seat.

What guest took the seat at the head of the table?

The table was oblong. She'd taken the seat closest to the kitchen. And he was screwed. Failing to come up with a reason to move the second place across the table, Simon set the pitcher of milk next to the toast and took her chair, leaving his nearly blind right eye as his leading man.

KNOWING THAT SHE wasn't going to get away without his sending out a search party unless she convinced the doctor that she was fine, Cara ate every bite of cereal in her bowl. At least swallowing no longer hurt. She had a piece of toast. And felt guilty for doing so. She was only prolonging a life meant to end. She wouldn't take her own life. Her mother had taught her well, and killing yourself, no matter how imminent death might be, was wrong.

Karma, Fate—they could use you right up until your last breath. Even the way you took your last breath could be used—to help someone else. You had to let nature take its course. And she would. Just as soon as she could get away from her current predicament.

"That was good, thank you." Her manners, another reflection of her mother, were ingrained.

Funny how she was thinking of Mom so much. Must be because being in her company again was so imminent. She felt comfort and then knew guilt again. She didn't deserve comfort. She was scum of the earth. Worse than Shawn and…

"You're shaking."

Cara came out of her personal hell to see the doctor studying her. With that way he had of tilting his head a bit to the side. She'd noticed it the first day. Kind of liked it.

She would pay for her mistakes by Fate's plan. In Fate's time. Peace settled over her again.

"Finish up your juice and we'll get you settled on the couch," the doctor said, nodding at her glass. His voice was…tender. She responded to it. Knew she shouldn't. His kindness was wasted on her.

"I was planning to leave today."

With a small frown, he shook his head. "We agreed you'd stay until you were better."

"We said a few days." Funny how absence of fear freed up voice. She didn't know the doctor. She figured he had a death on his conscience. And that he was hiding away from something. There were six months' worth of soap and other supplies in the big laundry closet at the back of the bathroom. He'd been gentle and respectful in his care of her. Professional. But it could just be until she was well enough to serve another need.

Men had those needs. Didn't seem to matter

what was going on in their lives. And one as hot as he was, a doctor, no less, probably wasn't used to going without.

Still, she knew no fear. Had nothing left to lose…

"…you're still weak, as evidenced by your shaking, but after two days in bed, with only a bit of soup to eat, you will be weak. You've been badly beaten. Repeatedly, in my opinion. Your body is pulling all of your energy into the healing process. For this reason, I cannot, in good conscience, let you wander out there on your own. I will, however, drive you to the closest town if there's somewhere else you'd rather be."

Town! Shawn could be there. Her heart pounded. Shawn couldn't know she was still alive. She couldn't go back to him. She'd rather kill herself. Shawn…he knew her weaknesses, her issues. Her mistakes… He'd use them against her…

So much for no fear. The same sense of purpose that had come over her the night she'd convinced Shawn she had a brain bleed took root again.

Sitting up straight, she said, "I'm fine. Really. Let me prove it to you. I'll…" she looked around "…clean the cabin for you today. I'll stay busy all day. And when you see that I don't pass out or have a heart attack, you agree to let me go."

"You are not cleaning my cabin." He glanced around, turning his body as though he had to inspect every corner of the building. "In the first place, it doesn't need to be cleaned. I have a system...a schedule." He shook his head, as though he wasn't sure what he was saying. Or maybe why. And then, with more of the gentle bossiness she was used to, he said, "What kind of a doctor would I be if I let you overextend yourself, cleaning up after me?"

The words reminded her of his earlier statement. Something about not being able to afford another life on his conscience.

"I'd like you to spend the day out here, on the couch, sitting up, except for naps if you feel the need, with some light activity. You have no broken bones, but you're still badly bruised. And the blows to your face were severe. We need to give the swelling some more time to dissipate, inside and out."

She hadn't studied her face in the mirror. Had actually avoiding even looking at herself, other than to focus on individual cuts as she'd tended to them. She'd felt all of the bruising, though, and the bumps, as she'd washed her face in the shower. She'd felt the sting as the soap and water sluiced over some of the deeper cuts.

"I put the salve on the wounds after I washed, just as you instructed." Antagonizing him, in any way, would be counterproductive.

He nodded. "I can see that."

"Thank you for the butterflies. The cuts are healing nicely." Unlike some of the other cuts

Shawn had inflicted over the years, calling them surfing accidents and then insisting that she didn't need medical attention. Of course, he'd taken advantage of her doctor phobia on that one. She didn't go to them.

Except for...well, Mary had helped her find... had gone with her...

Mary. Sweet Mary. Sometimes she wondered if part of Shawn's appeal all along had been the younger sister he'd protected so fiercely. From the time they were ten and fourteen it had been just the two of them, growing up in foster care.

She hoped that Mary, her sister-in-law, best friend and salvation, was going to be happy now that Shawn had no reason to be upset with her.

"You're tired. Let's get you to the couch."

Blinking, Cara realized she'd been fazing out while the doctor had been watching her. Maybe he was right. Maybe she did need a bit more rest.

Just a short nap.

"I feel badly leaving you with the dishes." She'd had an earlier thought that she'd do them before she left...

"I wouldn't have let you do them if you tried, so this just saves us wasting your energy on another argument," he said as he led her away from the table.

She didn't want to lie on the couch with him sitting there. Didn't want to sleep in the open...

"I'd be less of an intrusion if I napped in the

other room," she said, and when he paused, added, "I promise to sit on the couch the rest of the day and follow your instructions without argument."

She didn't want to spend another whole day in his cabin. Prolonging the inevitable. But she needed the bed. Her head was starting to hurt and she was feeling a bit nauseous, too. She shouldn't have had that last piece of toast.

"I'm going to hold you to that promise," the doctor said as he saw her to the door of the room and let her walk alone to the bed.

"I know."

He stood there until she was settled on the four-poster she'd made that morning with a cover from the trunk over her.

"Sleep well, Cara."

She kind of thought he'd smiled at her as he left the room.

Clearly, the man needed her to be a success-ful project.

CHAPTER FIVE

THERE WAS NOT a hell of a lot to do in a cabin that had only one main room and only burner-phone contact with the outside world. He'd been so busy sending himself on hikes, even on the one day it had rained since he'd been there, and bumbling blindly around the interior of the place, making his right eye work—or else—that he'd failed to consider that the hours would be long and excruciatingly empty with a patient sharing the space.

He offered her the option to choose a book from the library he'd brought up with him. It covered an entire wall of the cabin. She did, and they read for a while. Until lunch, which she'd offered to help him make. He hoped his refusal didn't come out sounding as desperate as it felt. He'd been looking forward to the ten minutes alone in the little kitchen that it would take him to grill up some cheese sandwiches.

Out of habit, when they first sat down, he studied the bruises and cuts on her face, making certain there was no sign of infection.

"You really don't have to look at me right before you eat," she said. "I'm fine with you looking away."

"You say that as if you wouldn't find it painful to have someone look at you and need to look away."

Her shrug touched him. The ease with which she blew off pain bothered him, too.

"You're used to walking around with bruises on your face."

"You can see the scars, Doctor. They aren't all that noticeable when I have makeup on, but you know this isn't the first time I've felt this way. Which is why I know I'm fine. I've never taken even so much as a morning off from work in the past."

"You weren't left for dead in the past. Hadn't faced a night of exposure. And you're right, I've seen the scars. A couple of the cuts you have right now, most particularly the one on your lateral left cheek, had I not butterflied it, would have left a much deeper scar than the ones already there."

"I thanked you for them. The butterflies."

"I'm not looking for thanks." He wasn't looking for anything. But he got kind of frustrated when she silently finished half a sandwich. Some answers would be nice.

"I'm of the opinion that these current injuries are worse than those left from previous beatings."

She didn't respond.

"How did you go to work…on those mornings you didn't take off?" His conversational skills definitely rusty, he filled his mouth with sandwich.

"Shawn owns a surfing school. I run…ran… the business end. Taking registrations, billing, scheduling, that kind of thing. A lot of it I could do from home."

He focused on the way the bruise to the right of her lip moved when she spoke. It was showing no signs of the yellowing that would tell him it was healing with the rest of them.

He didn't have to know her story. Her health was the only thing that concerned him. Still, they had to do *something*. "So, you hid out until you looked better. What about the scars?" he asked even as he remembered her mention of makeup.

"I didn't always hide out," she said. "Everyone knew that I sucked at surfing. As many times as Shawn tried to teach me, I just couldn't make myself stay up on the board. Anytime I had bruises, he'd just say I'd tried to go surfing again."

"And doctors believed him? What about the reports…"

"No doctors," she said, her tone firm. Then she glanced at him, almost apologetically, it seemed, and said, "I'm not real fond of those who work in your profession."

Interesting.

"No offense," she added, biting into the second

half of her sandwich. "You've been great. I feel fine. Well enough to leave…"

He raised his eyebrow, glad that the right side of his face, including the eye itself, still moved along with the left.

"…I know," she said after a second under his silent look. "I promised I'd stay at least until tomorrow."

They finished eating. He didn't ask why she disliked doctors. She didn't talk about leaving. He let her help him clean up—because it consisted of throwing away the napkins on which he'd set their sandwiches and washing out the glasses they'd used for their tea.

All that was left, then, was moving back to the living area—she on the couch, he with his book in the easy chair next to a side table with a lamp. He could read just fine. He could do most things just fine.

His right eye wasn't getting the exercise it needed, though. Every hour mattered.

CARA COULDN'T STOP looking at him. The first time had been an accident. He'd turned a page; she'd looked up and caught his eye. Sort of. He hadn't been focused on her, but she'd been in his line of vision. Usually a person would have fully focused, once caught out with that kind of sideways glance, right?

Without even a hint that he'd seen her, he looked

out the window to the left of him. She'd waited for him to say something. Eventually he'd gone back to his reading.

And so had she.

She wouldn't have expected that a woman so close to leaving the earth would care at all about broadening her mind, but the book she'd chosen—mostly because he'd been waiting for her to make a choice and it had been right in front of her—dealt with international espionage. Nothing she had any familiarity with whatsoever. The writing style was good. And the story was actually interesting enough to take her mind off the interminable wait.

Except for the break she took every ten minutes or so to look at him. Mostly, he was reading. Or staring out that window.

Maybe he saw something in the dry desert landscaping in the front yard that she was missing. Lots of sagebrush. Trees, because they were up on a mountain. But it was mostly rock and dirt with patches of weedy grass. Rough ground, all of it.

As she well knew. Cold ground, too, where it wasn't exposed to direct sunlight.

He was doing it again. Turning his eyes enough that he had to see her watching him. Saying nothing.

He definitely had his secrets.

But that was fine. So did she.

Santa Raquel, California

LILA WAS IN her office, tending to a pile of paperwork—state compliance forms—early Friday evening. It had been two days since the near all-nighter she'd pulled pursuant to Edward's call for help. She'd slept nearly twelve hours straight on Thursday after work, but she still didn't feel rested.

Weariness had been slowly creeping up on her over the past few weeks, interspersed with bits of almost excitement-laced hours of energy. So unlike her. If things persisted, maybe she'd call her doctor.

The Stand was unusually busy. They'd added twenty more beds over the past year and still were almost filled to capacity. So much violence. So much pain.

It was no wonder she was tired.

And yet...with her right hand hovering over a signature line, she paused, took hold of her mouse in her left hand and opened a private folder on her computer. From day one she'd been saving pictures—taken with permission and for her personal use only—of recovered residents, survivors who were living happy, productive lives. Some of them for the first time.

As her gaze passed from one to another, she was filled again with the same sense of peace, knowing that she was not only where she was needed, but where she needed to be. Wanted to be.

Her gaze came to rest on the digital picture collages she'd made of the children who had come through the Stand—some with their mothers and a few alone. Looking at those smiles settled her entire being. She hadn't been able to save her own little girl. But there was no doubt in Lila's mind or heart that from her place in heaven, her own sweet girl watched over every single one of the TLS children. Lila and her baby girl were in partnership on this one.

People thought she lived alone. That, other than work, she spent her entire life alone. She knew some of her closest associates had concerns about her lack of outside life. She knew that, with loving hearts, they wondered about her. And every day, when she went out on the premises and offered smiles, when she brought calm to traumatic situations and gave peace to destroyed hearts, she also knew that she wasn't alone. That she didn't live alone. She and her baby girl, her precious daughter who'd only made it to the age of twelve, were in this together...

A knock sounded on her office door, and the pen she'd been holding over a form left a jagged mark on the signature line.

"Come in." With her left hand still on the mouse, she quickly clicked out of the folder.

An impressive-looking suited man stepped

halfway into her office. His short graying hair was impeccably in place, as was the silk tie inside his buttoned jacket. His features, while handsome, weren't outwardly remarkable. Her stomach jolted anyway.

"Edward! I thought you'd gone. You have your dinner tonight…" Dr. Edward Mantle had been invited by a group of doctors he'd met at a recent hospital charity event to join them for their bi-weekly boys' night out.

She'd thought he'd left without stopping in to say goodbye.

Not that he was required to do so. But he'd been in court that morning. She'd just kind of expected, since she'd been a rather major part of this journey with him and his family, that he'd fill her in.

She'd kind of expected him to let her know how lunch went with Joy, too. Instead of taking his new-to-him granddaughter overnight right away, they'd decided to try several more day outings first. Because he was from Florida, not familiar with Santa Raquel and staying in a hotel, Lila had been more involved with him than she might otherwise have been.

Most of her participation, however, had been exactly what she'd have done for any other child who'd just lost all of the family she'd ever known in a horrifically traumatic experience.

"I sent my regrets for this evening's gathering,"

Edward was saying. "You got a minute, or would you like me to catch up with you later?"

"Of course I have a minute." Pushing aside the forms, Lila set down her pen and rose. "Have a seat." She indicated the couch and took the armchair perpendicular to it. Her families always came first.

"I've just left Joy," he said. Lila was not pleased by the rush of…lightness…at his remark. He'd come straight to her. As though they were somehow partners in the whole Mantle/Amos trauma.

In a sense they were, of course, partners. With boundaries. Professional boundaries.

Her only job was to facilitate as happy an outcome as she could. To be looking out for Joy's well-being first and foremost.

She wasn't faltering there. Joy came first. It was just…she cared, more than she felt comfortable with…about Joy's grandfather's feelings, too.

A widower whose only child was missing and presumed dead, the man was completely, utterly bereft.

Lila knew what that felt like. The loneliness. The burying of your own daughter. The loss of family. Of love.

And this wasn't about her.

Edward wasn't saying anything. He'd just left Joy. And was sitting in her office, on her couch, his elbows on his knees, rubbing his hands together.

The doctor who'd, overnight, left his practice

in Florida to fly to California to find his daughter and take charge of his granddaughter, was clearly at a loss.

He'd come to her.

Her job was to comfort.

Leaning forward, Lila touched the top of his hand. *Touching was not her job.* She sat back but had his attention.

"Tell me about lunch with Joy."

She needed to know what had happened in court that morning, too. Shawn Amos, Joy's father and Cara's husband, was supposed to have been indicted. And Chantel Fairbanks, a Santa Raquel detective and a member of the High Risk team that had been formed through The Lemonade Stand to help prevent domestic violence deaths, had put in a request for a meeting with the inmate before he was transported back to prison.

Chantel had wanted to speak with Shawn Amos, one on one, alone in a courthouse conference room, to see if she, a female alone, could get any more of a reaction out of him than any of the officers—both male and female—who'd questioned him repeatedly at the police station and in prison. But Joy came first. Edward had taken her to lunch.

"Not much to tell," Edward said, looking at her, then back at his hands that were plastered together. "I took her to Uncle Bob's." A burger joint on the beach with an oversize sandbox. A favorite with most of the Santa Raquel kids Joy's age. "When I asked her if she wanted to play in the sandbox, she shook her head…" His tired gaze settled on Lila and she couldn't help but look for the light of quiet strength she'd come to associate with him. Finding it, she nodded at him to continue, clasping her own hands together to keep herself from reaching for him again.

"Did she hold your hand as you walked inside?" Lila asked. They'd been working on it all week. Edward holding out his hand to the little girl. Repeatedly. Hoping she'd take it.

He shook his head.

Joy went with Edward when she was told to do so. But she'd only ever spoken directly to him when she'd been defending Julie Fairbanks—a TLS volunteer whom Joy seemed to have adopted as a surrogate mother. She'd told him that he could not be her grandfather if he didn't believe that Julie was the author of the children's books Joy had clung to since arriving at the Stand.

Julie had penned—and drawn—the stories, but until Joy's announcement, only the child and a few others had known that the twenty-nine-year-old philanthropist was also a successful author.

Until Julie worked with Joy, the little girl hadn't spoken a word after she'd been brought to The Lemonade Stand. Julie, through Amy, the character in her books, had connected with the child enough for her to tell them that she'd witnessed her father beating her aunt and mother. That her mother had told her aunt to take Joy and run, and that the aunt had hidden with the child behind an old dog pen. From there, Joy had seen her father haul her mother away by her hair.

The aunt, Mary Amos, had then run with Joy to the neighbors for help, after which the woman had been rushed to the hospital where she'd later died.

Joy spoke to those caring for her at The Lemonade Stand now. She spoke to Julie and to Hunter, Edward's nephew, fairly regularly, too. Spoke when spoken to. Or to make requests. But other than when she was at Edward's and crying out for others, she never spoke to Edward.

"I ordered a burger and fries, and she ate every bite," he said in the reserved way he had, taking his time.

Lila could see how strangers might see Edward as somewhat cold. And had no idea why she was so certain that a solid core of warmth ran deeply through him.

"That's good, Edward." Lila's job was to help this family help the child, she reminded herself as she leaned forward, too, needing the widower to know he wasn't alone. "If she wasn't somewhat comfortable with you, she wouldn't have a healthy appetite."

"I took her to the toy store. I told her she could have anything she wanted."

"Did she pick something?"

He shook his head again. "We walked every aisle."

"That must have taken a long time."

His grin made her heart leap. Because she needed so badly for this family to find healing. "Two hours," he told her. "She touched a lot of things, studied some, but each time I asked her if she wanted it, she shook her head."

"We don't know what kind of conditioning she's had," Lila quickly pointed out, not wanting to let go of that smile. "Oftentimes, after an abuser has hurt his victim, he overcompensates by buying things."

Edward nodded. "I know. I've read everything you've given me since Cara first went missing weeks ago. I just… I've never so much as frowned at Joy, so I didn't think…surely children of abusers have others in their lives who buy them things just because they care about them."

"Most do, of course. But until you win Joy's trust, you aren't, in her mind, in the category of those who care about her."

He knew what they were dealing with. He, like everyone else caring for Joy, was in counseling with Sara Edwin, one of the Stand's full-time counselors.

"When we got back here, I read to her. She sat next to me and watched as I turned the pages."

"Amy books?"

"Of course."

"Good." Lila nodded.

"I couldn't bring myself to leave her."

"Did she seem distressed, having you there?"

"No."

"Then this is progress."

His gaze was direct this time. "I know. But I fear that I'm being selfish, as well. If I'm staying because I can't bear leaving, is it her I'm putting first, or myself?"

"The fact that you're asking the question is your answer. You can't help loving her, needing to be with her. If you didn't, you wouldn't be good for her. Joy needs to know that there is someone who adores her, who will be there for her, no matter what. Someone who belongs to her. If you were forcing your presence on her when she showed signs of distress, that might be different."

His smile was larger this time. Filled with the warmth that he didn't often show—at least, not in the time she'd known him. She smiled back. It just came naturally.

And was something she did with others, too. So why did her heart suddenly feel such an acute stab of guilt? She was crossing a line that could not be crossed. Ever. With anyone. Anywhere.

"Have dinner with me." His question intensified her guilt.

"I can't." She blurted the words. Completely

unlike herself. Stared at him, afraid of what he might see within her.

"But I've got some wine and cheese in my suite here," she said, effecting as much of her usual calm as she could muster. "I'm…staying here tonight…" she said—the truth, but she wasn't staying because she had to. Only because she'd been planning to use the evening to catch up on the paperwork she'd just shoved aside on her desk.

"The wine—it can be tea, if you'd prefer— and I've got what's left of a platter of meats and cheeses from a function earlier today. I'd been planning to indulge myself with it in lieu of dinner."

She'd just invited a man to visit with her in her suite. What in the hell was happening to her?

Her suite at the Stand. Where she was always on call when she was in residence. And was often called. As opposed to alone with him, like a date, out…in the world. Where it was possible they could end up either at his hotel or her condo. Wasn't going to happen, but the possibility made her more uncomfortable than wine and cheese at the Stand.

Okay…she had things more under control than she'd first thought.

"I'd like that very much." Edward's warm glance—not quite a smile, but bordering on personal—sent her into a tizzy all over again. As much as Lila ever got in a tizzy.

"Please, don't misunderstand. I am not issuing an invi…"

His hand on hers cut her off. "I understand, Lila." He looked her directly in the eye as he said the words. "I'd like to tell you about court this morning, if I may, and we both need sustenance. I would greatly enjoy a glass of wine to take the edge off a dreadful day, and will in no way compromise the friendship you've shown me by making more of it than it is."

Her heart dropped. Jumped up and…just that, up and down, over and over, pounding in her chest. His words took her air, and brought it back in a whoosh. Ridiculous.

Unprovoked.

He considered her a friend.

And she wasn't in danger of breaking her promise to herself.

The promise to never, ever, let anyone get close enough that he or she could be hurt.

Lila would rather be dead than be a danger to another living soul again.

CHAPTER SIX

Prospector, Nevada

HIS PATIENT ASKED if he minded if she went to
bed to read as soon as the dinner dishes were
done on Friday. Boxed macaroni and cheese with
hotdogs and peas were his offering that night.
He'd prepared it all. She'd eaten everything on
her plate. And cleared and wiped the table while
he'd washed up.

If he were planning to keep the cabin—to ever
visit it again once his eye was better—he'd put
in a dishwasher. Telling her he thought it was a
good idea that she lie down, though it was still
early in the evening, he watched her walk away.
The woman bothered him.

He knew she was hurting. The way she held
her book…turned pages…when she'd wiped off
the table…her left wrist was bothering her. And
her neck or shoulder was, too.

She was tired, but had been sleeping well, so
he let it go for the night. He'd have a look at her
in the morning. And in the meantime, he was past

due for his drops. Six and six, every day, a.m. and p.m. Two drops each time.

In the bathroom, he tried not to notice the towel his patient had used that morning as he grabbed the drops from the zipped leather duffel under the sink that contained antibiotics, cold medicine, pain relievers and anything else he might need.

The drops were prescription. To relieve pressure on the eye. Pressure caused by swelling. Pressure that could prevent him from regaining his eyesight. Or could cause the process to happen more slowly.

Positioning himself in front of the mirror above the sink, he focused on his nose. Reached up over his head with his left hand, careful to keep his arm visible in the mirror to the only eye that could guide him and held open the lid of his right eye. The right hand had the easy part: lift until his hand was exactly half an inch from his nose and squeeze gently.

A drop fell to his cheek. Just under his eye.

Cursing his vision, he leaned his head back a second time, kept his nose in view in the mirror, measured the distance from the dropper and squeezed again. The drop hit his lower lid. He lifted his hand only slightly and tried one more time. He got the corner of his eye. He'd failed to measure from his nose that time.

If his damned nose wasn't so big he could see the right eye from the corner of his left, could aim better. You'd think, after weeks of daily drops, he'd be a pro.

Especially for a surgeon with hands as steady as his were.

It was a mental block. He'd thought, when he'd first diagnosed the problem a while back, that the acknowledgment would take care of it. It hadn't.

And so, after letting his arms rest for a moment, he once again got a fix on his nose in the mirror, raised his left arm over his head, slid his hand past his forehead to open his right lid and lifted the dropper to squeeze gently. Missed for a fourth time. His best was two attempts. His worst was nine. But he'd had a beer that night…

"What on earth are you doing?"

Two drops fell in quick succession, trailing down his right cheekbone. Arms coming down, Simon held the dropper and turned to face his patient. Still in her jeans and T-shirt, but minus the zipped sweater she'd had on all day, she was watching him.

He might have noticed her approach if he'd had peripheral vision in his right eye.

"Putting drops in my eye," he said when he'd determined that doing so could be for something as simple as dry or itchy eyes.

"I'd have thought a surgeon would have a steadier hand." She looked slightly down as she said the words. Such a funny combination of sassy and demure. Not that he was interested in her personality.

Or in anything other than her health. And then her departure.

"My hand's plenty steady." Childish of him to rise to her taunt, but her remark about not liking doctors was still ringing in his ears.

"Then you're just a bad aim."

"I blink."

"No, you don't."

He didn't think so. But he was damned well not going to tell her that he was temporarily blind in one eye. He'd come to the cabin to get away from the naysayers. Those who didn't believe he'd ever see from that eye again. Those who thought that his recovery meant accepting the blindness and moving on. He didn't want to hear another person tell him there were many things he could do besides be a surgeon. He couldn't afford to listen. To let doubts creep in. He was going to see again. It was a matter of will, now.

So many times, the difference between a patient surviving or not depended not on medical skills or science, but on the patient's will to live. Lucky for him that his patients were so young—they almost all had that will. In spades.

"You want help?"

As opposed to having her stand there watching him play his nightly game of drop ball?

"Yes." He handed her the dropper. Told her he

needed two drops, directly into the middle of the eye. Then bent down and leaned his head back so she could deliver them.

"Wow, you didn't blink either time. How do you do that? I always blink when something's coming at my eye."

She was getting chattier. Good sign in terms of her recovery.

"Thank you," he said, taking the dropper from her. She didn't leave. And he realized that she'd been coming to use the restroom.

"If you'd like to leave your clothes outside your door when you go to bed, I'll throw them in the wash again," he told her. "Tomorrow we can see about getting you a T-shirt of mine to wear, too. Or a flannel. It'll be long, but you can roll up the sleeves."

"I'll leave my clothes, thanks."

He had a feeling that having him do her laundry wasn't on the top of her list of desires, but what else could she do but sit around in the hospital gown he'd made for her or stand naked in the bathroom while the washer and dryer ran through their cycles?

Catching sight of the bruise closest to her mouth, he reached behind her neck and pulled her closer. Under the bright light of the bathroom he could get a better...

"Don't." She jerked away from him. And

stood there, meeting his gaze and then looking away. "I'm s—"

"No," Simon stepped back. "I am so sorry, Cara. My bedside manner is usually impeccable. I should have told you I'd like to have a closer look at your face…"

It was then that it dawned on him that she hadn't just been reacting to his pulling her forward, but that she'd thought he had something else entirely on his mind.

As if he'd take advantage…

"Why do you need a closer look at my face?"

"That bruise to the side of your mouth…its color is a little suspicious…" There'd been a slight cut there. If he hadn't cleaned it out well enough, an infection could have developed.

She stepped closer to him, but didn't look at herself in the mirror.

"Have at it, Doc," she said, sounding completely not at ease. So much so that Simon felt sorry for her.

The woman had a lot of spunk for someone who'd been a regular punching bag for her low-life husband.

He checked her bruise. Suspected that the swelling on the left side of her face indicated a minor zygoma—cheek—fracture but from all signs, including lack of displacement, nose bleeds or undue pain, he believed it was one that would heal itself.

As long as nothing happened to displace it.

He told her his findings.

Then left the bathroom to her.

But something had changed in those moments back there. Something that was going to have some impact. He'd realized something.

Something big. And problematic.

There was no way he was going to let her just walk away, to go back out into the world all alone, to go back to the life she'd led, and let that bastard hit her again.

Santa Raquel, California

EDWARD TOOK OFF his jacket, hung it over the back of a chair at Lila's small dinette. She'd seen him in golf attire a couple of times, but she wasn't used to seeing him in a dress shirt without his suitcoat on. Why he'd suddenly seem more vulnerable, she had no idea, and wasn't sure enough of herself where he was concerned to risk delving any further.

In the fourteen years since her previous life had ended, Lila had never, ever, not once, been even remotely tempted to notice a man's...attributes. Hadn't been physically activated by the sight of man for much longer than that.

She'd shown him to the small table instead of to the sitting area that was where she'd occasionally invited other special guests over the years, because the table had felt more formal. Now she wasn't so sure.

"I like your place," he told her. Looking around, she had to wonder. A man with his financial success...a man in general...couldn't possibly feel comfortable in her small, completely feminine apartment. The place really only consisted of one room divided into living room and kitchenette by the table at which they sat. There was a separate bedroom. And a bath. The entire place was decorated with lace and roses; prints of places she'd once dreamed of traveling to were framed on the walls. Her dishes were china. A gift from Brett Ackerman, founder of The Lemonade Stand.

Ashamed that it made her feel good to be able to impress him with her crystal wineglasses—wanting him to notice them—she opened the bottle and poured, carried both glasses to the table and then retrieved the deli tray out of the refrigerator. Pouring crackers into a lacy cloth-lined basket, she reached into a drawer for two rose-and-lace napkins—ones that matched the placemats on the table—and slid two dessert plates out of another cupboard.

All was done with silent, deliberate movements. Edward Mantle needed a friend. And Lila had to find her peace.

"Did you decorate this place yourself?" he asked as she sat down across from him, careful to keep enough of a distance that their knees didn't touch.

She and Sara had shared a meal at the table a time or two. Mostly, she sat there alone.

"Yes." She took a sip of wine before he could think about offering a toast. Afraid that he'd toast to their friendship and her heart would react again. Or that he wouldn't. And her heart would react again.

"It reminds me of a cross between a tea room my mother used to go to when I was a kid and the Florida room my wife had at home."

His wife. Cara's mother. Lila didn't know much about the other woman except that she'd passed away when Cara was in high school.

"Do you still live in the same house?"

"No." He shook his head. "Cara was already exhibiting signs of extreme anger and rebellion by the time my wife passed and I felt that getting her out of that environment, reminders of the eighteen months she spent watching her mother slowly fade away, would be better for her. She loved the beach so much and our old home was a twenty-minute drive…"

"Your house on the beach… You bought it for her." Edward had first mentioned the house in front of Joy, thinking he'd pique the little girl's interest, but the gambit had failed miserably. Joy had withdrawn at the mere mention of the beach.

"Yes."

"How long did the two of you live there before she moved to California with Shawn?" Ran off with him was more like it. Edward's daughter had disappeared into the night without warning or word. As Lila understood it, the two of them had been barely speaking at that point—Cara blaming Edward for her every unhappiness, accusing him of hating Shawn.

"We lived there together for two years," Edward said, no rancor in his tone. "Her room is still just as she left it."

That news—evidence of Edward's hidden emotional depths—didn't surprise Lila.

Cara had met the guy who ran a surfing school shortly after her mother died—Edward had been certain the school was a front for drugs, but the more he questioned, the more Cara pulled away, saying that he didn't want her to be happy.

Once they were out of the state, Shawn had contacted Edward and let him know where they were living, that they'd married on the way across the country and that Edward was not to contact his daughter.

Edward had insisted on speaking with Cara—which he had—and Cara had, not kindly, reiterated her new husband's words. She'd been eighteen at the time. Shawn had been several years older. They'd opened a surfing school in California.

From what she understood from Edward's nephew, Hunter, Edward had hoped the business was legitimate, that Cara was healthy and happy. Cara hadn't contacted him in years—or responded to any of his efforts to contact her. When Shawn Amos had warned Edward to leave Cara alone, he'd said that Edward did nothing but make her unhappy. And apparently Edward had begun to take all of the blame for the breakdown between them upon himself. He'd been too distant—too involved in his career for most of her childhood—was all he'd said to Lila.

"I was so certain that Shawn was the biggest problem between Cara and I," the man said now. "She was young, grieving, lashing out and was far too vulnerable. I should never have moved her to the beach."

"If she was as rebellious as you say, she'd have found some other way to put distance between you…"

"I tried to tell Cara that there were things about Amos that weren't quite right. He was too controlling, for one thing. She had to text him every time she got home from somewhere. And every night before she went to sleep. And he refused to come to our house for dinner. Or hang out with any of Cara's friends. But any time I said anything that could be even slightly construed as a criticism of Shawn, Cara shut down on me."

Lila understood his need to talk. To confide in someone. What she didn't understand was the strong urge she had to take his head to her breast and run her fingers through that short, graying hair.

"What happened today when you saw him?" That was the real question now. Neither of them had touched the food. Or their wine after the initial sip.

"I only saw the back of him. He was in an orange jumpsuit with his hands cuffed behind his back. He never turned around. Was in and out in less than a minute. He was indicted on charges of first-degree murder and kidnapping. Pleaded not guilty, said that he would be hiring an attorney to replace his court-appointed one, was remanded and held without bail, and they led him away."

About the best-case scenario, given the current circumstances. But Edward's frown, his fingers rubbing across his palm over and over, indicated otherwise.

Lila's stomach tightened. "Did Chantel speak with him?"

Something had happened. That much was for sure. And Edward had internalized it, whatever it was. He'd dealt with it by staying close to the granddaughter who, like her mother, didn't give any sign of returning his affection. One might think that Cara had soured her daughter against Edward, except that Joy had not known, until she'd been told several weeks ago, that he'd even existed.

"He agreed to speak with Chantel," Edward

said now, his fingers still busy against his palm. When Lila barely caught herself before reaching out to take that hand in her own, she slid her hands under her thighs.

"The first thing he did was ask Chantel if anyone had found his wife. Chantel was convinced that he was honestly worried about Cara. That he has no idea where she is. She said he had tears in his eyes when she told him that no one had reported seeing her."

"So…if Shawn didn't kill her, this means she's probably still alive." Lila tried to keep the excitement out of her voice. She was relied upon to instill calm.

Edward merely shrugged. "If he didn't kill her, where is she? And why hasn't she contacted anyone? By all accounts, my daughter doted on her daughter. From everything we've heard, Cara would die before she'd abandon Joy."

"Maybe she thinks Joy is safe with Mary."

He shook his head. "It's been all over the news in both Nevada and California that Shawn is in jail—partially due to the alert put out about Cara's abduction and the vehicle they were in."

"Maybe she's in the hospital someplace with amnesia…" She was grasping. But she had this strong urge to ease his pain. To give him hope.

When she knew that her responsibility was to help him accept what was and find a way to move forward.

Hope was the basis of all healing. But relying on false hope meant avoiding that healing. She, of all people, knew that.

"There's more." He sounded the same as he had all along. But she was sitting close enough to see the nuances on his face, the tightening of the cords in his neck as though he was struggling to hold back tears.

It was then that Lila knew Edward needed a friend that night. And that she was going to have to get whatever was going on with her under control, because she couldn't turn her back on a family member in need.

CHAPTER SEVEN

"SHAWN CLAIMS THAT he didn't hurt Mary. He admits that he and Cara were fighting. Mary grabbed Joy and was taking her away so that she wouldn't witness the altercation between her parents. He says that Cara lunged after her, to keep Joy with her, and that she tripped, knocking into Mary who lost her balance and fell face-first down their front steps."

"Mary's injuries were consistent with being hit. They weren't consistent with a fall."

Edward nodded. "When Chantel asked him to explain why there weren't scrapes or bruises on her legs or back or shoulders, he says that Cara, in an attempt to save Mary, fell with her and took the brunt of the impact."

"An explanation for the injuries to her when she's found."

Jutting his chin, Edward said, "He's either a psychopath—and, if so, I fear for my daughter more than ever—or he's telling the truth, according to Chantel. She said that when they initially told him his sister was dead, tears rolled down his face. He'd have to be a damned good actor to cry on cue like that."

Lila took a sip of wine because she simply didn't know what else to do. Nothing felt right. "So, you think now that he didn't hurt Cara? That she's gone of her own accord for some reason?"

"He says that when Cara saw how badly Mary was hurt she panicked. She begged him to take her away like he did when they left Florida. He said that he went a little nuts himself at that point, leaving his sister like that and running off with his wife. He says that he didn't want to lose Cara and that's why he took his friend's van. He says he can't imagine life without Cara. Chantel believed he meant it."

Lila didn't want to believe any part of the scenario was possible. Not for Edward or for Joy.

"How does he explain being alone in the van when he was found?"

"He says they'd pulled off to the side of the road to get some sleep, and when he woke up she was gone. Vanished. He has no idea what happened to her, but suggested that maybe she'd gotten out of the van to relieve herself. He says he looked all over the area but never found her."

"And what about Joy's account? What about the monster she talked about hurting her mommy? She said the monster's name was Daddy."

Edward nodded. Shrugged.

Could they convict a man solely on the testi-

mony of a seven-year-old girl? By the time Mary
had shown up with Joy at the neighbors', Mary
had been bleeding profusely and starting to slur
her words. They hadn't been able to get much
out of her. Who was to say that Cara and Shawn
hadn't run off, as Shawn claimed? Mary had died
before she could tell anyone what really happened
that morning in the Amos home.

"Surely the authorities believe he killed his sister or they wouldn't have indicted him."

"There was enough evidence for a grand jury
to indict. That doesn't mean a prosecutor will be
able to prove enough to get a conviction. Not unless we find Cara. Or Joy can lead us to more
clues. There were no medical or other records to
establish a pattern of abuse. If the case proceeds,
it could come down to watching the defense tear
apart Joy's testimony."

"They wouldn't put her on the stand. Most particularly not to testify against her father."

Edward shook his head. "They'd tape a session
with her. She wouldn't know it was for court or to
get her father in trouble."

And that clearly wasn't what was bothering Edward.

"Did Chantel indicate to you what she believes
about all of this?"

"She said she didn't honestly know. That since
she's never met Cara, and since I've had virtually no contact with her for the past ten years,

we have no way of knowing what she's like now. What she's capable of doing. Or could have done."

"But…"

He shook his head, his look intense as he met her gaze. "She has shown a history of turning her back on family, on me, her father, without looking back."

"I understand that," Lila said, knowing exactly what to say now. "But look at Joy, Edward. That little girl is sweet and precious. She didn't just get that way. She's a product of your daughter's love and care."

"What if Mary was the one who raised her?"

Lila shook her head. "Joy very clearly said that her mama told Mary to take her."

"She's seven. She could easily have confused or transposed the situation in her mind, making it what she needed it to be."

He was a man of science. She wasn't going to help ease his torment with her current line of thought.

"What do you feel inside, Edward? Do you think Cara stumbled into Mary, rolled with her down the stairs and left her to run off with her husband?"

Edward continued to meet her gaze. His eyes looked…weary now. And moist.

"Why would she do that?" she asked him. "Why would she run off and leave the successful business they'd built?"

"They left his school in Florida. Just up and left."

"To get away from you, it sounds like. So, why now?"

"Because they could see how badly Mary was hurt and they were frightened. Didn't know if Cara would be sent to jail."

"Why leave Joy?"

"They'd be harder to trace without a child."

"So why, after Shawn left with her, would Cara suddenly leave him?"

"She wouldn't."

"So, where is she?"

He didn't answer. And didn't look like he felt any better, either.

Lila could only give him what she had. "Do you believe she did this, Edward?"

"No. But…"

Lila shook her head. "No buts right now. If you believe Joy over Shawn, then you need to focus on that. Focus on helping Joy. On finding Cara. And keeping Shawn behind bars."

Because that was what Edward needed. Focus. He nodded. Took a sip of wine. And, eventually, gave her a long slow smile that scared her to death.

Prospector, Nevada

CARA WOKE UP Saturday morning with a sense of purpose. Feeling a thousand times better than she could remember, more rested and alert than she'd felt in a while, with energy pulsing through her veins. She'd...

Nothing. Lying inert, on the verge of wakefulness, she hadn't known any better. All it took was a move of her sore wrist, a touch to her face, and she was fully awake.

There was no longer a purpose to her life. She was in a life she had no right to continue living.

Because of what she'd done.

So maybe she was physically better. That strength, while wasted, gave her the ability to look beyond the immediate pain. To think clearly.

To face the horrible truth.

With a pre-dawn grayness shining in from the window across from her bed, she couldn't keep her mind at bay any longer. She'd committed murder. If Shawn found her, she either had to go on living with him, putting up with the more and more frequent blasts of violent anger, tiptoeing around so she didn't inadvertently set off an attack...

Or he'd turn her in.

It all came pouring back to her. He'd given her the option in the van that last afternoon they were together. However long ago that had been now. She wasn't sure anymore. Had lost track of time and days sometime during her weeks of captivity with Shawn. He'd told her that as long as she stayed with him, she'd be safe. He'd keep her safe. And if she tried to leave, he'd turn her in...

Except Shawn hadn't kept her safe. Not for years and years.

Maybe not ever.

No one had kept Cara safe. Not since Mom got sick. And then Mom hadn't been kept safe, either...

Which was why she'd promised herself she'd always keep Joy safe.

And then Shawn had started hitting Cara harder.

Another memory flashed. When she'd first awoken in that van, her entire body hurting, she'd been looking for Joy, inconsolable in her panic. That was when Shawn had told her that they'd lost Joy forever because of her, because of what she'd done. She'd wanted to die right then and there, but he wouldn't let her. He'd kept telling her how much he needed her. He'd held her as she'd sobbed...

"Cara? You awake?"

Still reeling, Cara turned her head toward the door. If she pretended to be asleep would he go away? Or come in and wake her?

"Yes."

"It's time for your antibiotic." For a while there he'd been waking her to take her pills. The day before, she'd been up to use the restroom before the pill was due. And now he stood outside the door and called to her?

What had changed?

"I'll be out in a minute," she told him, throwing off the covers and grabbing...nothing. She'd left her clothes outside the door to be washed the night before. Was wearing the makeshift gown he'd crafted for her.

"I left your clothes just outside the door for you," he said, almost as though he could read her mind. Who knew what she might have told him when she'd been out of her head with pain?

She didn't think she'd said anything. She hadn't been out of her head. She'd been beaten to a pulp and exhausted. "Thank you," she called back and, giving him a second to retreat, went to reach her arm around the door for her clothes.

The underwear was there, the bra and jeans, and three shirts. Hers and two others. T-shirts, both of them. A purple and a blue. From different years for the same Heart-Run. They'd be too big for her.

But better than the bloodstained T-shirt of Shawn's she'd had on under her sweater jacket.

She chose the purple one. Because, in the color world, purple was known for bringing spiritual peace. For assisting in honest, deep, true thought. She'd lost any hope of good Karma having her back. She was well and truly on her own now.

She had to be able to count on her own mind.

As she pulled the shirt down over her torso, she suffered a stab of guilt. Purple was a healing color. Violet vibrated at the highest frequency and, as such, healers believed it to be a potent tool. Cara might have an aversion to doctors, but she'd done a lot of reading. Studying. Learning.

For Joy's sake and for her own, too.

Joy.

Her heart caught, her throat tightened. Tears sprang to her eyes. And her mind closed in.

No. She'd lost any right she'd had to think of…

She had no business healing. So the purple shirt was the wrong one.

Taking it off, she replaced it with her own. Bloodstains were her style now. She couldn't pretend otherwise.

With a last look around the room that had offered solace to a criminal, she went out to face the doctor. To convince him that she was just fine and could be on her way that morning.

As soon as she got back out on the mountain, she'd figure out what that way would be.

CHAPTER EIGHT

THE FIRST THING Simon noticed when Cara came out of the bedroom was that she'd foregone his clean shirts for her washed but bloodstained one.

She wasn't settling in.

He took her message in stride.

Other than the one cheek, her face looked better. So much so that he could begin to make out natural features. Her expression remained bland, giving the same nothing away he'd been getting since he brought her inside, but he figured the pain of facial movement alone would explain some of that.

In his usual jeans and flannel shirt, Simon handed her two pills—an antibiotic and a pain reducer. She took the antibiotic.

"In exchange for putting drops in your eye," she told him, waiting, apparently, for his acquiescence.

"I've already done them this morning." Six tries. Not good, but not bad, either.

Her nod didn't give away anything of what she was really thinking. Now that she was up and about, her reticence bothered him.

Made him curious.

Probably because he'd made his life so damned small she was consuming it. That would explain why he'd lain awake the night before trying to figure out how to keep her from leaving and either returning to the bastard who'd hurt her and left her for dead or being found by him.

"I made oatmeal and toast," he said, taking two bowls from the counter and bringing them to the table, then going back to retrieve the plate of buttered toast.

She'd used neither milk—probably because it was reconstituted from powder and pretty crappy—nor brown sugar the last time he'd served the dish, so he didn't bother with either.

Mouth open, as though she was going to argue, Cara looked away, pulled out the seat by the kitchen and sat. Ahead of her now, he'd set the opposite side for himself. Because everything about the morning was planned.

"I know you're anxious to be on your way," he started, more nervous than the conversation warranted. He was a grown man with a mission—one that he'd been neglecting for the five days she'd been there—not a schoolboy lacking confidence.

Her nod was directed more toward her bowl than him.

"I'd advise against you doing anything as strenuous as hiking out of here," he told her. "With that facial fracture, slight though it is, something as little as a branch to your face could cause serious, permanent and possibly life-threatening damage."

He wasn't her jailer. She was a free adult.

And so was he. An adult with a troubled conscience with which it was already hard to live.

"I'll be careful." She ate as slowly, as deliberately, as always. She had to be in pain, but didn't wince. Didn't pause. Because for her, living through pain was habit. Taken in stride. It wasn't the first time he'd had that impression. But it strengthened his conviction as his appetite dissipated.

"I, of course, can't keep you here," he said, putting down his spoon. "But neither can I let you just walk out into the desert…possibly back into the hands of the man who hurt you. I'm sorry, Cara, I can't do it."

Her gaze shot to his then. Wide-eyed. Filled with fear.

"I'm not going to hold you hostage," he quickly assured her. "You're free to go. But if you do leave, I have to call the authorities. To alert them to the fact that I am aware of a domestic violence situation. As a doctor, I'm under legal obligation to do so."

Not technically. He wasn't licensed to practice medicine in Nevada—his helping her was legal only under the Good Samaritan law. And because initially it had been an emergency situation, and she'd refused outside medical care.

Her gaze didn't waver. The panic was there, almost blindingly so, reminding him of a deer in headlights.

"I mean you no harm," he told her. "To the contrary. Nor am I particularly welcoming of the company. I'm here alone by choice. My reasons for that choice have not changed."

TMI. Not in his plan. But neither had that stark fear been.

She blinked.

"But I can't let you just walk out of here."

Putting down her spoon, she wiped her mouth with her napkin.

"I'm happy to take you anywhere you need to go." Hell, at the moment, he'd be happy to drive her to another state. Hopefully one in which she'd feel comfortable getting help.

"There are shelters," he continued, "places a woman can go to be safe from situations like yours."

She didn't seem to be the least bit comforted by the news. Obviously, she knew about domestic violence shelters. She was an educated woman.

"No matter how powerful you might think your husband is, the law is stronger…"

He hoped to God it was. Believed it was.

"I'll testify to the state in which I found you. To the things you said when you were half-comatose with pain and exposure…"

"No."

No to him testifying? To going to another state?

He supposed he could forcibly pick her up, put her in the car and drive her to the police station. Trying to picture how that would work without him somehow restraining her—which he absolutely was not going to do—he rethought that option.

"I said that I wish to be alone to reassure you that I'm not taking this stance out of any selfish reason, and that's true, but I didn't mean to imply that you are not welcome to remain for whatever length of time it takes for you to be ready to face your future."

"Until you've determined that I've healed enough to leave, you mean."

He shook his head. "I know that's what I originally said, partially because I was so eager to have my solitude uninterrupted. But…I realize now…I can't just send you back out there. Not without alerting someone. Your husband is still out there. He knows where he left you. There's every chance that he could find you again."

"He's not going to try."

"You sound sure about that."

"I know Shawn. He left me for dead. He's washed his hands of me."

"Then why are you afraid for me to go to the authorities? To take you to the hospital? To a shelter even?"

"Because he'll be watching, to make certain

that I don't show up someplace. He'll stay in the area. Keep tabs. He knows my social security number. My driver's license number. All of our accounts are joint accounts. He knows all of my passwords."

It was a lot for her to say all at once.

And there was more she wasn't saying. He was certain of that. He was also certain that, for his purposes, keeping her safe until she was healthier and rested and he could talk her into getting help, he didn't need to know her secrets.

The less he knew, the less involved with her he'd be. The better able to tolerate her presence for however long it took and then get on with his life.

"But if we go to the police, they'll arrest him and you'll be safe."

"For how long? Until he posts bail?" She shook her head.

"He left you for dead. They might not post bail."

"Then I go to court and it's his word against mine. I have no proof that he did this to me."

"It's obvious he's done it before…"

"Surfing accidents. He has witnesses. I suck at surfing," she reminded him, as though that was only one of her many failures.

He listened, and his conviction grew. In leaps and bounds. Beyond anything he'd imagined during the long night.

"But you want to leave. You'll have no resources, can't access any bank accounts. What's your plan? What would you do?"

Her silent stare was more answer than he could translate...except to know that whatever she'd thought to do, she knew he wouldn't approve.

"So, it seems to me that your best option is to stay here long enough for him to figure you for dead."

"And then what?"

"We take you to a shelter in another state."

She didn't like the idea. Her frown told him so.

"As soon as you're ready, we go."

"How long do you plan to stay here?"

He'd considered that there were things she'd want to know. Things he had no real reason not to tell her other than that he was adamant about getting away from the well-meaning disbelievers who were trying to get him to accept his right eye as blind for fear that they might make him lose faith and give up when he knew that all he had to do was keep working it, keep up the drops, keep believing...

He had clouds, not blankness. His optic nerve was alive.

And being around someone who couldn't even tell...

It helped.

"I'm on indefinite leave." He gave her the answer he'd come up with in the wee hours of the morning. Less was best.

He'd give as little as she'd accept.

Her frown deepened, but there was no fear in her eyes now. Odd how he was learning to read her in such a short time—this woman he really didn't know at all.

"You facing a malpractice suit?"

"No." Though he'd considered making one up. With her stated distaste for doctors, it was an excuse he figured she'd easily buy.

He wasn't out to sell her on anything, though. Or sell himself out, either.

"My medical record is exemplary."

He couldn't help but wonder what had turned her off doctors. Couldn't help but wonder if she'd gone to a doctor for help in the earlier days of her husband's beatings and had somehow ended up back in the abuser's hands.

Not necessarily through the fault of a doctor, but if the system had let her down...

All the more reason he had to show her that there were good guys in the world. Maybe, if he could show this beaten-down woman that he could be counted on to do the right thing, his ex-wife's damning accusations wouldn't ring so loudly in his mind—wouldn't leave so much weight hanging on his back.

Sitting completely still, Cara was studying him.

"You could be lying."

"Yes."

"Why are you on indefinite leave?"

Her brown eyes—they seemed larger in her face now that the swelling was dissipating—seemed to pin him to his seat. And then, as he might have predicted, she glanced away. Escaping back into the world she guarded so carefully.

"Personal reasons."

"If I am to stay here with you, I need more." She swallowed. Licked her lips. Didn't look at him. "I need to know what you're running from."

"I'm not running," he told her quite emphatically. "Like you, I'm healing."

All night long he'd tried to come up with something, and there it was…in the space of a two-second answer. Just waiting for him.

She could ask what ailed him, but he knew she wouldn't.

She watched him, though, as he cleared their bowls and then the toast.

"I expect to help." She didn't sound injured. Or weak. "I'm a good cook. I don't mind cleaning. I can sew, too, if you have anything that needs to be mended."

So…was she…

"I feel that we should take turns in the bed."

"No." He had his limits. "I'd go nuts cooped up in the bedroom all night, fearing waking you if I needed to be up and about…"

True. What was also true, and he didn't share, was that with her getting well, he wanted her behind a closed bedroom door when she went to bed at night. The sight of her the night before, standing outside his bathroom, the touch of her gentle fingers on his flesh as she'd put drops in his eyes— she'd ceased being a patient in those moments.

"I will do your eyedrops for you."

He'd been determined to get down to one try for each drop. But in the scheme of things it was little enough to give up to keep her safe until he could get her to go someplace safer.

He thought of her fingers on his face. In the bathroom.

"Here, in the kitchen, pills and drops, at breakfast and dinner." A schedule. One he could chart— mentally at least.

"I don't want any more painkillers. I don't like what it does to my head."

"You're going to be a lot less comfortable without it."

"Truthfully, Doc, I feel better today than I've felt in…a while."

Her pain had to be at a six. The face fracture alone…

Which made him think this wasn't her first zygoma fracture. Or even her worst. He wondered about her sense of smell. About pain in her jaw when she chewed. He wondered if her features would be uneven when the swelling finally departed.

"Why didn't he ever hit your stomach or your mouth?"

Probably not a doctor-patient question—he

regretted asking before he'd even completed the words.

"Stomach because organs are precious. And my mouth because he likes kissing."

The bowl he'd been scrubbing cracked in two.

"But he didn't mind doing that to your face?" he asked, discreetly picking the two pieces of earthenware out of the sink and throwing them away.

"He only did it when he got jealous. It kept other guys from looking at me."

She said the words so matter-of-factly he thought, at first, that he'd misunderstood. But when he replayed them in his mind, he knew he hadn't. He glanced over. Her back was still to him. She hadn't moved.

"You said this bastard owned a surfing school?" He justified the question by telling himself that if he was going to keep her safe from the man's future clutches, he had to know facts.

"On Ventura Beach."

An hour north of his own home on the California coast.

Wait. She'd seemed familiar with Los Angeles Children's...

"Do you have kids?"

She'd said it was the two of them in the van, but she hadn't expressly said there weren't others present. If the bastard had her children...if...

"Not anymore," she said. And with that, she

stood, excused herself and disappeared down the hall toward the bathroom.

Leaving Simon white-faced, his entire world spinning. Her mistrust of doctors…familiarity with the medical field…*not anymore*. She'd had a child. One a doctor hadn't been able to save? Because her husband's fist had caused too much damage to littler bones than hers?

The pieces all fell into place.

Did she not trust the hospital to keep her safe because she'd taken her child to them and they hadn't been able to save that small life? Or prevent his or her father from doing further damage? Damage that had eventually been fatal?

It made sense. Something had happened to make Cara, a woman who'd clearly been beaten over a long period of time, suddenly pretend symptoms that would allow her to escape her husband's clutches. Something so horrible that she'd been willing to die just to get away from the man.

Or maybe she no longer had a reason to remain with him.

Whatever had happened, two pertinent facts resonated with Simon.

He had a life to help save.

And he was going to have a woman in his cabin full-time.

CHAPTER NINE

Santa Raquel, California

LILA MCDANIELS WAS not comfortable Thursday morning. She'd very deliberately chosen one of her less fashionable suits—all of which, new or old, were gray or brown—with a plain dark beige blouse. She'd pulled her hair into its usual bun. Her makeup, just a light foundation to protect her skin, was no more and no less than usual. Her shoes were the same serviceable thick-soled walkers she'd been wearing for years. No jewelry. She sat in her usual chair in the office she'd had at the Stand since the shelter's inception. There was nothing about that morning to make her feel in any way different from any other day in her life.

And yet…as she sat at her desk in midafternoon, she was…not at peace. Edward had been in a few hours before. She'd seen him each of the six days since he'd had wine and cheese in her suite, even if just for a few minutes. They'd talked at length the previous night, too—when, for the third time, he'd had to bring Joy back to The Lemonade Stand. A third night they'd tried and failed to have a grandfather-granddaughter sleepover.

Lila felt the failure acutely.

Even though nothing that was going on with him was her fault. He'd be the first to say so. He couldn't tell her enough how much he valued her friendship.

Actually, he'd only mentioned it twice, but she recognized that, for a man as reserved as Edward, twice was a big deal.

She valued his friendship, too. More every day, it seemed.

And that was the crux of the problem. Things were getting out of hand. Beyond, apparently, her ability to step aside and be neutral. What did she do about that?

She'd been asking herself the question for the past week. Before that, really. And had no answers. She had no boss to go to. No superior to whom she could defer this case.

And she wouldn't defer it even if she could. Joy and Edward needed her help. And she was damn well going to give it.

Closing her eyes, she pictured her own little girl at seven. It was the year she'd gotten sick. And there'd been nothing Lila could do to help her.

Was that why Joy's situation was personal to her?

Was it possible it had nothing to do with Edward at all?

The knock on her door shook her out of the reverie she was falling into far too often these days. After her meeting with Edward that morning, she'd called Julie Fairbanks to ask her to stop in for tea. She'd had to wait for the busy philanthropist to return from a children's charity board luncheon in LA. And then to have an art therapy session alone with Joy immediately afterward.

Julie's drawings of Amy helped Joy communicate. They seemed to give the little girl security. Julie, more than most of them, was bearing the brunt of responsibility for the sweet, dark-haired girl. A victim of abuse herself, of violent date rape and years of forced cover-up, Julie had only just begun to venture out of the suite in her family mansion for more than just board meetings. She'd been volunteering at the Stand less than a year when Joy had been brought to them. She wasn't as used to setting heart boundaries as the rest of them were.

And she was being asked to give the most heart.

Because, through her children's books, a mute Joy had bonded with her. They'd thought that as soon as Joy opened up, began sharing her fears, Julie would be able to take a step back, to slowly fade from Joy's life.

Knowing that no matter how much she grew to love the little girl, she would still have to let her go, Julie had still been willing to help. Lila admired her.

And hated what she was about to do.

Hated that she had to ask even more of a woman who'd lost so much—both of her parents, who'd died shortly before the rape, her youth and ability to trust, her ability to enjoy sex...

Not an infrequent visitor to Lila's private sitting room, Julie, still dressed in the black dress pants and black-and-white tweed jacket she'd worn to her luncheon, helped prepare their tea. It was a good thing she knew where the little lemon cookies were and the plate they went on, because Lila was suddenly dealing with a flashback to the last time she'd had someone in her suite. Edward.

She hadn't sat at the little table since.

Julie, who'd never sat at the table, didn't even seem to notice it there as she carried the tray into the sitting room and placed it on the small claw-footed coffee table set before the two rose-upholstered antique chairs.

She waited for Lila to pour. The familiar motion, the beautiful setting, brought Lila back to her calm. Her purpose.

"How are you?" Lila asked, not shy about getting right into Julie's skin as she met the younger woman's gaze. With Julie, that was what it took. Though unpaid, Julie was still Lila's responsibility while she was at the Stand.

"I'm good." The blue-eyed, dark-haired woman smiled. A real smile. It gave Lila's heart a boost to see it.

"More specifically, tell me how things are progressing with Hunter."

While the woman's new romance shouldn't be any of Lila's business, in the moment it had to be.

"He wants to get married…" Julie blurted, but not happily. Lila paid attention to the expressions on Julie's face. The new glow of happiness that, just a couple of months ago, she'd despaired of ever seeing there. The fear.

And the resolve, as well. Lila wasn't there to judge Julie. Or even to counsel her. She was there to find out if Julie could help them.

But first she had to be convinced, beyond a reasonable doubt, that helping them wouldn't be unduly detrimental to Julie. Because that was Lila's own code.

Lila had sacrificed one human being's best interests for another once before in her life. Her son for her daughter.

Never again.

"Tell me about it," she said now, needing to know how Julie was handling her struggles. If she was progressing…

"I want to marry him so badly," Julie said. "But I can't. Not until I know I can be a real wife to him." Tears filled her eyes, but she didn't look away. Sometimes Lila didn't know where Julie found her strength, how she managed to face her fear, take hold and forge forward. It was a remarkable ability. One she wished she could give to every single woman who walked through their doors.

Lila nodded, understanding. In a way, she even related personally to Julie's feelings. Aware of her own limitations, she knew she would never have another close personal relationship.

For her, it was a definite never. For Julie, though, there was every possibility that…

"He's so good to me," Julie was saying, smiling now through her tears. "So patient and sweet and funny."

The woman was in love—with a man Lila greatly admired. Hunter's almost uncanny ability to sense when people were feeling stressed, his way of lightening moments without really even realizing what he was doing had, in Lila's opinion, saved Joy's life.

The fact that the man was also Edward's nephew didn't really have anything to do with how fond she was of him, Lila assured herself silently. They were related by marriage only—Hunter's father had married Edward's sister, neither of whom Lila had ever even met…

"Edward says that you've stayed at Hunter's place." He'd told her that morning as they discussed plans for Joy.

"He stays at mine more often. I think, eventually, he'll move into the mansion with me. It's my home. It's far too big for just Colin and Chantel, even with a baby on the way. Three families could

live there without ever seeing each other if they
didn't want to. My grandfather built it for just that
purpose, to house his entire family and yet let everyone be independent..." The speed with which
Julie's words flew had Lila reaching out to hold
the other woman's hand. She gave it a squeeze.
And then let go, returning her hands to her lap.

"It's okay for you to find security and happiness in your home, Julie. You and your brother
are blessed to have been given the opportunity
to have that home."

"It's just that...I hid out there for so long. I...
don't want...people to think that I still need it
that way. Or that I'm unable to be healthy somewhere else."

"What does Hunter say?"

Julie grinned. "Are you kidding? He loves it
there." She paused and then added, "He slid down
the banister last night."

Feeling so genuinely happy for the couple, Lila
took a moment to let it be. And then said, "With
your studio in your home, it makes perfect sense
that you two would live there."

She was pretty sure she was going to ask for
Julie's help.

Julie nodded. "I want to ask him to move in
with me," she said.

"What's holding you back?"

"I know he'll push for marriage again. You
know Hunter. Once he knows what he wants,

there's no stopping him. But I just keep looking down the road, you know? He's all het up with love right now, with the newness of it all—but what happens later? When we're used to each other and have a routine and maybe even start to take the relationship a little bit for granted? What happens then if I still can't make love with him? At some point he's going to want to make real love to a woman. And…he wants children."

"Don't you?" Lila couldn't imagine a woman more suited to motherhood than Julie.

"Of course I do."

"There are ways to make that happen without traditional sex," Lila pointed out.

Julie nodded. "We've talked about that. There's always artificial insemination."

Julie didn't sound all that happy with the solution, but at least she and Hunter were talking. There were no elephants in the room between them, apparently. Lila was feeling better and better about Julie's recovery, her happiness, and about the Joy plan, too.

"He's… Every night Hunter has some new idea—some new way to get me to relax and feel physical pleasure," Julie said. Because intimate talk among residents was not only common, but crucial to healing, Lila didn't even blink.

"Are any of them working?" Lila's sudden prayer was based solely on a surge of hope for Julie's sake alone. The young woman, who dedicated her life to helping others, deserved her own happiness.

"Somewhat," Julie said, her cheeks coloring a little bit. "I've been able to feel desire…it just shuts down before we actually get anyplace with it."

"Give it time," Lila told her. "I'm sure Dr. Larson is telling you the same. The fact that the feelings are there means you aren't incapable…"

Julie nodded. Then gestured to the untouched tea and cookies. "Should we have some of this?" she asked.

"I have a question to ask you first." Lila had made up her mind. "But I need your word that if you have any hesitation, any at all, you tell me immediately."

"Of course."

"Edward had to bring Joy back again last night." The man was taking the failure hard. Edward had made a comment about there being something elementally wrong with him. First his daughter and now his granddaughter wanting nothing to do with him.

He was a man who loved generously. Unselfishly. Lila one hundred percent believed that Joy needed him. They just had to find a way for the two hearts to meet.

"I heard," Julie said. "Hunter told me when I talked to him on my way back from LA. Edward's taking it pretty hard."

Lila nodded, feeling…guilty…for already having firsthand knowledge, and for the fact that she wasn't telling anyone about Edward's middle-of-the-night calls to her personal cell phone.

"With Shawn in jail and no sign of Cara, we need to get Joy out of The Lemonade Stand and settled into a family environment as soon as possible. The longer she stays here, the more we delay her ability to resume her life."

Julie nodded. "Hunter wondered if Edward was going to take her back to Florida with him. His dad and Betty are there. I know Betty would love to help raise her." Julie would no longer be the little girl's surrogate.

But it wasn't the younger woman's potential grief that stopped Lila's heart. Or had her mood taking a sudden nose dive.

Edward was going back to Florida eventually. She knew that. Needed that.

"I'm sure he will, at some point," Lila said, forging ahead. "But not until she's comfortable enough to go with him happily. To that end, we came up with an idea…"

Julie waited, her expression open. Lila knew a moment of real envy. And then fear. What in the hell was wrong with her? Why, after all these years, was she suddenly faltering?

"We believe, if you and Hunter were close by, Joy would be able to make it through the night away from the Stand." Lila dove right in. "With

Hunter being Edward's family, it would be easy to explain to Joy that she's spending the night with Edward, but that they're staying with family instead of at the hotel. We feel that taking her to a real home, and also with you and Hunter present, that we would give her the best chance at success."

Julie nodded. "Fine. I'm in. I'm assuming you'll want to do this at Hunter's house? I was actually thinking, you know, when I ask Hunter to move in with me and all, if Edward was still here, that maybe he'd move out of the hotel and into Hunter's house. It's really a lovely place. There's a heated pool… Joy could swim…"

"I need to make certain that I'm being clear, here. We aren't asking you to spend time with her, or be a part of the evening. We just need Joy to know that the house belongs to Hunter and that the two of you are close by. Her care will be left solely up to Edward."

"I understand." Julie nodded. "Hunter and I have already talked about the fact that I'm giving so much of my heart to Joy when, in the end, someone else will be her mother. I'm going to miss her horribly when she goes, of course. It'll be hard. But I have Hunter, my family, my Amy books. And…I love that little girl. If I can help her be happy…whatever it takes…"

Lila smiled. There. Things had fallen nicely into place, as they'd obviously been meant to. That was it, then. Edward's family would be there for him and they were all going to be just fine. She was quite close to being able to let go.

CHAPTER TEN

Prospector, Nevada

THERE WAS SOMETHING off about the man. Odd. Every morning Cara stood over him as he sat in a chair at the table before breakfast, peered down into his eye and administered drops. He never blinked. His gaze never connected with hers, either.

She found his ability to focus so completely kind of impressive. Figured that it might come from being a pediatric thoracic surgeon.

Working on the hearts of children…just the thought of it made her shudder.

Every morning he'd have breakfast ready by the time she left the bedroom. She did the dishes. And prepared lunch, after which he'd clean up. Dinner was determined over lunch. Drops and pills before breakfast and dinner. Every morning and every afternoon he left the cabin to spend a couple of hours outdoors.

She figured that was for her benefit, to give her space, and always showered during his morning walk.

As she sat alone in the cabin every day, Cara told herself that the doctor's outside adventures were for his benefit, as well. She had no idea what he did out there. He never came back with anything. He'd been out the morning he'd found her. Maybe long walks were part of whatever process he was going through.

While the doctor was out, Cara also cleaned the cabin. One chore each day. Dusting. Sweeping. The bathroom. And she read.

They both read. A lot. She read instead of having to make conversation. Why he did, she couldn't say.

And by the time darkness fell each night, she was exhausted. More, she supposed, from holding at bay the demons inside her—the sense that she was in a surreal wasteland—than from any physical malady.

The doc was still concerned about her face. Telling her every night, as she excused herself to her bedroom right after dinner, to remember not to lie down with the left side of her face against the pillow. She could have told him she'd slept on her back for more years now than she could remember.

She also could have told him that all of his doctoring was wasted on a body that wasn't long for this world.

Except that she wouldn't.

And she wasn't sure, exactly, how the big plan

for her would play out now. When Shawn had left her to die she'd been ready. Had expected to go quietly to sleep and pass over. She'd been found, instead, and now she was too healthy to just lie down and die.

Every morning and every night she lay in bed and asked Fate to make her way known to her. She begged for merciful quickness. The longer the doctor kept her with him, the more she rested, the more she healed and the more confused she grew.

As a bad person, she had no future to build. That was a given. Because of Joy…what Cara had done…she had no life to live. And yet, there she was.

Trapped by a man's conscience in a situation that meant either going to the authorities or staying with him until she healed enough and was ready to go to the authorities.

She was never going to be ready.

Unless that was the Karma she'd earned for herself. To spend the rest of her life in prison.

A fate worse than death. But was it her fate?

Sitting on the couch, she saw the doctor at the edge of the yard, leaning a stick up against the back of a big sagebrush. Should she tell him she was ready to go to the authorities?

The thought took her air. Sent a searing pain up her neck and into her head. She closed her eyes, letting it pass. Waited for the sudden nausea to dissipate. Clearly, the authorities weren't the right answer.

Not yet, anyway.

Eyes opening slowly as the room ceased to spin, Cara's first sight was the doctor walking toward the front door of the cabin. His steps were sure. Strong. Confident. Just like him.

Could he be the reason she was still alive? Were the fates using her, just like they'd used Mom? Through all of the procedures, the pain, Beth Mantle had maintained that when she was meant to go, the fates would take her. And until then, she'd assured Cara time and time again—with her frail and shaking fingers still sifting through Cara's hair, like she was the one meant to give the comfort—you never knew who Fate was helping through you.

Cara had been so sure that her mother had it all wrong. That it had been the meds talking. That the fact that her mother had beaten the odds and was still alive was because she wasn't meant to die.

And then, one night, after Cara had sat with her, read to her and they'd joked about the syringe she'd get for breakfast, Beth had simply closed her eyes and passed away.

No goodbye. No *This is it, Cara*. No warning. Just gone…

The door swung open.

"You look pale." The doctor came toward her. A surge of…comfort…washed over her so acutely Cara couldn't speak. Could only watch and wait as he reached her, gently slid a hand behind her neck, tilted her head and...studied her face.

With his free hand he lifted her wrist. Felt for her pulse.

"What's your middle name?" Her need to know was sudden. Inexplicable. Like she didn't know him well enough, or really know him, until she had his full name.

"What?" He dropped her wrist, but still was looking at her face. Touching softly here and there.

"I... That first day...you said your name. I saw your badge. Simon L. Walsh. What does the L. stand for?"

Dr. Simon L. Walsh.

He was the doctor insisting on watching over her. Not a man she would ever really know. Or who could ever know her.

"Lee," he said. "My middle name is Lee."

"You've never asked my last name." Why was she doing this? Forcing the issue so that he could turn her in and end this thing?

He stood back. Probably thinking about her face. And if the frown was anything to go by he wasn't wholly pleased.

She didn't give a damn about how her face was healing.

"I know your last name. It's Amos."

Heart pounding, she was glad he'd let go of her wrist.

"You left your driver's license on your night-stand the second night you were here. I saw it when I brought in your pills."

He'd known for days. And...

"You could call the authorities at any time. You could turn me in."

"Turn you in?" He frowned. "I don't want to turn you in, Cara. I want you to be willing to get help. The proper care that you need and deserve."

"But..."

"You said that first day that you had no other family. That there was no one." As he said the words, she vaguely remembered such a conversation. In the haze of the first pain- and sleep-filled hours she was in her bed. His bed. That she was borrowing. Temporarily. Just until she could figure out what she was supposed to do.

"If there's no one looking for you, other than your husband, there was no need to alert anyone where you are. And, to the contrary, a very good reason not to do so."

Peace settled over her as he took a seat in the chair she'd come to think of as his, where he read medical books in the morning. Fiction in the afternoon.

His methodical ways were part of what made him odd. And yet...they were a strange kind of comfort, too. Like the smell of him the morning he'd carried her in from what she'd thought would be her deathbed...

"I'm assuming it's his name?"

"Whose?" She was truly perplexed, glancing over to find him sitting there watching her.

"Your husband's."

Oh. "Amos? Yes." Fear shot through her as soon as she said the word aloud. Had Shawn already gone to the authorities?

Had he told them what she'd done?

Mary. Sweet Mary.

No, wait. Shawn wouldn't go to the cops. He'd have to tell them about hitting her. It had all started that morning when a guy at the fast-food restaurant where they'd taken Joy for breakfast had smiled and held the door for her as they'd been leaving...

The memory was brand-new to her. Right there. Clear as day. As though it had been there all along.

Mary had been there. Had seen that Cara hadn't flirted with anyone. She wouldn't let Shawn lie and say that his jealousy was Cara's fault for encouraging the guy...

Her heart rate slowed as she thought of her sister-in-law. And then sped up again. Mary was hurt. It was all Cara's fault.

She couldn't get a clear picture. Didn't know

why she had that impression. And let it go. Let the haze return.

Memories brought pain. Searing, unbearable pain.

She didn't need them. She knew that day had turned her into a criminal. They'd been on the run for a reason. Even if she hadn't done anything herself like he'd said she did, and she wasn't all that sure she hadn't, she'd gone with Shawn. They were accomplices in whatever had happened. There was no getting beyond that.

"Here, take this." The doctor, Simon, was standing in front of her, handing her a pain reliever and a glass of water. It wasn't until then that she realized she had tears falling down her cheeks.

"You looked pale when I came in. Your pupils were dilated, equally, and not alarmingly, so not indicative of brain bleed. Your pulse is slightly higher, indicating discomfort. Why not just tell me you have a headache and accept some relief?"

She'd always preferred to deal with the pain so she could keep her wits about her. "It's my night to make dinner."

"I'll get dinner. You take this pill and rest."

For once, she didn't even want to argue with him.

THE BASTARD'S NAME was Shawn Amos. He'd assumed, of course, but hadn't known for sure. The entire time Simon had been in the kitchen, preparing a stir-fry, he'd been hearing Cara's voice say that name. Amos.

Her husband had given her the name. A man who knew Cara far better than Simon did.

Who legally had more rights to Cara than Simon did.

His thoughts tumbled around, more akin to the way his mind had been working since the attack than the methodical, chart-like process he was used to. Still, he'd gone twenty minutes and prepared most of the dinner without once noticing that half his sight was nothing but clouds. Without closing his good eye just to see if there'd been some change.

Without even thinking about his blindness.

Looking around the corner at the woman sound asleep on his couch, Simon once again heard her voice say that name and felt an intense wave of anger…which was immediately at war with the protectiveness that welled up inside him.

Simon's first instinct upon having confirmation that *Amos* was her abuser's name was to call someone to find Amos. To arrest his ass and lock him away for the rest of his life.

And if he did? How could he be sure that Amos actually would end up in jail? If this was a first offense…

And how could he prove that Shawn Amos's fists were what had done the damage he was tending?

Most particularly if Cara wouldn't testify.

That was the key. Getting Cara to trust enough to let someone help her.

Like…she was letting him help her. The realization struck him. The woman trusted him enough to put her life in his hands. She trusted him to care for her. Not to hurt her. And not to break his promise to her.

Could it be that his job, then, was to continue nurturing her until she could trust him enough to let him take her someplace where they'd know how to help her with Shawn, where the law could protect her and where she would be safe until she could resume her life?

He didn't hate the idea. Just as he didn't hate having her around as much as he'd expected he would. As it turned out, he had all the time he needed outside to exercise his right eye in private. Was fairly certain that he was seeing more shadows in the clouds when he was in bright daylight.

Used to being in busy hospitals, Simon had never been a loner. And Cara was…easy…to be around.

Liking his plan, liking that he had a plan, Simon quietly set the plates on the table in the places that had become, in his mind, his and hers.

THE PAINKILLER HAD HELPED. Cara felt much better when she came to the table for dinner. Her head still hurt some—the usual tension headache—but not nearly as badly. Not the migraine kind. She was relaxed.

And surprisingly hungry.

"This is good," she said, enjoying the doctor's cabin version of stir-fry. Reaching for the bottle of soy sauce, she added a little more to the mixture of chicken, vegetables and noodles on her plate.

He shrugged. Reached for the soy where she'd put it, just to the right of him. If she'd known he wanted it, too, she could have just handed it to him...

The bottle flew to the floor.

Heart pounding, she jumped up. Moved toward the kitchen to grab a wet towel.

"I'm so sorr...umph." She ran into the doctor.

"Oh, my God." The words came out. The fear in her spread. "I'll clean it up," she said quickly. "You go ahead and sit in my place. It's my fault. I don't know what I was thinking. I placed it too close to the edge of the table..."

Warm wet towel in hand, she was heading down to her hands and knees on the floor when male hands pulled her upright. Held her in place.

Both of her arms flew upward, covering her face, causing the towel in her hand to whack him on the chin. "Please," she said, even though she knew begging didn't help. "I'm sorry. I'll clean it up."

She was going to offer to replace the bottle.

But she couldn't.

She had no money. No way to get money. She was living off him for free. Had been for well over a week. And…

"Cara." The doctor's voice called to her; his hands gripped both of her arms. He'd fight her until he had both of her wrists in one hand, and then he'd…

"Cara."

He'd cared so gently for her face. Wanted so badly for it to heal. She buried her head further in her arms. Trying not to cry. A sign of weakness. Which seemed to bring out the male instinct to conquer. "I'm sorry," she said against her chest.

And…the hands on her arms…left. They were just…gone. She thought of the soy sauce still on the cabin's linoleum floor. Needed to clean it up but was afraid to move. To incur wrath.

"Cara? Look at me please. I need to see your eyes." He was a doctor. Had been checking her pupils since the day she met him. She had to get the floor cleaned up.

Dropping down, wet towel still in hand, she wiped up the sauce. The doctor was there. She could feel his presence, but she couldn't see him. Not even his feet. Standing, she stumbled once on her way to the sink. Rinsed the towel well. And again, to be sure she wouldn't streak the floor with leftover soy, and went back to make certain there would be no sticky residue.

Hopefully, he was sitting back down. Eating. Before his dinner got cold.

The floor was clean. Cara rinsed the towel again, her panic easing as the warm water flowed over her skin. Calming her. It would be a bit before the shaking stopped.

Actually, she had no idea how long it would be. This was the first time she hadn't been physically injured along with the shaking.

"Can I please look at you now? If I promise not to touch?" The doctor's voice came from a few feet away. Calm and reassuring. As always.

And she realized what she'd done.

CHAPTER ELEVEN

IT TOOK EVERY ounce of Simon's strength not to take Cara Amos into his arms and hold her until she stopped shaking. Instead, he stood in the kitchen, attempting to keep enough distance to help her feel safe, yet close enough to catch her if she fell, and let her guide his actions.

When she raised her head—to stare at the bottle of soy sauce now back on the table—and he saw her pupils were dilated in a fight-or-flight response, he struggled to remain still. To pretend as though having a woman act this way with him was perfectly normal.

"I'm sorry." Her words were calm—as though they came from someone else.

"You have nothing to be sorry for. It was an accident."

"I..." She looked from the chair he'd vacated to the spot where they'd collided on her way from the sink.

"I was getting up to help you," he said. "I'm the one who knocked the bottle off the table."

"It didn't break," she said now, still sounding normal in spite of the almost childlike statement considering that they both knew the bottle had survived the incident much better than she had.

"No. The lid just popped off."

"I didn't put it on tightly enough." Her gaze hadn't left the bottle.

"Cara."

Arms wrapped around herself, she stood there. Shaking. But looking as though she was somehow trying to restrain the reaction.

"Cara, it's okay."

She nodded.

"Please come back to the table. Sit with me."

If nothing else, she'd given him the very clear sense that she'd do whatever he asked to please him so he wouldn't hurt her. The idea made him sick to his stomach. But he used it just enough to get her safely to her chair.

Then he handed her a glass of water. "Here," he said. "Please take a sip or two."

When he sat back down rather than towering over her, she did as he'd asked.

"Eat when you're ready," he told her, his mind reeling with what he'd just witnessed.

He, a man who could take a scalpel to the chest of a child and remain calm, had just about lost the contents of his stomach thinking of what must have happened to her to make her react as she had.

He was in way over his head.

He wasn't sure how much time had passed, how long they sat there, silently, him watching her staring at her plate. Long after the food had grown cold, Cara lifted her fork. Slowly, methodically, she lifted every bit of stir-fry into her mouth. While he sat helplessly, she stood, wordlessly carried the dishes to the sink, washed them.

When she reached for the cupboard where he'd been keeping his eyedrops, he lowered himself in his seat as he always did, tipped back his head and waited while she carefully placed both drops in the middle of his unseeing eye and resisted, as always, the need to blink so as not to lose any of the much-needed antipressure salve, and then went for her pills.

Whether she admitted to being in pain or not, he was going to insist that she take a pain reliever with her antibiotic.

"It's your last one," he said when he handed her the antibiotic. "Today was day ten."

She wanted to act as though nothing had happened; he was fine with that.

She nodded. Took both pills. Swallowed them.

"Thank you," she said. "Good night."

Turning, she walked with straight shoulders across the cabin, entered her room and quietly shut the door. Closing herself in with whatever hell lived inside her.

He should have told her he knocked the bottle off the table because he'd been forcing his right eye to know exactly where she'd placed it. Damned fool. He should have emphasized that the accident had had nothing to do with her. And everything to do with the fact that while he'd heard her set the bottle down, had seen part of her arm as she'd placed it on the table between them, he hadn't been able to see *it* and had been too proud to turn his head and make that obvious.

He considered a light knock on her door to quickly confess, but decided her distress at his invasion wouldn't be worth it.

Cara was a smart woman. A rational one. Once she calmed down, thought back over the incident, she'd know the bottle on the floor had been just what it was. An accident.

What remained to be seen was how she treated him now that he'd seen her inner struggle. Now that he'd met her demons.

Simon had a feeling that, in some ways, his seeing that was going to bother her more than if he'd done what she'd first feared and hit her.

THE NEXT MORNING, Simon had breakfast prepared and waiting, as usual, the second Cara opened her door. She wished him good morning, as usual. Said, in answer to his normal question, that she'd slept well. She ate everything in front of her. Took her pills. Administered his drops and did the dishes—as though nothing had happened the night before. Not trusting himself to just let it lie there, to let her deal with her trauma all alone— to not try to help somehow—Simon fled.

Outside and out of sight of the cabin, patch on, walking stick in his right hand and his left arm extended in front of him, he proceeded to face the challenge he knew he could master. Getting his right eye to see what was right in front of him.

SHOWERED, DRESSED AND too restless to sit, Cara spent the morning cleaning. She swept the cabin. Washed the linoleum floor on her hands and knees. Made chicken soup for lunch—homemade, not canned. It wouldn't be as good as what she made at home, but she boiled frozen chicken for broth, cut the chicken off the bone and put it in the broth she'd skimmed. And remembered Joy standing in the kitchen…between the stove and the back door. Mary had been with her. Just that. A flash. But she knew it was from their last day together. Before she and Shawn had had to leave.

When tears plopped into the pot, she brushed at her cheeks. Her pain might be real, it might even tear her apart, but it didn't make up for what she'd done. Adding dehydrated onions to the water, she stirred, alternately trying to avoid any more flashbacks and trying to recall any moments she could find that included her precious baby girl.

Joy's presence had changed Cara. Had made her life meaningful—given her purpose.

Adding frozen peas to the soup, sparingly because the doctor had far more canned goods than frozen, she stirred. Shied away from the memories that haunted her but searched desperately for them, too.

For the rest of the morning, she waited, on edge, for anything else that might come to her, but by the time the doctor returned to the cabin for lunch, she had nothing but frustration to show for it.

Afraid he'd bring up the night before over lunch, she was pleasantly surprised to find that he was just as willing as he had been at breakfast to let her eat in peace.

She tried to read while he cleaned up. To appear engrossed so he wouldn't talk to her. But the second he left for his afternoon time outside, she missed him.

Or rather, dreaded the idea of another set of hours stretching ahead of her with nothing but mental torment to offer.

She might never remember all of the details of the day that had virtually ended her life. Might never know how she'd felt as she'd crossed the line from worthy human being to criminal. But one thing was for certain, she couldn't just sit in a one-room cabin with a book on her lap for another afternoon.

From the moment the doctor had carried her into the cabin eleven days before, Cara had not ventured back outside. He'd suggested she might like some fresh air. Assured her he trusted her not to run off—as if she would. He'd call the cops and what chance would she have—a beach and city woman—against mountain men who not only knew the terrain, but probably knew all of its hiding places, too?

The doctor had suggested that she go outside while he was actually at the cabin, as opposed to when he was outside himself. In case she felt faint or had a problem, she could call out to him. She figured he also wanted his time alone. But the desert was vast enough, the mountain ranges forever enough, that they could both be out without her impinging on his private sabbatical.

Zipping on her sweater jacket over the doctor's blue T-shirt, she turned down the propane on the room heater and took her first breath of fresh air in eleven days. And then took another. Its cool touch filled her lungs as she lifted her face to the warmth of the October sun. At home it would be in the seventies. Up here—northern Nevada, the doctor had told her once when she'd asked where she was—the temperature wasn't all that different. Sixties, maybe.

Studying the road that led away from the cabin, seeing, for the first time, the dark SUV that the doctor must have driven up here—the vehicle he'd said he'd take her to town in, she supposed—she turned in the opposite direction. No sense in taking a chance on reaching the end of that drive and ending up on a real road where someone might see her.

She'd seen the doctor come from the east side

of the property—that morning and once before, too—so she headed west. She wouldn't go far. Just enough to get some real exercise. To clear her mind of the garbage invading it.

To rid herself of the panic that had been with her since the night before.

At some point the doctor was going to want to talk to her about it. She knew him well enough to know that. He wasn't the type to just leave well enough alone.

She didn't want to talk about it. Partially because she hated the person she was around Shawn. Partially because she hated that she'd become a woman who instinctively cowered when her own mother had been so brave.

And partially because she knew the doctor would want to fix her, and there was simply no point.

Cara walked without purpose and yet felt good to be doing something. The exercise felt good. Being outside felt good. Was she wrong to enjoy some moments in a condemned life?

Filled with confusion, she decided she wasn't hurting anyone and kept walking. The landscape was odd—desert and yet, up here in the mountains, she crossed patches of straggly grass along with rocks and packed dirt. The trees weren't anything she'd have imagined, either. While there was a lot of openness and sagebrush, there were also areas of pine trees and, over in the distance, some odd-looking oak kind of trees, too.

She had been captivated by a huge oak in the middle of the several-acre property of the Savannah bed-and-breakfast her family had visited for a week when she was a child. The oak had had a low-slung branch and she'd spent an hour or two each afternoon just sitting on that branch reading her heart out.

She remembered her mom and dad tempting her away with a railroad museum, a tour of some historic fort, a wildlife center, even a ghost tour. She'd been about twelve and hooked on a series of books about babysitters. She'd loved that old tree, the solitude she'd found there. The romantic feel of it all.

She'd done all of the other things, of course. Her folks couldn't leave her at the bed-and-breakfast alone, but each afternoon, before dinner, she'd been allowed to go out to that tree.

Almost upon the grouping of trees now, she stopped when she heard a sound. What kind of wildlife even lived out there? She hadn't thought to ask the doctor. She'd just figured that since he went out twice a day every day that being out was safe.

The sound came again, seemingly from the trees just ahead. Rustling. And...a grunt? More curious than anything now, she continued forward.

What did she have to lose?

Even as the thought entered her mind, she shook her head. She knew she was in a no-win situation, a no-win life because of choices she'd made, but that didn't mean she relished the thought of being eaten by a bear. If there were even bears out there.

The sun's warmth comforted her face as she pressed on. She couldn't hear any birds, but the silence encompassing such vastness was, in itself, a kind of comfort to her.

The rustling came again. Definitely ahead and just to her right.

What if it was a deer?

She'd love to see one up close.

Deer were more afraid of her than she'd ever be of them. From what she remembered her father saying once, that was true of most wildlife. With the exception of maybe alligators.

A worry when she was growing up. But not in the northern Nevada mountains.

Progressing slowly, she continued to watch in front of her. The minute she sensed danger, she'd turn and, just as surreptitiously, walk away.

Were there mountain lions out here?

Again, if she didn't corner it or it was a cub, she should be okay.

Filled with an odd sense of adventure, of discovery, she took another step. It had been so long since she'd been free to just…do. To reach out. To explore.

Catching a flash of movement, Cara stilled, assessing the landscape. Yes, a flash of...color. Not brown. Not fur. Blue and red. Plaid.

Exactly like the shirt the doctor had worn to the table for lunch.

CHAPTER TWELVE

CARA CONSIDERED HER OPTIONS.

Should she let him know she was there?

Probably better that she just turn quietly and leave. He was being so generous to her, not only in providing medical care but in feeding her. Giving her a place to sleep. Hot water in which to shower. Everything she touched every day—the soap she used, the toothpaste—all of it was coming from his pocket, not her own.

The least she could do was leave him some privacy.

She hadn't moved, afraid to do so in case she alerted him to her presence. In case he was angry to have his solitude impinged upon.

No…the doctor wasn't the get-angry type. Or rather, if he did get angry, which surely he did— everyone did, even little Joy had had her temper tantrums—he would have the ability to control himself.

As she did now. As she'd taught Joy. As her mother had tried so hard to teach her. Even when your anger was justified, losing control of it, spewing it, was wrong.

He'd taken enough steps that she could see more of him now—an arm out in front of himself. His left leg. Feeling guilty, and yet curious, too, she watched from her frozen stance. He was walking like a zombie. One stilted step at a time. A stick appeared, then his right leg and the rest of his body. He had a patch over one eye.

What the heck? Was he weirder than she thought?

Nothing like she'd thought?

A guy who liked to play pirate games with imaginary friends? Fascinated, and horrified, too, she stood there and watched as his left arm moved directly into an oak tree branch. The force of the branch stopped him.

Waiting to see what would happen next, she wondered if she should take this time to disappear from his life, remembered the authorities, and came up with nothing else. She really started to worry when the man who'd been so proficient, so precise, with her care, took a step back. Threw down his walking stick, dropped his left arm to his side. And walked straight for the branch.

Had he lost his mind? He'd seemed so...normal—more laid-back than usual, even—at lunch.

She waited for him to stop and stared as he drew closer to the branch. It was big enough to break his nose and if he didn't stop soon...

Her heart pounded and her breathing got short,

but six inches before his nose hit that damned tree he stopped. Just…stopped.

He didn't reach out for anything. Didn't *do* anything once he'd reached his destination. He just stood there.

And then, with no warning, the crazy man let out a hellacious yell, jumped up with his fist in the air, hit his fist on the branch up above and started laughing. Bent over with laughter.

Unless… Was he hurt?

Cara sprinted forward…realizing too late that she was outing herself, and saw, as she drew closer, that her first assessment had been the correct one. He was laughing.

Like a damned fool.

Did he keep some kind of peyote out there? Was that why he was on sabbatical? Because he had a substance-abuse problem?

It was the only thing that made sense. He'd said his problem was personal. And…

She was almost upon him.

"What on earth are you doing?"

She wasn't passing judgment on him. Operating on the hearts of children had to take a lot out of a man. No one could blame him for succumbing to something that would help him deal with the stress that had to come with his job.

But if he was there to get better, he was doing a lousy job of it.

So…maybe as he was helping her she could help him…

He hadn't answered her. Hadn't even straightened up yet.

She was almost upon him. "I'm sorry for trespassing. I know I shouldn't be here. I'll go…just… are you okay?"

If he wanted to fry his brain it was none of her business. Lord knew what she'd done was far worse.

Slowly rising, he pulled the patch off his right eye, spun almost as if on military command and faced her.

"I am on a mission."

The words made no sense. Unless… Were they playing soldiers now?

"Okay." She took a step back. "As long as you're all right, I'll just head back this way…"

She turned. Took a couple of steps. Wondering if someone could be high enough to be hallucinating without showing any other physical signs, and then come back down again by dinner…

"Cara."

She turned, but hesitantly.

"The soy sauce bottle last night. It wasn't your fault."

So, not quite hallucinatory.

An odd time to bring up the subject she'd been hoping they were going to avoid like the plague. She should have stayed inside.

Or turned back when she had the chance.

He seemed to be waiting for a response, still sans eye patch, so she nodded. Not quite sure what she was dealing with, and knowing what she didn't want to deal with, she just stood there.

"I mean it," he said.

Yeah, she got that. She'd overreacted. Maybe she'd placed the bottle too close to the edge of the table. Maybe he'd just missed when he'd tried to grab it. Didn't really matter.

No use crying over spilled milk, Mom used to say.

Though this wasn't quite the same thing. She got that. Recognized that her mind was babbling. She even knew why. He was making her uncomfortable.

She had no idea what to expect. Who she was dealing with. She felt powerless and helpless and was getting closer to a panic attack by the second. She nodded again.

"I'm temporarily blind in one eye."

Cara stared. Dumbfounded. Of anything she'd expected, even giving her wildest imagination free rein, that hadn't been even close.

"I can't see out of my right eye. That's why I knocked the bottle off the table last night. I couldn't see it."

He couldn't see…

The eye patch had been on his left eye. The arm out in front of him. The stick. The daily treks.

A surgeon with only one eye…

Temporarily.

"Did it just happen?"

"Right before I came up here."

Wow. She tried to imagine it…dedicating your life to repairing the hearts of little children and then suddenly being unable to do so. She felt the threat of tears.

Had a feeling he wouldn't want any shed on his behalf. She didn't know how she knew that, or why she thought she knew it, but…

"That's why you're here."

"Yes."

She nodded. "Thank you for telling me."

She should go. Still, she stood there. Taking it all in. Maybe the laughter had been hysterical. Because he'd walked smack-dab into a tree and then had been able to get there without hurting himself.

Was he doing some kind of blind training, then?

Learning to live with what he had left?

She remembered something else.

"Sometimes when we're, you know, both in the…cabin…reading…you look at me and say nothing. It's because I'm in the line of vision on your right side and you don't see me."

"I look at you?" He frowned.

Tilting her head, she smiled. "Obviously not, but it looks as though you are." If she were him, she'd want this whole thing to go over with as much ease, as much lightness, as possible. Without her being insensitive.

"All this time, you've been thinking I'm watching you?"

"Not all the time, but, sometimes, yeah." She shrugged. Grinned again. "It's been kind of eerie, actually."

"And you didn't say anything."

As she'd seen it, she really hadn't been in any position to say anything. Would rather avoid a possibility than forge headlong into something she couldn't handle.

Wow, not at all what her mother had taught her. Had she really changed so much?

Not liking how he was watching her then, as though he could read her thoughts, or worse, her feelings, she asked, "What was it, a tumor or something?" And regretted the cavalier way she'd asked as soon as the words were out of her mouth.

For all she knew, the man had something terminal. Just because he had all his hair and looked far more delicious than any man should look, didn't mean that he wasn't on meds. Or that he hadn't opted out of invasive treatment.

"Is that what the drops are for? To try to shrink a tumor?"

Growing up as the only child of a doctor and a retired registered nurse, she knew too much for her own good. And not nearly enough.

"I don't have a tumor."

When a flood of relief made her weak, Cara took a step back. She and the doc…it wasn't personal. Couldn't be personal. She had no life left to offer anyone. But if she did…if they'd met in another universe…

"What happened?" Something compelled the words, anyway.

"An…accident. It resulted in pressure on the optic nerve. There's only a small window of time that surgery to relieve the pressure will be successful, and unfortunately I was just outside that window."

"So…you're permanently blind, then."

The news hit her like a blow. Crazy as that was. She'd thought he said *temporarily* blind.

"No!" Her head popped up at the vehemence she heard in his voice.

"I had the surgery. When the optic nerve dies you have no vision at all. Everything is blank. Black. Within minutes of surgery I regained some ability. I saw light. Or a light, cloudy mass."

"So your sight will return to you." Another surge of relief. What in the hell was the matter with her? She'd have thought she was PMSing except that she wasn't due for another two weeks.

And had to figure that one out, too. It wasn't like a single man was going to pack feminine supplies for his sabbatical. And since she'd arrived with nothing…

"That's the hope."

"The hope?" She needed this story to have a happy ending. Probably because she had no chance of one. And knew that her emotions were out of whack for the same reason.

Her head knew that life was done. But until her life was physically over, her heart was going to do what a heart did. And the emotional center in her brain was going to help it along. Which was why her mom had been so vitally alive and able to tend to her five minutes before her death.

She got it.

"It could be six months to a year before we know exactly how much sight will return. There's a lot of pressure on the eye. The drops are to reduce the pressure."

She nodded.

"And the eye patch?"

"As with any muscles you don't use, the eye muscles can atrophy. I'm making certain they don't."

He stood there like some kind of god or king of the land. So completely sane. Strong. Good and kind. And injured, too. What kind of man exercised an eye for hours a day, every day?

Her emotional center reacted again.

She had no idea what to do about it. Or with it. All Cara had ever wanted in her life was to love and be loved. Living with who she'd become…a criminal, a killer…that was going to take some getting used to. She shook her head.

The doctor nodded. And she realized he'd seen her shake her head. As though she doubted the veracity of his words.

"It's working," he said now, a note of excitement in his voice. He came toward her, and when he kept walking back the way she'd come, she walked with him. "I've been certain that I'm starting to see dark shadows in the clouds. Big absences of the same amount of light. And today I've just proved it! I saw the branch. As a shadow only, mind you, but I saw it. I walked right up to it, looking with my right eye only, and knew when to stop so I didn't hit my face." He was grinning.

Cara couldn't help but grin right along with him.

CHAPTER THIRTEEN

"SHARE A GLASS of wine with me?" In celebration
of the first major victory he'd had since clouds
had replaced blackness right after surgery, Simon
had taken steaks out for dinner, thawing them in
hot water. Just as they were sitting down to eat,
he thought of the bottles of wine on the top shelf
of the pantry and suggested they open one.

"Okay." Cara didn't look all that happy.

Standing halfway between her and the pantry,
he said, "We can forgo it if you like." Her comfort
meant far more than his celebration.

A cause for some consideration. A couple of
weeks ago nothing had meant more than regaining his eyesight.

"I'd actually like a glass of wine. It's just…"
She shook her head.

"What?" He really wanted to know.

"Shawn's ugly side came out with a lot less
provocation when he drank."

The entire world faded away—a feeling he'd
only ever known during surgery—as Simon focused on her. She'd opened a door—reached out
to him. One wrong move and he could lose her.

But a right one…

"I'll have tea," he said, looking her directly in the eye. Needing her to know that he was promising that he would never, ever raise a hand to her. Or anyone.

She had nothing to fear from him.

"No… Simon…it's okay." She seemed to stumble over his name. Hearing it on her lips caused him to stumble.

"I'd really like a glass of wine, actually. We need to celebrate your moment. That's what…gets you to the next good moment. Honoring them…" She looked down, as though she'd said more than she wished she had.

While he was standing there wanting more.

"I'm fine, Simon, really. I know you aren't going to hurt me. I won't react that way again."

"I can handle it if you do," he told her. "But he didn't just hit you when he was jealous, did he?"

"It started out that way." Her chin jutted but then dropped. Right along with her gaze.

Simon wanted to pick them back up for her, hold them up for her, but, of course, he couldn't. He had to settle for, "What you're dealing with… it's way out of my area of expertise, but I know that there are things beyond your control…things that will take time…just know that you're safe with me."

She stared at him, as though she'd seen a ghost.

Simon wanted to stay right in that stare, to be a part of her. He went for the wine, instead.

There was only so much he could do. It wasn't like they were in a relationship. Or intended to be in one.

He was looking out for her. Almost as if she were only a patient. Glancing at her still-swollen cheek, he figured he was right on the mark.

He'd do what he could to help.

The rest would have to come from her.

Or not.

"YOU DON'T WEAR a wedding ring."

Sitting in his chair in the living room, a glass and a half of wine under his belt, Simon hadn't seen the statement coming.

Just like he hadn't expected Cara to sit with him after dinner. It was the first night since she'd been there that she hadn't immediately excused herself to her room.

They'd talked about northern Nevada. He'd been surprised at the number of questions she asked. She wanted to know everything.

And the reason he'd had answers to give her, from topography and wildlife to weather averages, was because he'd been the same way. Had read everything he could find on the internet before he'd purchased the place.

And…she was watching him. Still on her first glass of wine, but it was almost empty.

"I'm not married," he told her. Her curiosity was natural. She was, for the moment, living with him. Alone. If he had a wife…the wife might be a consideration.

He watched for her reaction. Wanting his married state to matter to her, more than just for curiosity's sake. Even knowing that his wanting made no sense.

There was no room in his life for a woman. Not in the near future. Maybe not in the foreseeable future.

"I was," he told her, as it suddenly occurred to him that Cara needed to know that he was not open for anything more than what they currently were to each other. "She wasn't happy with my part in our relationship. It ended…bad."

"Do you think you were a good husband?"

"I know I tried to be."

"Not the same thing, is it?"

"Probably not." But in his defense, he'd done everything he could possibly think of to be there for Emily—even when the love was gone.

"How long have you been divorced?"

Be careful what you wish for. The thought sprang unbidden to mind as Cara's questioning nature, which he'd admired moments before, turned on him. He might want to reconsider the next time he thought about opening a bottle of wine. It seemed to loosen her tongue.

Funny how less than two hours before he'd been wanting access to her thoughts…

"A little less than a year."

Funny how he still wanted access to them. But sensed that if he turned the questioning on her, the evening would end.

"Do you miss her?"

"No."

"Not even a little bit?"

"No." He supposed he should. If he'd ever really loved her at all…

"Was she a nurse?"

That question kind of amused him. Straight out of a novel or a porn movie—the whole doctor-nurse thing. He was surprised that she'd be one to stereotype. Everything else about her was so unique…

"She's a high school guidance counselor." *Was.* Past tense. Now she was in jail. Awaiting a trial that would start sometime after the first of the year. Even as late as summer, his lawyer thought, based on court-ordered psychological evaluations and medical reports. Simon was going to have to go back to testify. He'd made up his mind that he wasn't going to court until he could see again. He had to give Emily that much—the chance at a lighter sentence.

"How long were you married?"

He sipped from his glass. Thought about the

glass and a half still left in the bottle. If the questions continued, he might need it. "Two years."

"Shawn and I have been married ten."

His mind calmed. Not because he wanted to hear about her with the bastard. But because she'd offered him something of herself.

If answering her questions brought him answers, then bring on the questions.

"You were a child bride," he said, trying to sound completely unaffected and yet casually interested. He had a lot of compassion to give. Just wasn't all that versed in giving it to big people.

"Eighteen." That piece of news brought a slew of unanswered questions. Starting with her parents. She'd said she had no one but Shawn. Had she been orphaned? In foster care? A runaway?

"How old were you when you got married?"

Simon almost grinned. Simple math at that point would tell her it was only three years ago. She wanted to know how old he was…

"Thirty-three." Eight years older—thirty-six to her twenty-eight.

"You waited a long time."

"Becoming a thoracic surgeon takes time and focus. I didn't have enough left to be fair to any relationship."

She sipped. Studied him. As though she found his answer overly interesting.

He wondered if she wasn't a drinker at all. If the wine had gone to her head. Made sense, considering that when her husband drank she had to be on guard.

"Is that why the marriage failed so quickly? Because you spent too much time at work?"

Her gaze more piercing, Simon felt as though he was a little bit on trial. Had no idea why he would be. But said, "No. It failed because what I thought was love turned out not to be."

He'd never put it in words before. He'd suspected. More so, lately. But as he said the words, he knew them to be true. "I wasn't in love with her."

He'd admired the hell out of her. But, in a very different way, he'd fallen for her six-year-old daughter. He'd needed to be there every minute for her. To do everything in his power to help her survive. And then thrive.

In the end, he'd failed Opus, too. A failure that had sent Emily over the edge.

"I'm sure you thought you were, at first," Cara said, looking at the last sip of wine she was swirling in her glass.

He picked up the bottle on the table next to him. "You want a little more?"

She held out her glass but gave him a look that let him know she was waiting for an answer.

And he knew…she was seeking knowledge. Because she needed it. Not about him. But about life. About relationships.

"I did think I was, at first," he said, meeting

her gaze head-on. *Talk to me. I want to help. I'll do anything I can. I promise.*

Words he'd said aloud. To a little girl who, in the end, he hadn't been able to save.

Cara wasn't a child. He didn't love her like a daughter. And yet…his need to be there for her seemed eerily familiar to him.

"I was so in love with Shawn I'd have believed the moon was made out of cheese if he'd told me it was."

The way she said it, the almost haunted look on her face, made him wonder if there were things the man had told her that she regretted believing.

He wanted, in the worst way, to ask if she loved her husband still. He might not be all read up on domestic violence, but he knew enough to know that abused spouses often went back to their abusers. That the pattern of need and love and abuse was made so much worse by the emotional hold the abuser often had on those he hurt.

He wanted to ask. But didn't dare.

"It took me a while to figure out that what I felt for Emily wasn't love," he said.

"Maybe it was." With her legs curled up beneath her on the couch, Cara looked like she belonged there.

He pictured her like that on his sofa at home, sometime in the future. And knew it was the wine playing with his brain.

No more wine with her.

Just this night. This bottle.

"Maybe in the beginning you really did love each other."

He couldn't lie to her. Not for answers. Not for any reason. Simon said nothing. Just left her statement lying between them.

She sipped her wine. Was quiet for so long he thought their night of conversation was through.

Regretted that it had ended so quickly. And knew that it was right that it should.

"I don't know when I quit loving Shawn."

Thank God! He couldn't remember being happier hearing any other news. Took a sip of wine. Held his glass in both hands while he watched her.

When he feared she really would end the evening, he said, "Maybe it was the first time he left a bruise on your face."

Great bedside manner, Doc. Couldn't you have put that more delicately?

It was just that every time he thought of the man, which was pretty much every time he saw those scars and swollen features, he grew angrier.

Not in a go-kill-someone way—though he wasn't averse to trying if the man dared show his face anywhere near Cara ever again—but because he needed to make it better for her.

Because he knew he couldn't. It wasn't within his power.

Like when he'd had a patient he just hadn't been able to save.

Like Opus…

Cara was shaking her head. "It wasn't then," she said. She sounded so calm, so sure, he believed her.

"When, then?"

With a brief shake of her head, like she was startled, she blinked and looked at him.

Damn. Had he lost her?

"I'm not sure," she said. And he wondered if maybe it wasn't the question that had startled her, but that she didn't know the answer.

Maybe she needed to know.

Maybe he needed to help her figure it out.

It would be a hell of a lot easier if he knew how. Of course, sometimes even when you knew, it still wasn't enough.

"I… He used to be… I felt so…loved by him, you know?" She was looking at him, but he wasn't sure if he was supposed to answer.

"I felt…secure. Like…no matter what…I could count on him and he could count on me."

He nodded. Pretty much figured that was what marriage was about. Until it wasn't. And then what?

"But then… Shawn was possessive. I used to love that about him. Loved that he cared where I was at all times. That he needed to know when I was home safely. That he loved me that much. That I was that important to him…"

Earlier questions about her childhood returned.

Where were the parents who should have given her that sense of being important?

Not that it was any of his business…

He sipped. Waited, in case she had more to say.

"Then he got weird about it. Like, if he thought a guy looked at me in too personal a way, if I spoke to the guy, he'd think that I wanted him or something. But not all the time." She shook her head.

More time passed. She sipped again, but the wine in her glass wasn't going down much.

He wondered if she should get some rest. Didn't want her to go. Thought maybe he was overstepping, wanting to know more.

Wasn't inclined to suggest that she call it a night.

He wondered about making a run into town. Picking up some things for her. He didn't want to leave her at the cabin alone, but if he taught her how to use the .22…

"I don't know when it happened…" She was speaking slowly. "I think I know why, though."

Not because the man had hit her? He had to know, too. "Why?"

"Because I couldn't trust him anymore. Not like he'd be unfaithful to me. Or even lied to me. He never did either. But because I couldn't trust who he was. Because none of it was pre-dictable. It didn't make sense. Because I never knew what would make him jealous. Or why he got jealous. Or even when. He didn't always go off on me right away. It might be a week later... maybe I set a bottle of something down on the table and for whatever reason he knocks it off, or someone else does, and he explodes on me for setting it down."

It was as though a bolt of lightning shot through the dimly lit room. She'd just told him why she'd reacted as she had the night before. Or how her fear had been so instinctively, instantly, automatically born.

"Sounds like walking on eggshells," he said, feeling inane.

She nodded. "Yes. All day. Every day. You could be going along, feeling good, and suddenly the monster comes out of the closet and lashes into you..."

Her face shadowed then. In a way that cut him clear through.

"I'm sorry." She stood, leaving her glass on the table. "I'm taking up too much of your evening."

It was almost as though he'd known her retreat was coming. He didn't stand. Didn't do anything to stop her—in spite of the instincts that were pushing him to go to her.

"I'm fine, Cara. Stay if you wish."

She shook her head. "If you don't mind, I'd like to use the restroom and then go to bed."

She'd already done his drops. Was no longer taking any pills.

"Of course I don't mind," he assured her.

But he did.

CHAPTER FOURTEEN

Santa Raquel, California

DARKNESS HAD FALLEN, dinnertime had come and gone, and Lila hadn't noticed. In a brown pant-suit, coming from a bungalow in the middle of the second cul-de-sac along the winding flow-ered walkway that ran through the grounds of The Lemonade Stand, she was thinking about the nineteen-year-old woman whose boyfriend had brought her to them because he'd suspected that her father was abusing her.

He'd been right—though not as he'd thought. Harold Abernathy hadn't been having sex with his daughter, he'd been punishing her for her sexu-ality. Binding her breasts. Putting a locked belt over her genitals. And whipping her every time he suspected she'd talked to a boy. Taking in the low-voltage lighting along the path, the spotlights on the flower beds, Lila thanked God for loving boyfriends.

"Lila, there you are." Molly Wilmington, one of the women in Joy Amos's bungalow, came up the walk. She was in a sweater and housedress, and her arms were wrapped around her middle. "We called Sara and she thought I should contact you, but we haven't been able to find you…"

Switching mental gears, Lila smiled at the woman. "I'm here now, Molly, what do you need?"

"It's Dr. Mantle, ma'am. He was upset when he left, and we thought Sara should know. She was going to call him. I'm not sure if she got through or not. I've been busy looking for you. She thought you might like to be told…"

The woman, a widow in her sixties who'd been abused by a nephew she'd taken in, was going to be leaving them soon. The nephew was in jail and she had family in Arizona who desperately wanted her and had already found a condominium for her to purchase. She'd finish her counseling there.

She didn't need the tension that filled Lila at the mention of Edward's name.

"Do you know why he was upset?" she asked, carefully schooling her voice as they stood in the fifty-degree air.

Molly nodded. "I was sitting right there," she said. "You know Joy's been spending nights with him at his nephew's house."

Of course she knew. Three nights, to be exact. With Julie and Hunter in the background. Sleeping over, saying good-night, but not spending any time with the little girl at all. All three nights had been successful. Edward would be going it solo soon.

And then he and Joy would most likely be heading to Florida.

Just like Molly's imminent move to Phoenix.

Residents moved on. It was a requirement. They were interim family at the Stand. Which was the only kind of family Lila could be to anyone.

"He asked her if she wanted to go home with him tonight. She said yes, and when he held out his hand to her, she even took it. I thought he was going to cry. It was just...so wonderful."

The older woman's eyes filled with tears. Lila might have joined in the moment if not for the fact that she needed to know why Edward had been upset.

"It just takes time," she said, instead of asking the question she wanted to ask. "It just takes time."

Molly nodded. Sniffed. Nodded again. Their residents were emotionally fragile. Every one of them, in one way or another. She honored that. Gave Molly the understanding she needed. A warm smile. And patience.

"Anyway, Joy asked him if Julie could read her her bedtime story. Edward told her that Hunter and Julie weren't going to be there tonight, and Joy pulled her hand out of his and said that she didn't want to go. When she asked him if she had to, he said no. Of course not. But he left right

afterward. He seemed…different. You know…
like…not emotional at all, or something…"

Nodding one more time, Lila thanked the
woman.

"I just, if you don't mind me saying, I see the
way you look at him and…it's just…you know,
being older, it doesn't take away our feelings. Our
desire to be loved. Or to have someone to share
the ups and downs of our days."

It took Lila a second to realize that Molly was
trying to counsel *her*.

"I know we aren't friends," Molly continued. "I
just want you to know that if you ever need one,
you'll have my number in Arizona. You do so
much for everyone here. You've given me my life
back. Given me hope for a new and better future.
I'll never forget that. Or be able to repay you for
the kindness you, in particular, have shown me."

In a completely uncharacteristic move, Lila
reached forward and hugged the woman.

For a second there, she'd been tempted, honestly tempted, to admit that she did need a friend.

The second passed and Lila was already on her
cell phone, calling Sara by the time Molly had
made it back to the door of her bungalow.

"MAY I SIT DOWN?" It took everything Lila had to
keep the relief out of her voice. And the tremor
of emotion, too. The fact that Edward hadn't
been answering his phone, that he had several

people looking for him, worried about him, wasn't on him.

He hadn't asked The Lemonade Stand to take him on. He'd only asked for help for Joy.

He didn't glance her way. Didn't even seem surprised that she was standing next to his barstool in the upscale hotel where he'd been living.

He stood and she feared that he was going to walk out on her. Wanted to be able to compel him to stop. But knew she couldn't.

She had no hold over him.

"There's a booth," he said, pointing to a high, padded-leather seating area by windows that faced the ocean.

Behind the booth was a natural rock fountain, several feet long with live greenery throughout.

Edward had invited her out many times since they'd met over these many weeks that his granddaughter had been with them. They'd been on outings with Joy and Hunter and Julie, but she'd never been alone with him anywhere but at the Stand.

She watched the ease with which he lowered his tall, manly body into the booth. Noticed, of all things, the wrinkles on the back of his suit coat. Gray. To go with his silver, white and gray-striped tie.

Edward was always impeccably put together. Probably more so than necessary. What did it say about her that she really liked that about him?

Resisting the urge to check the pins in her bun,

she slid in across from him. It didn't matter that the light makeup she wore had long since faded away. Or that her chin was starting to show a hint of wrinkles—one on each side. She was there as a professional.

At the very most, as a friend.

Not as a woman.

He ordered a scotch on the rocks. She *wanted* a daiquiri—strawberry banana—but asked for a beer. Not a time to look feminine. And she was driving.

When they discovered that neither of them had had dinner, they ordered a couple of appetizers to share. They both named their top two choices and found them to be the same—bruschetta and stuffed mushrooms. She was not going to make anything of that.

And wasn't going to consider why she'd chosen to struggle to read the menu rather than wear glasses that made her feel old.

"You haven't been answering your phone," she said as soon as they were alone, afraid, when she heard herself, that she sounded accusatory. "I say that only as an explanation for why I'm here," she hurriedly added. "I tried to reach you several times."

His head shot up then. "It didn't... I should have thought right away... But you wouldn't have sat down and ordered if... Joy... Nothing has happened, has it?"

The unusual stuttering, along with the stark fear in his gaze, confirmed what she already knew. Edward's emotions, while not much on the surface, ran deep.

Reaching out a hand to cover his, she assured him, "She's fine." When he turned his hand over to take her fingers in his, she realized what she'd done. Pulled back.

"Sara was concerned with the way you left," she told him, deliberately bringing in the counselor's name. "When she couldn't reach you, she called me."

Lila had called Hunter, too. And Julie. Before she remembered that they were in LA at a theater event that evening—and spending the night. Edward had purposely chosen that evening for a solo run with Joy. At Hunter's house instead of Edward's hotel.

Maybe she'd overreacted, coming here...

"I'm glad you're here," he told her, meeting her gaze. He looked tired. The all-the-way-to-the-bone kind. It had to be getting to him—his only child still missing. His granddaughter's rejection. Being away from the medical practice that gave him purpose.

She didn't know how she'd make it one week without The Lemonade Stand.

Their drinks arrived and she took a sip of beer. She didn't drink often, and beer almost never. But that night it tasted good.

"I'm not getting it right, Lila."

"Getting what right?"

With one hand on his highball glass, he gestured with the other. "The whole parenting thing."

"You just need to give it time. Things take time." Seemed like it had been years since she'd gone a day without repeating the phrase.

"What time? Joy's been with you almost two months. It's not healthy for a little girl to be living like that. She needs family. A home. Normal school with regular kids…"

He stopped, shook his head. "Not to say that the schooling there isn't great or that the kids are abnormal, but the situation… The security to protect victims from abusers, the counseling… Kids shouldn't have to be faced with that every day."

"It's okay, Edward." Lila smiled. "I knew what you meant. And I agree completely. State-run facilities are only allowed to keep residents six weeks," she told him. "With good reason. Because we're privately funded, we have more leeway, but we don't want any of our residents to make a home at the shelter. We're just there to help them recover, get back on their feet, start anew…"

"It's time to get her out of there and she doesn't even want to spend the night alone with me."

"She held your hand today, Edward!"

Lila remembered several weeks back when Edward had celebrated for two days because his granddaughter had looked at him.

He looked over at her, emotion shining, and then shook his head. "I can't tell you how that shook my heart, feeling that little hand slide trustingly in mine. It was like I was thirty-two again and my Cara was back, trusting me to keep her world safe and secure. 'Come on, Daddy,' she'd say…"

With a quirk of his lips, he took a long sip of scotch.

"It's clear that Joy, and Cara, too, are your whole world," Lila said, the words coming straight from her heart. A heart this man had touched. "You've put your entire life on hold, your career on hold, to be here."

He nodded. Sipped again. Then, with his hands clasped on the table, he leaned forward. "It just isn't enough," he told her. "I'm not enough."

"Don't say that."

"Who am I kidding here, Lila? I drove my own daughter into the hands of a fiend." Intensity shouted from the softly spoken words.

Lila hadn't been there. She'd never met Cara. But… "From what you've said, you did everything you could to protect her from him."

Edward shook his head and then sat back as their food was served, leaving Lila disappointed at the interruption.

That night, sitting in the hotel bar with him, she felt like someone she didn't know. Living a life that was not hers.

They talked about Santa Raquel. About her welcoming, close-knit people. About the cooler water in the Pacific compared to the warmer Atlantic waves he was used to.

He talked about taking Cara to the beach when she was little. And about all of the times he'd missed doing so because of work.

And she listened, soaking up every tidbit he would give without her asking. She'd already given him any answers she had.

And yet, when their plates were empty and cleared away, she didn't want to just get up and go.

She'd only finished half her beer. Figured she could nurse it a little longer. And wasn't sure she should.

"You going to be okay?" They'd resolved nothing. Joy and Edward needed more time. Life didn't often come with easy answers.

As she asked her question, Edward caught the bartender's attention and held up his glass. "I just need to drink tonight," he said. "And before you get the wrong idea, I'm not much of a drinker. Never have been. But tonight..."

She'd thrown away part of a bottle of wine the last time they'd had a drink together. She knew he didn't make a habit of consuming alcohol. She also didn't judge.

But... "Be careful, okay?" she said. She meant to reach into her purse. To take out enough bills to cover her half of their impromptu meal. Instead, she looked straight into his eyes. Afraid for him.

He took hold of her hand as though reaching for a lifeline. "Sit with me while I drink?"

How could she do anything but nod?

CHAPTER FIFTEEN

WHEN EDWARD HAD said he needed a night of drinking, Lila had been picturing multiple glasses consumed in quick succession. A picture with which she was intimately familiar—growing up, and later, too. Which was one of the reasons she'd agreed to stay. She knew what to expect, and how to handle what could come.

She just hadn't expected the man to nurse his second scotch like she was nursing her first beer.

"I've been looking back a lot," Edward was saying toward the end of that second scotch. "Trying to see with fresh eyes, with open eyes. Clearly, I failed Cara. She didn't feel safe coming to me when she was struggling. I broke her trust, somehow."

Lila had nothing to contribute but a willingness to listen and a desire to be there.

He met her gaze. "Frankly, the more I look, the less I like what I see."

She knew that feeling. Too well. "We are our own worst critics." She told him something it had taken her a long time to learn. "Taking an honest look back is hard," she continued, not as the managing director of a women's shelter, but as a person who'd been there. "It's also sometimes the only way to move forward. To learn what went wrong so that, best-case scenario, you can fix it. And if you can't do that, at least you can prevent it from recurring."

"Exactly," he said, his eyes growing dim as he took another sip and signaled for another drink. "I won't do to Joy what I did to Cara."

No! That hadn't been where she was going with that.

"You love her, Edward. All that little girl needs right now is love and family. You're it. You're all the family she has. She needs *you*." Lila had never been more certain of anything than she was of that.

"I loved Cara, too. I'd die for her."

She couldn't let him give up.

"So what went wrong? When did it go wrong? Were you ever close to her? When did it all change?"

She asked him questions she'd been asking herself on and off since childhood. Questions for which she'd found answers. For her, the quest had led her to be alone. Because she was who she was. But Edward... The man was a healer—and not just as a profession.

"Everything changed when Emily got sick," he said without any pause at all. "She and Cara were so close..."

He talked about how his little girl had always been a bit of an introvert. How she liked to be with her mom more than hang out with friends. How she'd been Emily's little shadow. She'd loved to read. And to cook. To go with her mom to volunteer at the church and deliver meals to those in need.

"She loved to play, too," he said. "But quietly. Board games and hunting for treasures on the beach rather than riding bikes, climbing trees or playing in the waves. Which was why it was so off, from the very beginning, that she was so taken with Shawn Amos. He ran a surfing school! Cara not only didn't like surfing, she just wasn't the athletic sort." He grinned. "Emily and I used to love to watch her try to bowl. She'd get the stance just right, the approach, the delivery, her ball would go right down the middle—and knock over a pin or two. There just wasn't enough force to make anything more happen…"

Another hour passed as Edward talked about his lovely family—and it was a pipe dream to Lila, the picture he painted. Listening to him… reliving it with him…gave her a bit of what it felt like. She didn't want him to stop.

The dimly lit room had long since seemed to fade away. People came and went, quiet conversation buzzed. There was no sense of urgency. It was as though they had all of the hours they might need or want.

"I couldn't believe it when Emily was diagnosed with kidney disease. There'd been no sign. No symptoms. I should have seen, should have known... I'm a doctor, for God's sake. I walked around in a conscious coma for weeks—I couldn't fathom living without her. Had no idea how to do all of the things she did around the house. And absolutely no clue how to be to Cara what Emily had been."

"Did she go right away?" Facing the end of the beautiful story was harder than she'd expected. She'd known it was coming. The hard part was where she came in.

He shook his head. "We had eighteen months. She went through a transplant. Dialysis. A second transplant. That's where Cara really started to pull away..." He sounded as though he was only starting to figure out that part.

"Why do you think that was?"

He shook his head. "I wasn't... I don't know," he said, frowning. "I'd found a new doctor. One who gave us a better than ninety percent chance of success if she had a transplant from a live donor with a clean match. Turned out, I was a match and I gave her one of my kidneys. I got out of the hospital long before Emily did, and when I got home Cara was...different. Angry. It's the first time I can remember her yelling at me. I was shocked.

"But I knew what she'd been through, poor thing. She was only seventeen. Trying to take care of everything while both of us were recovering. My sister, Betty, was there, of course, but Cara insisted on taking care of her mother herself, as much as she could.

"Thing was, the disease, it attacked my kidney in her body, too. It was like Cara blamed me for that. I spent more money than I had looking for other things we could try. Brought in everyone I could find who could give us an ounce of hope. Emily went along with all of it willingly, but Cara… She was so kind to her mother. And could barely talk to me with a civil tone."

"She was blaming you."

He shrugged. "I guess. Because I wasn't a good enough doctor to save her mother."

Lila shook her head. "Who knows what goes on in a hurting child's mind? But I'd guess it was more because she needed someone to blame and you were safe. You'd love her anyway."

His lips started to tremble as he said, "She was right about that. I'd give anything to see my baby girl again. Just to know she's alive…"

And then he shook his head. "After that…I was lost," he said, looking at Lila. "I told myself I moved us out of the house, bought the place on the beach for Cara's sake. But, looking back, what if I did it for my own? I just couldn't bear to keep that house. Emily was everywhere. I was failing to function…"

He stopped, tears in his eyes. "I was selfish, is

what I was," he said. "I took her from the only sense of security and love she had. I ripped her away from everything she had left of her mother. And I worked every hour in the day, telling myself that every life I saved was a tribute to Emily…"

Leaving Cara to wander the beach alone. Prey to anyone who'd love a vulnerable, grieving, beautiful young lady.

Lila saw it all so clearly. Maybe she had it wrong. But she didn't think so.

"You were in survival mode," she said aloud. "The situation was out of your control. It sounds like your Emily was an incredible woman. Both you and Cara loved her to distraction. And the two of you managed to share her well, too. Losing her… There was no way either of you were going to come out of that unscathed. You did the best you could, Edward. And that's all Joy needs from you now. Your best."

"She needs me to love her enough to give her what she needs," he said. And then, expression completely serious, said, "I've been thinking about talking to Hunter and Julie about adoption. They both so clearly love her…"

Lila could think of a few reasons why the idea might be perfect. Life coming together as it should. The best-case scenario. And reasons for concern, too.

"They've only been together a number of weeks." She went with the concern. "The relationship is so new. Neither of them have been in a committed adult relationship before, and to take on a child so soon, most particularly one who is dealing with emotional trauma…"

Even as she said the words, believing them, she knew that Julie would take up the challenge in a heartbeat. And had a feeling Hunter would, too.

Which would leave Edward…where?

"Would you go back to Florida, then?"

He shook his head slowly. "I can't imagine leaving her behind. Not after losing Cara. My practice is there. My home. My whole life, really. I said I was thinking about asking them. I didn't say I'd definitely made up my mind to do so. Sometimes I think that if I just take her to Florida, get her away from here, away from the horrors…"

He frowned. "See what I mean by not being good for her, just as I failed my own daughter? I took Cara away from it all and look where it got us…"

He looked so damned…lost…she couldn't help the sudden lurch in her heart—coupled with a driving need to help him.

"There are no easy answers, are there?" he asked, and Lila couldn't find the will to look away from him.

"No." She wanted to break whatever spell this remarkable man had over her. She couldn't even bear to break eye contact.

"Come upstairs with me."

She heard her worst nightmare coming from his lips.

She didn't want to lose his friendship. Didn't want to lose this moment.

She wanted, in the worst way, to do as he asked. "I can't."

He nodded. Reached over and smoothed a hand over her face. "Dear Lila. I was certain I'd never again feel for a woman…in this way…"

Surely Edward wasn't telling her he'd been celibate, too? She shook her head, not trusting her own thought processes at the moment. "What way?"

"You're special, Lila." He shook his head. "Like my Emily was special…"

Like Emily. Like she could be—even for one minute out of time—a part of a beautiful fairy tale…

"I'm… I can't have a relationship with you."

His hand held hers now. She couldn't let go in spite of the mixed messages she was sending. "I know," he told her. "Your life is The Lemonade Stand. Mine is in Florida."

Yes. All of that. But so, so much more, too.

"You're a client."

"My granddaughter is a client. And you have become more to our family than the director of the facility where she lives. You, with Hunter and Julie, have become part of Joy's journey."

So his feelings for her…maybe they were gratitude. Nothing to be concerned about.

"I'm not in the habit of begging. Or even of asking twice," he said now, "but I sense that you feel some of the same things I'm feeling. Tell me I'm wrong and I'll never speak of this again."

She had to tell him. She knew it down to her core. The only decent thing was to tell him he was wrong. If she didn't, she'd be placing him in harm's way.

Because, while he searched his heart for things he might have done wrong, Lila didn't have to search. She'd put both of her children in harm's way. Left her son there. And then, she'd hurt him herself.

"Lila?"

He wanted her to admit she felt something for him.

She couldn't look at him and lie. Lila opened her mouth. Said nothing.

"We're not kids anymore, Lila. We both know the score. We know better than to build sand castles. So where's the harm in finding solace—and pleasure—in sharing this night together? One night."

Where was the harm? Her mind spun with all of the places harm lurked.

Her lonely body wanted him. Why it had chosen now to come back to life after all these years,

she had no idea. Hadn't expected ever to feel red-
hot desire again. Not at her age.

Sex aside, she wanted to be held. To lie in a
man's arms. To sleep there. Just this once.

She wouldn't hurt him that night. She was as
certain of that as she was that the sun would rise
in the morning.

"It can only be for one night." A flood of heat
soared through her body as she heard herself say
the words. "I mean it, Edward. From the bottom
of my soul. It can only be one night."

He smiled. Stood. Threw some bills down on
the table, took her hand and walked her out of the
bar, down the hall and to the elevator.

They didn't speak.

She didn't want to think.

The elevator door opened. He stepped inside.
Pushed the button for his floor. Held the door.
Looked at her.

And she got on.

CHAPTER SIXTEEN

Prospector, Nevada

CARA STOOD IN the waning afternoon light, holding up two tall boards. In the middle of the yard, she remained stock still, making no sound. Simon, with the patch on his good eye, was trying to find her.

Since she'd found out about his daily exercises, she'd been finding ways to help him exercise his eye muscles without risking running into anything that could do him serious physical damage. He'd told her, just the night before, that he thought he was making a lot more progress, making it more quickly, because he could concentrate fully on what he saw and not on having to be aware of his surroundings.

With her changing up the things in the yard, he never knew what he was looking for. Or where. He only knew the large radius in which he might find it.

His hearing was acute, she'd learned, and now she was standing beneath the hot desert sun, sweating in spite of the sixty-degree temperature.

She should have shed the new hoodie he'd brought before starting the exercise.

Even hot, it felt good to have on different clothes. When he'd first suggested picking up some things for her, she'd balked. What possible explanation could there be for a man living like a hermit on a mountain buying things for a woman? Then, the day before, he'd surprised her with a box. She'd been nervous when he'd announced that he was going into town for the second time in a week when he had been there, according to him, only once since he'd gotten to the cabin. Then he'd shown up with the box.

Three pairs of leggings, brown, blue and black. Two pairs of jeans. A pair of hiking boots. Four pairs of undies—silk and lacy and unlike anything she'd ever worn before. Matching bras. Socks. A couple of shirts. A sweatshirt. A variety of feminine products. And a can of Mace. He'd ordered them online at the kiosk at the shop in town and picked everything up when it arrived.

It didn't surprise her that he'd gotten her sizes right. He'd done her laundry. What had surprised her was the Mace. He'd wanted her to know that she was safe. At least long enough to get to the .22 he'd shown her how to use.

Daily target practice had been added to their agenda six days ago. She was getting to be a pretty good shot.

Not that she expected to need—or even use—the skill.

Or the Mace, either, for that matter. Still, she'd slept with it the night before. And had a flash of sleeping with a doll her mom had bought for her that had a storybook with it. The doll was little. She'd been little. She'd held it in her hand every night.

And then she hadn't. She had no idea what had happened to the doll…

Simon, who'd been making his way around the yard, was coming right at her now. She'd told him if he found her to stop two feet in front of her. She waited. Holding her breath.

He hit the two-foot mark and just kept coming. Slowly. Methodically. A couple of inches from her he stopped. Just as he had by the tree.

Pulling off his eye patch, Simon stared her right in the eye—so close she could smell the soap they shared on his skin and see the darker line around his irises.

"So, I have to be up close to see it," he said, stepping back. "But I'm seeing. That's the important thing. That and the drops."

Cara had the sudden urge to scream at him.

She held back tears. Handed him the two boards she'd been holding and walked into the cabin.

"Cara?"

She heard him calling behind her but didn't stop. She went to her room. Her sacred space. He hadn't set foot in the room since her second day with him.

"Cara!" She heard the concern in his voice. Took a deep breath. Another whole week had passed and she'd come no closer to knowing what she was going to do. What was supposed to happen with her. How her life would end.

Under the doctor's—Simon's—tender care, she was more rested, healthier, physically stronger than she'd been in years. When he'd gone into town the week before he'd stocked up on real food. Fresh food. She'd been eating like a pig.

Because she'd insisted on using her cooking skills to please him, he'd eaten even more than she had.

She wasn't sure, but she had considered that she was slowly losing her mind. The desire to scream at the only man who'd ever truly taken care of her was proof of that theory. Her emotions, usually so…controllable…were completely out of control.

Memories were returning every day. Snippets of things she'd long forgotten. Hadn't even known she'd forgotten. Things like that little doll. Until she held the Mace she'd had no recollection of that doll.

But knew that she'd bought one for Joy. And that her little girl had loved it.

Joy…

Shaking her head, Cara picked up the Mace. Squeezed it tight.

"Cara."

She didn't answer. Didn't want him to know that she was losing it. Knew she was safe behind the door.

And then the door moved. His head peeked around. "There you are. You had me worried."

"Sorry. I…just got hot…standing in the direct sun." And she was still sitting there in her hoodie. A normal person would have taken off the jacket.

"What happened out there?"

"Nothing. You saw the boards before you ran into them. That's good!"

He needed to believe so. What was it to him if she thought differently? Pointless information, that was what.

He came into the room. If she told him to go, he would. She had no doubt. Instead, she scooted over on the bed, leaving room at the end for him to take a seat if he wished.

After hesitating a couple of seconds, watching her, he did.

"Talk to me," he said.

It was an odd moment. They'd been living in this small cabin together for more than two weeks—sharing a bar of shower soap, a tube of toothpaste, every meal and a washing machine—and yet, other than the night they'd had wine, they'd never stepped over the clear, yet unspoken, boundaries.

"You sure you want that?" She gave him a sideways glance. The man was gorgeous, even when he was pigheadedly stubborn. Some woman was going to be very lucky someday.

"Yes. Why do you ask?"

She shrugged. "What we've got going here… this weird waiting game we're playing, putting off what's going to happen to me while you heal…it works because I've got nowhere else to go…and because we don't let it get messy."

"Messy?"

"You know…your stuff is your stuff. Mine is mine. We don't commingle it." Except the shower soap, the toothpaste and the food.

"I want to know what happened out there, Cara."

She shrugged. So he was going to push things. So maybe it was time. She couldn't hang out there sponging off him forever. The healing time he was giving her… It was a waste. She knew it. She was just too weak to put an end to it before he forced the issue.

Was this it, then? Him forcing the issue? She'd kind of envisioned more of a standoff at the car— him driving away, either with her or without her, and going to the authorities. He'd told her it was a twenty-minute drive down the mountain into town. So even if he used his burner phone and called the authorities the second she refused to get in his car, she'd still have twenty minutes' lead on them…

Yeah, and he'd stay right there in the yard after making the call, too. He'd stay with her until the cops arrived. To keep her safe...

Another losing venture he'd taken on. Along with his eye, in her opinion. Not that she was a doctor. Or knew a damned thing about eyes.

Now, if it was his kidney he'd been struggling with, well, she could give him a dozen textbooks on that subject...

The thought came unbidden. The bitterness attached to it shamed her. How could she possibly, *possibly*, begrudge one single thing she'd learned while caring for her mother? She'd absorbed it all willingly. Gratefully. So thankful for every second they'd had together...

"Cara."

He'd go if she told him to, she kept reminding herself.

So, why wasn't she telling him to go?

"I came in because I almost hollered at you."

He blinked. Pulled back with obvious surprise. "Yelled at me? Why?" And then. "Oh, because I got too close. You should have said something. Next time, do like you've been doing and just leave something in the yard. You don't have to stand there..."

"I can't lug anything big enough far enough for you to not figure out what and where it is."

"I don't care." His voice was gentle. "I'm not having you go backwards for..."

"Stop." She couldn't bring him down with her. "It had nothing to do with how close you were," she told him. "It could have, if I hadn't been watching your approach, if I hadn't known why you were getting closer. If I hadn't been silently cheering you on…"

She broke off, regretting the last statement. Like she was personally invested in his success.

Simon didn't jump on it. He was frowning. "Then what? What did I do?"

"It's what you aren't doing," she said. "And really, it's none of my business, and it's not like I'm an expert or anything…"

She couldn't do this. If he wanted to live in his little lie bubble, that was his choice. He wasn't hurting anyone.

"What aren't I doing?"

"It's none of my business."

"Then I'm making it your business."

He was a couple of feet away, on the end of the bed, and it felt like he'd touched her. His gaze held hers. So sincere.

Why hadn't she met him ten years ago? Or before that, while her mother had still been alive?

Shaking her head, Cara remembered that sometimes asking why was nothing but a dead-end road.

"Cara. Please."

He'd taken her in. Cared for her…

"It's just…you might have the best eye guy in

the world, maybe you paid him a lot of money and his surgery success rate is phenomenal, but I think he's promising you the moon and stars when all he can give you is clouds."

Then again, if Simon hadn't come up to his mountain cabin to heal, he wouldn't have found Cara. Maybe it was like Mom said…you never know, with every breath you take, who you might be serving.

Of course, saving the life of a criminal was kind of a dead end in itself.

God. She just couldn't get over it. Couldn't see herself that way. And yet, as the days passed and she grew healthier, as she started to remember more about that horrible day, there was truth to things Shawn had told her.

And things that didn't bear remembering. She'd rather go to her grave than remember the moment when…

She shook her head again.

And realized that Simon was staring at her.

"What?"

"I didn't ask you to help me." He looked…disappointed. In her.

"I want to help you." Just as she'd been grateful for—and maybe selfishly hogged?—every aspect of helping her mother. "I just… I don't see any progress from last week. You stopped just inches before the tree, too. And if someone is promising you more, if you're building your whole future on what some doctor has told you…it just makes me want to scream. That's all."

"I saw the shadow, Cara. That means the optic nerve is not dead."

He was missing the point, but she absolutely didn't want to piss him off. Looking down at her hands she said, "Okay."

"It could take up to a year before I'll know how much of my sight will return."

"Okay." Was he not mad at her, then? She was afraid to look.

"You don't believe I'll see again."

"I didn't say that. I have no idea if you'll see again. I'm not God. And I know nothing about eyes and how they work." She studied the base-board along the wall in front of her. And then the tips of her new hiking boots. "I just hate it when people are misled. When they place all their hopes on something because someone makes promises and then it fails."

"And you think I've been misled?"

She nodded. There. It was out in the open.

"Then you can relax. I do have a renowned eye surgeon, but he didn't live up to his repu-tation, in my opinion. His prognosis was more along the lines of 'find a new career' than any-thing else. He and most of my peers and people I've thought were close friends all these years. All they wanted to do was impress upon me all of the things I could still do…while promising their undying support."

Oh. What the hell, then…

"Science and medicine, they only do so much," he continued, watching her intently, though she knew he was only seeing her out of the one good eye. "The rest is in the hands of God, or fate, which often works through the power of the mind. That's the true healing force. And that's why I'm here. I *know* I'm going to see again. It's just a matter of patience, working the muscles and not losing belief.

"The first two I could do anywhere, but that last one… The only way I could be certain I wouldn't fall under the pressure of all of the renowned medical people around me and begin to accept less for myself was to get away from them."

She'd been relieved there, for a second, when he'd said that his doctor had told him not to expect that eye to see again. Right up until she'd realized that it wasn't the other doctors she had to be concerned about.

It was the doctor sitting right in front of her. The one who refused to accept that not every physical ailment could be fixed—no matter how good a doctor you were. Or how much you thought you had control over such things.

A doctor who reminded her of a doctor she'd once known. One she'd also lived with. One who'd gone to extreme lengths because he'd refused to accept the truth.

"My distance vision might not be improving yet, but I saw the dark shadow of you and the boards more clearly than I saw the tree last week."

He was, quite possibly, going to be the person to share her last moments on this earth. And this was how she repaid his kindness? By not believing in him, just like those people he'd run away from?

What kind of a person did that make her?

And what did her opinion matter?

"I saw you," he said.

Maybe he had. Maybe he was only convincing himself he had. Maybe both times his body had felt a change as something drew near and he'd made himself believe there was a shadow. Either way, she wasn't saying any more. Except, "Okay."

She looked at him, to make sure that he got the message that, though she didn't believe him, she wasn't against him. She wasn't going to be the one to blame for his loss of hope.

She kind of smiled.

He kind of smiled back.

CHAPTER SEVENTEEN

SIMON HAD THE hots for his houseguest. He couldn't pretend otherwise. He also had no intention of acting on the feelings. The woman was married—to a bastard Simon hoped she'd divorce the first chance she got—but for the moment...

She was also there under his protection. Because his conscience wouldn't let him just watch her go out into danger all alone. He couldn't prevent her from doing so. But as a doctor, he had the means to report the abuse he'd treated in an emergency situation. He wasn't doing so as long as she was with him. Because he was hoping she was getting emotionally stronger as well as physically and would soon be ready to let him take her to a shelter. To get whatever legal and psychological help she needed to be completely free.

He also wasn't going to further involve himself with a woman who didn't believe in him. And clearly, in spite of her reassurances, she didn't.

Knowing that she thought he wasn't going to see again was a blow he hadn't expected. Like finding the enemy had infiltrated your camp.

Still, aware as he was of his intense physical

attraction to her, he had to be very careful in the choices he made. Like the time she'd walked into the room and he'd suddenly been picturing her in the underwear he'd picked out for her—wondering which pair she was wearing. He'd left the cabin, chopped wood he didn't need and continued to chop until all sensation had left his body.

He laid it all out clearly in his mind as he prepared dinner that evening. Cara hadn't come out of her room since he'd left her there almost an hour before. She'd taken a book in with her when she'd retired the night before. Perhaps she was reading.

She'd been doing most of the cooking, but he'd offered to make his baked spaghetti earlier in the day and was keeping to that predetermined program.

He should never have gone into her room. Had only done so out of concern. The way she'd gone inside so suddenly…gone straight to her room. For all he knew, she'd suddenly fallen ill. Head trauma could take weeks to present complications. He'd had to be sure.

He hadn't had to stay. Once he'd known that she'd just been preventing herself from saying something she seemed to think she'd regret, he should have politely excused himself. Not badgered her.

Truth was, he was quietly, slowly going nuts with her living like a shadow in his home. Not just because of physical need. Because he had this insane desire to know what she was thinking. All the time, it seemed. It was almost a...compulsion...to know her better. To know her intimately.

Even when he knew he didn't want to know. Couldn't afford to know.

He *was* going to see again.

He chopped onion. Dropped it into heated olive oil, watched for translucency and vowed to think of nothing but dinner preparation until the meal was complete.

He almost made it. Cara came out shortly before the spaghetti was due to come out of the oven. He was preparing a salad from the fresh vegetables he'd picked up in town the day before when he'd retrieved her package. He'd spoken to no one except the clerk. Wanted no contact with the outside world until he was ready.

And now, until Cara was ready. He couldn't turn his back on her, stop seeing the good in her, just because she didn't believe he was going to see again. A lot of great individuals, giving, respectable, loving people, shared her belief. He needed her out of his life, but more than anything, he wanted her to have whatever time she needed to find the inner strength to break free from her fears and seek help.

She worked around him in the small kitchen, getting plates, filling glasses with ice, setting the table. He always sat to the right of her now. She

placed things on the table to his left. He hadn't
asked. She hadn't said, either, but he'd been noticing more and more over the past days how much
she fit herself into his routine, doing small things
to make his life more comfortable. Her awareness,
in the midst of the hell she had to be going through
inside, drew him to her as much as anything.

As had happened many nights before, they
ate without speaking. And yet the silence wasn't
uncomfortable. His need to know what she was
thinking got in his way a bit. Until it won out.

"Why do you have an aversion to doctors?" It
was a fair question. His determination was based
on the fact that he *was* a doctor and on their conversation that had ended so abruptly earlier that
afternoon.

Because he'd been consumed by a need to move
closer to her on the bed and had gotten up and
walked out without another word.

Her fork suspended above her plate, Cara
seemed to be studying the table. She took another bite. Chewed. Swallowed. And looked at
him, her long dark hair loose tonight, framing
those big brown eyes.

"My…mom…" She shook her head, her gaze
dropped. She filled her fork and took another bite.
Chewing seemed to be difficult.

So many times he'd wondered about her parents. Her past.

"What about your mom?"

Her gaze aimed toward the table, she shook her head again. Took a sip of tea.

"Are your parents still alive?"

She might leave the room. If she did, he'd do the dishes and settle down with a good book.

"I was thinking that it might be good for your eye to watch television," she said, eating a little more. "You know, with the changing lights, some bright some not, you might be able to distinguish some things."

She was trying to support him. Just as she'd said she would. He supposed it was better than telling him to his face to accept the truth of his changed circumstances, as his friends back home had done. Didn't feel any better, though, knowing as he did that she thought he was wasting his time.

Still, her trying… It meant something.

He couldn't let it mean too much or her beliefs could start to have an impact on him. Wearing off on him. Causing him to start having his own doubts…

But…she was trying…

Not having the heart to tell her he'd been watching television all along, after she went to bed, he nodded. "You've seen my collection of movies," he told her. "Pick one and we can watch it tonight."

She nodded. Took another full bite.

"Cara, are you parents still alive?" All of a sudden the information was critical. To satisfy something burning within him or because he somehow knew she needed help finding her way out of inner hell, he wasn't sure.

"My mom died when I was seventeen."

A year before she'd married that bastard. A small piece of her puzzle fell into place.

"And your dad?" Had she been raised by a single mom? Maybe her parents were divorced. Or…

"He's dead to me."

That one surprised him. Put him on alert, too. He'd heard that abuse was often a cyclical thing. Was that why Cara had remained with a man who hit her for so long? Why she hadn't stopped loving Shawn the first time he hit her?

Had her father's abuse maybe been more predictable? Was that why it had taken Shawn's unpredictability to make her stop loving him? His mind filled in blanks with possibilities. He wanted the truth.

"Why?"

She shook her head again.

"Tell me about doctors then. About your mom."

Her gaze, when she turned it on him, was vulnerable and determined in equal measure. "Why? Why are you doing this?"

"I want to help."

"I don't need your help." Her gaze dropped.

"I don't want your help," she said next. Set her fork down.

And looked at him again. "I'm sorry. That was

rude. You're… I appreciate…the clothes…caring for me…it's…"

Reaching out a hand, Simon touched her cheek. Just a light brush. "Tell me about your mom."

He needed to help her. There was no telling how much longer they'd be able to live like this…two capable human beings with full lives ahead of them, in a tiny cabin. He had a lot of money saved. Investments. He could hang out a long time, if he so chose. Years.

But he wasn't a hang-out-and-do-nothing type of guy.

Probably why he was obsessing about having sex with his housemate. Definitely why he needed her to get emotionally strong enough to seek help elsewhere.

Cara carried her plate to the sink, rinsed it and left the cabin.

WHAT IN THE *hell am I doing?*

She was probably just messed up, way more than she'd thought, but it was starting to seem like she was falling in love with the man who wouldn't let her get on with the end of her life.

She was a married woman.

A criminal.

Outside, Cara made it to a fallen tree at the side of the cabin and remembered him telling her—pointing out the log when they'd been in the yard one day that week—about first finding her. About nudging her with his foot, pushing her over, thinking she was a fallen log…

Which reminded her why she was there at all.

He was her doctor!

And it hit her…transference. She dropped down to the tree. Not caring if it was bug infested. Or if a mountain lion or other nighttime predator was close by.

Transference. That totally explained the bizarre urge she'd just had to lay her head on Simon's shoulder and beg him to take her back to the bed they'd sat on together that afternoon. To make love to her and hold her all night long.

Years ago, she'd heard her dad telling her mom about a patient who'd told him she was in love with him. Cara had been twelve or thirteen and hadn't liked—at all—that some woman fancied herself in love with her father.

Mom hadn't been concerned, though, citing a similar situation that she'd known about when she was charge nurse at the hospital where she'd worked before Cara was born.

Cara could remember having doubts, still, but she'd taken her cue from her mom and quit worrying about it.

Until Mom got sick. A memory came flashing back. Her father had been working late. Said he'd had a seminar to attend. Mom had had a particularly painful night and she'd been unable to sleep. The later it got the more agitated she'd become.

Eventually, Cara had gotten up and gone into her dad's home office. Had been trying to find a list of patient files on his computer. She couldn't remember the name of the woman who'd told him she was in love with him, but she'd known if she could just see it again…

She'd had some idea about going online and trying to find the woman. Maybe an address or phone number. Maybe she could just make sure that Daddy wasn't fooling around on Mom…

He'd come home and found her in his office, going through his things. He'd demanded to know what she was doing. When he was there, so strong and solid, she'd been unable to accuse him of infidelity. Made up some lie about…she couldn't even remember what.

What she remembered was that he'd known she was lying.

He hadn't punished her, though. She'd thought, then, that it was because he was guilty of something and relieved she hadn't found out. And if not that, then he just hadn't cared about her enough anymore to bother with discipline.

Wow…

Shaking, Cara sat there, looking back. Another lost memory returning. Had she been burying them for years?

Was this how Fate had chosen for her to go? By losing her mind?

As a mom, with a child she'd loved more than

life, she could imagine… Her father had to have known what Cara was going through with Mom sick. What if he'd gone easy on her because he'd understood?

She shook her head. But no matter how hard she tried these days to shake off what she couldn't handle, it continued to batter her.

Burying her head in her knees, she covered it with her arms—needing the pain to stop.

"Cara…"

He called softly from a distance, but he was coming toward her. She could hear him now.

Heart pounding, Cara raised her head. How much longer was she going to be able to resist him? Resist leaning on him?

It wasn't right.

Needing anyone wasn't right. Not now. She'd lost her chance to get help. She'd lived too long. Gone too far.

Oh, God.

The closer Simon came, the more Cara felt herself weakening. Succumbing to panic. Not the screaming kind. The kind where she needed comfort so badly she'd give in to its offer.

Shawn had been the only one she'd ever turned to before…

"Cara." Simon was almost upon her, compassion in his tone.

She knew it was wrong…

Having feelings for a man when she couldn't

even believe in the one thing that mattered most to him. When she was just like all the rest of the people who'd let him down.

Could she hate herself any more?

She'd been given a chance to build some good Karma. Maybe even earn herself a place with Mom. Maybe there she'd get to be with Joy again…

And she was going to blow it because…

Shawn had always told her she was weak. He'd proven it to her again and again and again. Every time he hit her and she stayed. Every time she kissed him.

Every time she'd cried on his shoulder.

In the end, he'd been more right than probably even he knew. She'd done the unthinkable.

And then, when he'd stood by her, as he'd always promised he would, she'd even lied to him— just so she didn't have to feel any more of his pain.

The log gave slightly as Simon sat down a foot away from her. She saw his tennis shoes, his jeans-clad legs. Wondered if he'd put on his denim jacket over the flannel shirt he'd had on all day.

She'd come outside without her hoodie.

"Here."

He handed her his jacket.

Staring at the garment, Cara was more frightened than ever. Was Karma telling her she could trust this man? That she was allowed to need him?

Had he read her mind? Because their paths were somehow connected?

Was she reading far more into his gesture than was there? Like she'd thought her father was having an affair because a seminar ran overtime?

Because she was shivering, she took the jacket. Waited for Simon to start grilling her again.

And waited some more.

He just sat there, not even moving.

Minutes passed. And more minutes.

Cara glanced over at him. Had he fallen asleep? Sitting up?

He was looking out toward the yard. Just sitting there, as though he had all night with nothing else to do.

Partially true, of course. But reading or watching a movie would be preferable to just sitting out there in the dark.

She thought about going in, pretty sure that he'd follow her. Considered what movie they might watch. What book she might read when she excused herself for the night.

The walls of the cabin seemed to close in on her at those thoughts.

Everything was closing in on her.

Thoughts, like an avalanche, getting louder. Blasting over the night's quiet hum.

When she could stand it no more, Cara opened her mouth.

CHAPTER EIGHTEEN

"WHEN I WAS fifteen my mom was diagnosed with kidney disease."

Simon didn't move as Cara's words filled the night air.

He'd taken a gamble, coming out to sit with her. For such a strong woman, she was fragile when it came to accepting help.

She named the disease, pronouncing the medical term perfectly. He wasn't all that familiar with it, but knew that it had to do with a body's rejection of its own kidneys. Killing healthy kidneys. And eventually taking its toll on other organs.

There was no cure, no known cause. It wasn't genetic, was a slow killer. And, from what he knew, had the potential to be incredibly painful.

"We knew she was going to die."

Cara's voice had changed. Almost like she was a girl of fifteen again.

"You were close?"

He'd told himself before he'd come out that he'd ask absolutely no questions. He'd be there if she needed him, but he wasn't to engage otherwise.

"Yes."

He was pretty sure she'd nodded. He wasn't looking.

"I was an only child," she said then. "Mom and I... We did everything together. She'd do laundry on Mondays and Fridays, and when I came home from school, I'd put it all away. Thursday was grocery shopping. She'd be waiting for me when I got home and off we'd go..."

The lightness in her tone made it hard for him to swallow.

"She wanted me to join Girl Scouts, to dance, or do gymnastics, to join a club at school, but I didn't want to. I really just wanted to be with her. She played games with me. She'd been reading to me since I was born and I loved to sit while she was sewing, or doing Dad's books on the computer, and just read..."

Dad's books. Confirmation that there'd been a father in the picture.

Cara's voice drifted off, leaving him there with her, as a little girl, sitting in her mother's study as she read.

"She taught me to cook." A full minute had passed. He wondered where she'd been. "But she didn't just have me watch her, she showed me how and let me try. By the time I was ten I had dinner jobs—salad and dessert. I got to pick the dessert."

It sounded like she was smiling. Simon was thankful for the night air cooling his hot skin. For the hard branch beneath his thighs, keeping him from sliding closer.

"I now know why I always wanted to be home with her…"

He almost asked…

"It was Karma's way of giving me every minute I could get."

The pain in those few words had him squeezing the log with his fingers. He could feel how badly she hurt. Couldn't imagine how she'd survived such a loss at a time in her life when a young woman needed her mother most.

His idea of a karma that would let her get so close to her mother only to strip her away was not nearly as kind as Cara's.

And to go from that to a man who beat her…

Yet…she'd done as her mother had done. Married and kept her husband's books. Was it that that had kept her with Shawn so long?

Had her mother also stayed and endured a husband's violent bouts of anger?

"And then a doctor… He just wouldn't give up. It was like he thought he was God or something. He talked her into a transplant. Of course the disease ate that kidney, just like it ate her own two healthy ones. She was back on dialysis for a while, and we knew it was only a matter of time until one or another of her other organs shut down on her, too. Her access got infected. Every time she went in for another procedure she came home weaker.

She was in so much pain, but wouldn't take meds because she didn't want to lose any of the time we had left together…"

With a sick feeling in his gut, he was getting it. Knew why she didn't like doctors. Terminal care was never an easy thing. Not ever. Did you try everything that was medically possible? Live in and out of hospitals in the hope that you could beat the disease? Or, at the very least, prolong the patient's life? Or did you accept fate and ensure as much good-quality living as you could? These types of questions were the part of Simon's job that he didn't miss. The part that he hated, in fact.

Cara had fallen silent, and he wasn't sorry. The glimpse she'd given him—the things that had led up to her decision to marry Shawn, perhaps even *driven* her to marry him—filled him with the same kind of pain he'd known during his time with Opus.

Sometimes, even though you did all you humanly could, it wasn't enough. He'd yet to figure out how to live with that. So could hardly help her do so.

"Then there was a second transplant." Cara's voice had taken on a note of bitterness. "The doctor had referred her to someone else, though, of course, he was right in the thick of all of it. He convinced Mom that this new guy had a procedure, something about tissue and organ transplants…by that time, I knew it was all just more

pain for Mom. There was no cure. But Mom...
she just kept agreeing. She'd go off to the hospital, and when she got home, always weaker than
before, in more pain, I would take care of her."

"What about your father?" The fact that he was
breaking his promise to himself to not ask questions didn't stop him from doing so.

"Working, of course. It's all he ever did. Some
days he'd be gone before I got up in the morning
and wouldn't be home until after I'd gone to bed
at night."

He needed her to stop. For her sake. He couldn't
take this pain away. "So...your mom...she never
got to see him, either." He was looking for a bright
spot. If the man had hit his wife, then at least her
last months hadn't been spent dealing with that,
right?

And even though her mother's care had fallen
solely on Cara, at least she also hadn't had to deal
with bouts of violence—predictable though it may
have been.

"Yeah, Mom saw him. He changed his hours
and traded shifts so he could be home with her
while I was at school."

Simon tried to fit that piece of information with
the rest of the scenario he was building. Figured
that every bad guy had some good qualities. But
wasn't sure that the explanation worked with
where he was going with everything.

But then, from what he understood, abusers

often truly loved their victims, too. Which was one reason victims went back…

"The second transplant failed more quickly than the first one. We didn't even get to have a hope celebration. You know, where we celebrated because we got a good report…"

A hope celebration. He'd never heard it put quite that way. A hope celebration. Only a close family would bother with such a thing…

"Then it was dialysis again, but by then, with two rejections, and the disease eating away at her, her other organs just started to collapse."

He knew that score. Too well. Professionally and personally.

"But the doctor… Do you think he just let her be as comfortable as possible for her remaining days? Let us have some movie and craft days… or just movie days?"

Simon was guessing not. And knew enough, from a medical perspective, to realize that her mom and dad had to have been involved in the choices for her mom's care. A doctor gave choices, he didn't make them.

The doctor had been giving them hope.

Simon got that. Had given it so many times. Had needed it for himself recently.

Unless… Could the guy have been putting this family through so much in an attempt to make more money?

His skin crawled. There *were* those in his profession who...

"Of course he didn't," Cara said a few seconds later. "He just kept talking about new procedures, new machines, new medications...right up until the day she died. She'd just been telling me, the night that she died, that if the new medication worked, she'd be able to last until some new dialysis thing was approved..."

The things people suffered, the lessons life taught them, framed their perceptions. Cara didn't believe in giving false hope in medical situations. Adamantly didn't believe. To her core.

Having her around him...not believing he'd see again...shedding doubts on him even if she didn't voice them...

And yet...this moment wasn't about him at all.

"She was in so much pain, had lost quality of life due to that pain and..."

She broke off again. He needed to hold her. There were times a doctor could put his arm around a patient or a member of the patient's family. To offer comfort.

When it came to human suffering, sometimes boundaries had to be a little fluid.

"This doctor..." He had to know this part. Had to know if the man had profited unduly, at a family's expense. If he'd been prosecuted. "Who was he?"

"My father."

Santa Raquel, California

LILA WAS STILL with Edward—out of bed, but just barely, when her cell phone rang. Hating herself for spending the night with him, even while reliving the most incredible experience she'd ever known, she was trying to get into her suit before he came out of the bathroom.

She'd only ever had one lover before him. Her high school sweetheart. Had no idea of the protocol for the morning after a one-night stand—most particularly one that had been so…satisfying.

Her cheeks burned when she thought of the things she'd let Edward do to her. The things he'd shown her how to do for him.

Legs in her pants, she shimmied over to grab up her phone.

Chantel.

Lila's heart was pumping hard for an entirely different reason as she answered, holding the phone between her shoulder and her ear so she could finish getting dressed.

The detective wouldn't be calling her at seven on a Saturday morning unless there was an emergency.

"Lila? I'm sorry to bother you so early, but I was gone yesterday and…"

"What is it?" *Who* is it? Her mind ran over their most recent resident releases—women who were still so vulnerable.

"Shawn Amos. His attorney argued him out of jail yesterday afternoon."

"He's free." She could feel her face whitening, thoughts of Joy foremost in her mind.

"Since yesterday afternoon. The prosecutor just didn't have enough to keep him locked up. He's not dropping the charges, but we're going to have to find more evidence before this goes to court…"

Edward came out of the bathroom, wearing a robe. She was in his room. His things were all around her. He was everywhere. She hurt for him so much she lost track of her thoughts for a vital couple of seconds.

Joy.

"I've already got a car on its way to the Stand," Chantel was saying. "I called security there first, made certain that Joy's in her cabin and the shelter has had no breaches."

Thank God.

That this would happen while she'd been…

She couldn't think about what she'd been doing.

She'd known it was wrong.

What? Who is it? Edward mouthed the words to her, holding his hand up to his ear as though holding a phone. As he raised his arm, his robe opened a notch.

She turned her back on him.

She couldn't care about him—other than as a family member of a very young resident. Absolutely could not give her heart to him.

For his sake—not her own.

Even now. Her youngest resident was at risk and she'd been off in a hotel room seeking her own physical pleasure rather than at the Stand, keeping her safe…

Telling Chantel that she'd be there soon, she rang off, her mind racing. She had to figure out what to say to Edward, Joy's grandfather. He'd need advice. A plan.

It was her job to have one for him.

And there she stood, practically with her pants down, completely unprepared…

She shouldn't be here.

"Shawn's out on bail." Not the least bit professional. Most particularly the part where she was upset by the news. Shaken by it.

His movements deliberate, he discarded his robe, reaching for a drawer. "I'm going with you."

Lila looked away, walked to the window, staring out at the ocean as he dressed.

"There's not enough evidence that Shawn killed Mary. With only Joy's testimony…and Cara still missing…"

"He'll know Joy can testify against him. If things happened as she says they did." He was much more calm than she was. Lila's thoughts settled.

"We can't let her off the grounds at the Stand," she said, finding herself somewhere in the muck she'd created. "I'll appoint round-the-clock security to her. Chantel has a car in the area, keeping a watch out."

She stiffened as his hands settled on her shoulders. She hadn't heard his approach. Turning, she saw that he'd already donned a suit and tie. She looked him straight in the eye.

"This was a mistake, Edward. It can't happen again."

He nodded. "We can talk later, if you'd like. Right now, I'm in your hands. Tell me what to do. How I can help. I've got money. Do we need to hire another private investigator?"

She hadn't known he'd hired one.

It stung, the ease with which he shifted the topic away from the two of them. But he was absolutely right to do so.

"Let's get to my office," she said, all business now. "Chantel's meeting us there. I'll call Sara on the way in and have her be there, too."

"I'll call Hunter."

She expected him to let her go ahead of him, to grab his keys and leave himself. Edward surprised her with a tender kiss on the lips first.

Then he let her go.

CHAPTER NINETEEN

Prospector, Nevada

ALMOST TWO WEEKS had passed since Cara told him about her parents. The first couple of days after that she'd hardly talked at all. And since then...their conversation had been easy, comfortable. Personal even—movies, books, general opinions.

They stayed completely away from anything emotional or relating to beliefs.

He had no idea how long it had been since she was in touch with her father. If the man knew about Shawn. He could even be looking for Cara. The couple of times he'd tried to bring up the topic of her father, she'd shut down on him—except to say that he wouldn't be looking for her.

But he knew now that her favorite color was purple. She didn't like peas. Her lucky number was eight. She loved dogs—had cried when Shawn made her get rid of the one a client had given her—but had understood that, with all of the hours they were gone, it wasn't fair for her to keep the pet. The dog would have spent more than half his life in a cage.

Cara wanted nothing to do with politics.

And always gave money when she saw someone begging—as long as Shawn wasn't right there. Then he gave the money.

She'd always wanted to go to college—Shawn hadn't seen the point. She knew enough to work in the family business. They'd made enough money to live comfortably. And college would have put them in debt.

She'd wanted to be a child life specialist—one with a degree in child development who advocated for the rights of children, usually in a hospital setting.

Simon had asked if she'd ever wanted children.

She'd excused herself to bed on that one. It had been the night before. He'd been missing her ever since. Acutely. More than made sense, considering it was only six in the morning and she'd been sleeping in the room next door all night.

More than should have made sense. Except that Simon had spent most of the night awake, sitting up on the couch, admitting to himself that he was falling in love.

With another man's wife. Someone who thought he was kidding himself that he'd ever see out of his right eye again—someone who didn't think he'd ever have his career, his life's work, back.

IF NOT FOR the calendar that Simon kept on the refrigerator, Cara would have lost all track of days. As it was, she avoided looking. She'd been with Simon more than a month and while she was fine right where she was, she knew the life was unrealistic—as was any life for her, other than jail.

Maybe, then, that was her lot? Rather than dying, she was to spend the rest of her days behind bars?

The idea panicked her. Oddly, though, not because she cared anymore about jail—she could sit around and wait anywhere. The idea scared her because it didn't feel right. She was sure now that Karma could have a job for her to do there. A way to use her useless life.

Maybe it was just the fear that Shawn would get her before they put her away that kept her rooted in nowhere land.

And maybe it was that she was the most selfish creature on earth, as Shawn had said so many times when he'd been beating her. Or on the way to beating her. Maybe she was still in the cabin in the woods, avoiding jail—or Shawn—because she wanted to be with Simon for as long as she could be.

Mom had always told her to listen to her heart and Lord knew she was trying. Confused, and frightened a lot of the time, resigned to the rest, she couldn't figure out what Fate was trying to tell her.

If only she could remember more than just horrifying snippets of that last day at home. If she could tell a court what she'd done— If she could understand why she'd done it, how she could have been so disassociated from who she knew herself to be...

But then, what did she really know?

Hiking on the mountain with Simon the first Monday in November—something they did every afternoon now—Cara's mind continued to attack her perceptions to the point that she considered asking Simon to check her into a mental institution. She didn't feel that far gone. But she didn't feel lucid, either.

Nothing rested comfortably inside her anymore. Nothing.

She'd been so certain her father had walked out on them emotionally when her mother got sick. His constant refusal to accept that she was going to die and let them build as many meaningful and happy memories as they could with the time they had left. The way he'd practically bullied her into more and more procedures...

Including giving up his own kidney so her diseased body could kill that, too...

She hadn't thought of that in years. And yet now she remembered how she'd felt when her parents had told her the plan. Her Aunt Betty had come to stay with her, but as sweet and loving as she'd been, her aunt's presence in her parents' place had scared the shit out of her.

That was when she'd realized she was on her own. That she couldn't count on either of her parents to always be there for her.

That her dad would willingly risk his life, that he was willing to die and leave Cara orphaned... the emotion welling up nearly choked her.

And then, as had been happening again and again during the weeks since she'd told Simon about him...she saw another side. Another view.

Edward Mantle had been trying to save his wife's life. Save his family. He was a doctor. He'd gone about the whole thing in the only way he knew how. By continuing to try.

Just as Simon continued to try to see.

Shaking her head as she slipped on a rock, trying to keep up with Simon's pace, she'd have liked to tell both men that Fate was much more powerful than any kind of science man might study or determination man might have.

And that Karma would be the final decider, no matter how much anyone did to fight the inevitable.

But wait... Karma was based on your own actions. You created your Karma. Good or bad.

So...she'd done all of this?

She slipped again. Looked backward and watched the trail of rock slide down the steep cliff they were climbing. Simon wanted to get to the top of the peak just behind the cabin. They'd started out with small, short hikes in other less-steep areas. They'd explored over a mile's radius around them—seeing no wildlife at all, but finding some coyote beds.

She'd heard coyotes howling during the night several times since she'd been there. Calling to their mates, Simon had said. He'd also said that bobcats could sound similar. That they roamed these hills. Which was why he always carried the .22 when they climbed. And never wore his patch.

The rocks continued to slide behind her. Cara continued to fall farther behind Simon. She was tired, but not so much that she couldn't make it to the top. She could follow those rocks bouncing to the bottom. She could slip. Fall. Not on purpose—she could not take her own life; it was wrong, Mom had told her. Which was why her mother had agreed to all of the medical procedures. She had to do all she could to live until her life was taken from her. That was when she'd know she was done.

But…

"Hey, you getting tired? We can stop for today."

Simon was back. Not even a little bit out of breath. Looking just too damn good in those jeans that hugged his butt and the flannel shirt that covered the arms, chest and shoulders that had once cradled her…

His eyes held the light of life as he gazed at her. His features alive and...filled with concern, too. He held out a hand to her.

More than anything, she wanted to reach out and take it.

"I was...just enjoying the view," she told him, climbing up to him on her own. "I'm fine. I can make it."

"You might think I'm going soft, but I've got this feeling that this climb is kind of symbolic for us," he said, looking up to the last quarter of the ascent. His face was just a foot away from hers. His right eye seemed to be looking at her, but based on their exercises, on what he described seeing on TV when he had his patch over his good eye, she wasn't seeing any sign of returning vision.

Not that she'd voiced her opinion aloud. After a while, he'd quit telling her about it.

"How is it symbolic for us?" she asked, her heart breaking at the thought of Simon not reaching the goal he was so determined to achieve.

"Our lives. We're both on our own uphill struggle right now, but if we keep going, we also both have what it takes to reach the top."

She didn't doubt that part.

"But what happens if we get up there and the view isn't what we expected?"

For the first time in ten years, Cara was thinking about Edward Mantle and seeing something entirely different. Over the past few days, she'd actually thought about contacting him.

Until she remembered the rest of her life—the time since she'd been his little girl. The things she'd done.

He'd be disappointed. Maybe even distraught. He'd try to fix something that she'd broken and that couldn't possibly be fixed. She couldn't do that to him. Let him think she'd run off to la-la land and was living happily ever after...

"You can get help, Cara." Simon hadn't taken another step. He was watching her with that assessing way of his—but even that seemed to have changed. "As soon as you're ready... I'd go with you. Be there for you..."

He'd go with her?

She stared at him. Started to shake from the inside out at the thought of a life ahead with Simon in it.

There wouldn't be one. The rational part of her knew that. But...what if he came to visit her in prison? Even only once a month. Life would be worth living for that. There would be a future to look forward to in that.

But would he really come? What if, after a year passed and he couldn't see, he gave up hope? Would he blame her for bringing her doubts into his world up here?

She could see herself, sitting alone at a table in

a prison visiting room, waiting, and having him not show up.

Not that her penance was about her.

When was she ever going to quit thinking about herself? It was just like Shawn had said…

But…how did a person listen to her own heart and not feel self? How did one not look after self?

Most particularly when one had the responsibility to look after self?

She shook her head. She was doing it so much she was getting dizzy.

"I wasn't actually thinking about me when I said that about the view not being what we expected." She hadn't been. But was afraid to continue the conversation.

Just as Simon respected the parts of her that were off-limits, she had to do the same for him.

"What were you thinking about?"

He'd asked. If she wasn't thinking about her own view… There were only two of them there…

He kept pressuring her to take his solution to her problem. Maybe she needed to return the favor. Maybe she wasn't being a good enough friend to him, letting him believe in the impossible rather than planning for the life ahead.

"What if your vision doesn't come back one hundred percent, Simon? What then? You don't seem to even consider the possibility. To have a plan B."

Sucking in his lips, Simon appeared to chew on them a minute. He gestured vaguely.

"Being a surgeon is all I know," he told her. "I can't do that with one eye. So I know the vision is going to come back. I'm being tested. I'll pass the test."

With that he turned and started to climb again.

Feeling an anguish she knew wasn't her own, but one that she now understood, she followed him. Staying up with him. Not looking back at all.

THE VIEW FROM the top was... It moved him. Standing up there with Cara by his side, Simon felt as though he could accomplish anything he set his mind to. Filled with his own power, his own strength, he knew that there was not a test too tough for him to face.

Bursting with the sense of it all, he said as much to Cara.

"So what if the test you must face is being partially blind in one eye?"

He was on top of the world. Could see the vastness of endless possibility spread out before him. He'd met a beautiful woman who was climbing inside his soul one step at a time.

And she didn't believe in him.

He'd known, of course. For weeks. He still didn't have any good response for her. Cara didn't deserve his anger. She couldn't help how she felt.

"What if it's like my dad?" The wind almost

carried her words away. She wasn't standing close to him. Wasn't looking at him. Yet he knew how much the words were costing her.

And so, when she continued speaking, he didn't cut her off. He just guarded himself against any impact from her words.

He had to persuade her to get herself help. To get her out of his immediate life.

"My mom had a terminal disease. She was going to die. He couldn't accept that, so instead of helping her and going through it together, with me, instead of easing Mom's suffering by letting her go naturally, he kept refusing to accept the inevitable, and in the end, we were left with nothing. No Mom. No family. He even sold our house, the home where we were a family, because he couldn't accept that she was gone…"

Simon had already lost his small family. Had his own home. His need to see wasn't hurting anyone. To the contrary, when he could see again, he'd be saving lives.

"It's the whole doctor thing," she said. Turning to look at him then. "Are you all alike? Thinking you've got some secret power the rest of us don't have? Stubborn to the point of hurting those around you?"

The short answer was *of course not*. But Simon didn't give it to her. Maybe a person who studied medicine, who believed in medical science to the point of dedicating his life to it, did have a certain sense of being able to save the world. Maybe not.

He hadn't been able to save Opus.

But he heard so much more in Cara's words than just her insight into his situation—much of which she knew nothing about. Clearly, she'd been doing a lot of thinking about her own life. And, based on the fact that she was beginning to see her father in a different light, she was making progress.

He rejoiced for her.

And knew a stab of pain, too. Because soon, very soon, Cara was going to be ready to leave him. He needed her to be ready soon. The feelings he was developing for her were getting out of hand. And there was no future for them.

He couldn't see himself ever, ever, ever marrying again—putting himself in a position where, if feelings changed, when people changed as they did, he'd be trapped by finances and laws and whatever home and life they'd built together. Forced to stay in an unhealthy environment. Until one of them snapped...

And it was growing clearer by the day that that kind of security was the only thing that would ever make Cara happy. She'd been seeking it since she was fifteen years old. There was no way he could ever ask her to live without it.

By all counts, their time at the cabin had to end. And so did their time together.

CHAPTER TWENTY

Santa Raquel, California

LILA WAS COMING from the clinic at the Stand the first Saturday evening in November—having just registered a new resident being treated by Lynn Bishop, the nurse practitioner who lived on site with her family—when she felt her phone buzz for a text message. Pulling the cell out of her jacket pocket immediately, ready to present herself where she was needed, she saw who it was.

Brett Ackerman, the Stand's founder, never called her. They communicated mostly through his secretary and occasional notes. More and more, since his marriage and the birth of his first child, he'd begun texting her.

She figured it was because time had become more precious to the new father and businessman whose charity accreditation company took him all over the country. And suspected his reason was more than that.

Ella, Jerimiah and I would like you to come to dinner tomorrow night.

They'd asked her to dinner several times. And their wedding, too. They wanted to share their young family with her. They, like everyone else, didn't understand that she couldn't be part of a family. That she was a danger.

Her answer to them was always the same as it had been to Edward Mantle.

That night, she faltered for a second. A hard second. But only a second.

I truly appreciate the invitation. I'm so sorry I cannot be there.

She'd meant to type *no thank you*.
But hit Send anyway.

WALKING DOWN THE hall to her office minutes later, Lila smiled at a couple of residents passing her on their way to the cafeteria. There was an ice cream social that night. She'd peek in if she got the chance.

The library door was open and she noticed an older woman, one of their newer residents, sitting in a plush leather armchair in the corner, engrossed in a book. Paperwork in hand, Lila stopped in. Said hello. Made certain the woman was truly after some reading time and not feeling lonely and then made her way to her office door. As she rounded the last corner, she saw

Edward push away from the wall he'd been leaning against.

Obviously waiting for her.

His tie was loosened, but his dark suit looked as crisp as usual; his wing tips had their usual sheen.

Desire pooled instantly.

She kept walking toward him, the same smile she'd just given the reading resident on her lips.

"How was Joy today?"

"She wants to go to Hunter's." He shrugged. "She wanted ice cream, too, so we settled for Julie and Hunter taking her to the ice cream social, and then I'll tuck her into bed."

The issue of Joy leaving with Edward, staying with him, had been temporarily tabled as Shawn Amos took up his life, had a winter surfing class going in the big garage where he stored surfboards and wet suits, and still claimed to know nothing about his wife's whereabouts.

He was only out on bail. The cops were watching him like a hawk, whether he knew it or not, and so far he had done nothing that could implicate him in anything.

Law enforcement officials and others were extremely suspicious of the fact that he hadn't asked to see his daughter. Technically, he could have visitation rights if he sought them out. Could possibly even fight for custody. He knew that Joy was currently staying at a shelter. Probably even knew that Edward had been granted temporary guardianship.

But he hadn't even asked after her.

Because he knew that if Joy saw him, she could unravel and reveal all kinds of things that he'd rather people didn't know? Could perhaps lead them to evidence that would convict him?

Or because he didn't want to confuse the little girl when she'd already gone through such a hard time and could very well lose him all over again?

Was he staying away for Joy's sake? For his own? Or just to buy himself time before he took the law into his own hands?

"You want to come with me to get some ice cream?" Edward asked as Lila unlocked her office door and dropped the folder in her hand on the desk.

Feeling drab in her gray suit suddenly, she put her hand up to her bun, pushed in pins that were already tight, stabbing her scalp, and dropped her arm.

"I…can't."

He nodded. "It's not like I can jump your bones in the middle of bowls of ice cream."

"I know." She smiled at him. Stopped herself. Wanted to go to bed with him so badly it hurt. And…

"I've been thinking," she blurted. "Maybe you should move into my suite here at the Stand."

She had thought about it. Several times. Always followed by an emphatic *no* for so many reasons.

His eyebrows rose, and smiling, he started to say something.

"Not with me!" Lila quickly clarified. "I would stay at my condo and sleep in my office if I need to stay over here." She could always access the closet and shower of her suite after Edward vacated. Or use any number of other bathrooms on the premises, for that matter. She didn't need a lot when it came to morning ablutions.

Soap. Water. Toothbrush. Brush. Foundation, which she kept in her purse. That was it.

"I'm not going to put you out of your space, Lila."

"Think about it a minute," she told him, though part of her really, really did not want Edward invading her space. Wanted that almost as badly as she wanted to know that he'd slept in her bed. Even if not with her.

"We could bring a cot in and you could have Joy stay with you." She pulled out the big guns. They were the whole reason the idea had occurred to her.

Him staying there, that was. Not him in her bed.

That had come before. Way before.

Long before she'd realized how deeply in trouble she was.

She'd had sex with him. Unprotected, delicious, adventurous sex with him. And she'd done it knowing she couldn't start a relationship.

At least, at fifty-three, she didn't have to worry about an unwanted pregnancy, to boot.

"In spite of her father being out of jail—in my opinion, even more because of it—Joy needs the sense of home and security we are trying to give her. She can't keep staying in a bungalow with a housemother forever. She'll have to continue attending school here, at least until we know more about what's next for her in life, but…"

Edward nodded, his expression serious, but not frowning.

"You know I'll jump at any chance that helps us do that for her, that helps me establish myself as a caregiver that she knows loves her and with whom she feels secure…"

Joy held his hand pretty much any time they walked together now. But given a choice, she still wanted to be with Hunter and Julie over him. Lila knew how much that hurt him.

He was going to accept. Her heart dropped. He was going to accept!

Edward would be living at the Stand. Not just coming to be with his granddaughter and leaving after dinner.

While Lila's heart soared, it felt as though the world was closing in on her.

"But I'll only stay at your place under one condition."

If he thought she was going to stay with him, that was out of the question. Most particularly at the Stand, where everyone she knew... Where people would know...

Not there. Not anywhere.

She took a breath when she could. Crossed over to her desk. Put the folder she'd dropped there in her In file. "What condition?"

She couldn't sleep with him again. Not even...

It dawned on her then that he wouldn't ask Lila to sleep with him with his granddaughter on a cot in the next room...

"I need to know why you spent one, I have to say, pretty spectacular night with me, but have been treating me more like a stranger than you did before. It's been two weeks, Lila. You have to know you have nothing to fear from me..."

"I'm not afraid of you." Not in the least. Which was part of the problem in a weird kind of way. She trusted Edward implicitly. Felt more safe and secure with him than she could ever remember feeling. Even as a kid. Especially as a kid.

"Then what is it?"

"I'm not interested in a relationship."

"Kind of late to decide that, isn't it? We're friends, at the very least."

No. She shook her head. He was a family member of one of her residents. Her caring...it stemmed from that...

But even as she tried to convince herself, she knew she was lying. Something she'd promised herself never to do again.

"What's wrong, Lila? I need to know that before I can move into your home. I need to know that I'm not making life more difficult for you. I just... I can't sleep in your bed not knowing why you refuse to join me there again."

His words took all of the air out of her lungs. They zapped her energy. Her heart. Sinking down to her chair, she closed her eyes. Tried to find her center—the place where she was always calm and her way was clear.

She'd been struggling to get there for weeks. Since before she'd slept with Edward. And every single second since.

She was going to tell him. It might not be right. It might not be best. It could be the end of everything she cared about.

But she was going to tell him.

Something had taken over since the moment she'd met Edward. Assuredly he was wrong for her.

But she was going to tell him.

She could lose her job. Lose everything...

Lila looked at Edward. She opened her mouth, feeling every muscle it took to do so. "The pattern of abuse often repeats itself from one generation to the next. My husband and I met in high school. We both came from abusive homes. We swore we'd make a home in which no violence existed. Who but two victims would be better able to make that happen?" She shook her head, but kept pushing the truth out as fast as she could. "He became violent first. I became his victim. Then my son did. I didn't leave. I didn't save my son. And, in the end, when the bottom of my world fell out, I beat my boy, too."

The words were said.

Her secret was out.

And Lila just wanted to curl up and die.

EDWARD GAVE HER little choice. The second she stopped speaking, he took her hand and led her through the door in her office to the suite beyond.

That was another thing. If he stayed in her suite he'd have to access it by going in and out of her office.

Her files were all kept locked. Her computer was encrypted. She trusted him. He'd passed all security clearance.

She just… In and out of her office…every morning and every night…

"Let me make some tea," he was saying as he pulled out a chair for her at her kitchen table.

"I can make tea."

"You lost all your color back there, Lila. You almost passed out."

Things had been a bit hazy for a second. She'd admit that. But, "I'm fine now."

If they could just move on, if he would keep her secret and they could act like those last words of hers in her office had never been said…

"I'll make tea." She stood up. Gathered together the familiar, pretty things she'd collected, surrounding herself with beauty to replace the love she'd never have again.

Edward sat. She made tea. Poured. Carried it to the table. She figured he'd need to know logistics. Need a key.

Maybe he'd want a coffeepot—coffee—in the kitchen. And a manly mug or two.

She served him his tea in the china rose cup. Brought some English biscuits, remembering the year she'd received an entire year's supply of them for Christmas. It had been the second year the Stand had been open. The box had come anonymously, but Lila had always known who sent it.

The son she wouldn't see. Couldn't see, for fear of feelings surfacing that might cause her to lash out at him. To hurt him or his family.

And he... God bless him, didn't push.

"Tell me about it."

About the biscuits? That had been years ago and...

"Tell me about you, Lila."

She stared at him.

"Please. Let me share this piece of you, as you shared my deepest regret. And then, if it's your wish that I leave you entirely alone, I will do so."

Why? She saw no point in putting them through this. Until she saw the pain searing the corners of his eyes and understood.

Edward had hurt his daughter. Had possibly driven her into the arms of the man who'd killed her. Understanding dawned then.

Their meeting…their connection…it had been no mistake. They were two souls looking to make up for mistakes they'd made—doing everything they could to atone…

"I already told you, I grew up in an abusive household." Maybe he hadn't meant for her to go back that far. She only knew she couldn't tell the story without it. "My father backhanded my mother any time she dared to disagree with him. She backhanded us. My older brother and me. Until my brother was killed in a car accident. Then it was just me."

He put his hand over hers. She slid her hand away. She wasn't looking for sympathy. "Then I met my husband…we swore to each other that the pattern of abuse stopped with us…"

Hard to believe she'd ever been that naive. And that arrogant.

"He's the father of your son."

"And my daughter." Oh, God. Sweet precious baby girl. The words just slipped out. She could handle the pain of her loss as long as no one else knew…no one added sympathy to weight already too heavy to bear.

"You have a daughter."

She looked at him.

And that was when she realized what safety

really felt like. "I had a daughter," she told him. Then, before she could crawl across the table and into his arms, climb on his lap and beg him to hold her, she continued.

"We kept our pact, my husband and I, to keep abuse out of our home—until our daughter was seven. She was diagnosed with leukemia…"

Feeling Edward stiffen, seeing the pain in his gaze as he looked at her, she knew she didn't have to explain the years of painful treatments. The months of despair followed by months of hope. Never quite relaxing.

"So many nights she lay awake crying, asking her daddy and me to make it all better…" She swallowed. "He started to drink. Lost his job. Bills piled up. We lost our insurance…"

It wasn't a new story. Or an isolated one, either. She'd heard it more than once since she'd come to work at the Stand.

"And he hit you." Edward's tone was hard. And filled with compassion, too.

"Yes. And then he hit me."

"But with your daughter sick, you couldn't leave him."

"We'd met a man at the hospital. His son had leukemia. He helped us. Gave my husband a job. We had insurance again. Our daughter was in remission. My husband told me every day how sorry he was. How much he loved us all. He begged me to trust him again, like I used to do…"

She'd tried. Maybe, given time, she'd have learned how to trust again…

Some abusers truly recovered. Some women loved them safely for the rest of their lives.

"And then our baby girl got sick again." Nothing would ever be as bad as those last months of her sweet daughter's life. "She was twelve then. Old enough to understand what was happening. What it meant when they said there was nothing more they could do. The beatings started again, but never in front of her. I had to stay. He kept his job that time, and I needed the insurance. My son tried to intervene on my behalf. He was a senior in high school then. He took some pretty severe hits, too. I asked him to just leave when his father got ugly. But I didn't leave for him. I didn't take him out of there. I stayed. And prayed that my daughter didn't know…that she thought she was dying in the circle of a loving family…"

Tears were pooling in Edward's eyes while she was shedding her own. They were streaming down her cheeks.

"The weeks and months passed," she said, needing to get it all out now. Then to figure out where she went from there. Needing more than ever for Edward to know why she could never love him. Or let him love her.

"Tension became a permanent part of me. And of our home. Until the day we buried our little girl. I came home from the funeral and my son walked in right behind me. He was only looking out for me. Worried about me, but something about having that big man towering over my shoulder... I don't know... I look back on it and I just can't make it right, can't figure it out... He reached out for me, and I just lost it. I screamed at him to get away. I started hitting and I just couldn't stop..." She was sobbing now. Sometimes it felt as though she'd never stopped.

Edward's silence left room for the anguish to just keep coming.

"I will never forget the look of horror on his face."

It was that look, that one single memory in a lifetime, that had sealed her fate.

"I took a sleeping pill that night. And did what I had to do for the next little bit. I got my son off to college. And when my husband kept beating me, I even pressed charges. I got myself into counseling. And now I'm here."

"And the founder of The Lemonade Stand...he knows about this?"

"Absolutely. Every detail." She wouldn't be there otherwise.

"Where's your husband?"

"In prison. He ended up in more trouble there, too, beating an inmate. He's now serving a life sentence."

"And your son?"

Lila shrugged. Then smiled through her tears.

"He has a good, healthy life," she told him. "He's married with a family of his own. Has a great job that he enjoys. A lovely home."

"So you see him?"

She shook her head. He still wasn't getting it.

"I haven't seen him since I hugged him goodbye when he left for college. I can't see him, Edward. I can't risk being an abuser in his life. Or in anyone's life. Don't you see? The pattern of abuse… it starts at home. Not every abused kid becomes an abuser. I didn't think I would. You just don't ever know. Until you've reached the end of your tether and find out what you do when you snap. You…you bury yourself in work. Me? When my emotions get too intense, I lash out."

And that was why she could never, ever be in a close personal relationship.

Not ever.

CHAPTER TWENTY-ONE

Prospector, Nevada

NOVEMBER WAS PASSING, day by day. Cara had taken to avoiding the calendar on the refrigerator altogether. Each night she went to bed knowing that one more day of her time away from time was gone. She was one day closer to having to do something.

Memories continued to haunt her waking hours—snippets, some so good they hurt and some so bad they teased at the edges of conscious thought and wouldn't quite appear—but she dreaded the nights, the dark silence, even more. In the night, her tension grew. Every minute that ticked by was another one gone.

And still, she was no closer to knowing what she should do.

What the hell should she do?

Most nights, climbing a mountain and getting permanently lost seemed like the best solution. Remembering that the option was open to her brought her comfort enough to drift off to sleep.

And then morning would come, the light of

day, and she'd be struck once again with the weight of hopelessness.

Mom had always told her to follow her heart. Her heart was telling her to protect herself.

But was it that selfishness that had driven her away from the man who truly loved her into the arms of a man who'd needed to own her?

The bitter reality was another horrible pill to swallow. If what she suspected was true—if, like Simon, her father had been struggling with grief—how must he have felt when his only child cut him off?

He'd lost ten years of her life. The birth of his grandchild…

Usually at that point, she shut down, got out of bed and started another empty day. Suicide happened when the pain was more than one's ability to cope. She remembered reading that somewhere.

She could not commit suicide. Her mother's life, her death, had to stand for something, and in Cara's mind, it stood for the value of life.

In the shower one morning a couple of weeks before Thanksgiving, Cara had to remind herself, again, that life was a gift. That her duty to the gift of life was to live it through to the end. To ensure that her life's purpose was fulfilled.

As the water battered down on her, so did her thoughts. How could she serve a purpose when she knew she'd done something horrible but couldn't remember actually doing it? Didn't know how she'd felt, what she'd been thinking. Didn't know why…

In that tiny stall, she stared at the razor Simon had given her. And thought about just being done with life. It would be quick. And efficient, too. The blood would just wash down the drain with the water. No mess.

With her eye firmly on the razor, she reached for the soap. Washed herself. The razor was there. Waiting to help her…

Daddy might be notified.

Wouldn't her taking accountability for her worthless life by taking away the need for anyone else to try to help her, or to feed her in prison, be better than his knowing that his only child was rotting away behind bars?

And Simon… He needed to be free of her. She was dragging him down. Distracting him from his course.

The blades of the razor were sharp. You didn't live with medical professionals without learning about critical veins. *Listen to your heart.* Her mother's words came to her. *Promise me, Cara. Anytime you have decisions to make…listen to your heart. It's good and pure, sweetie. Trust it.*

Had she been listening to her heart when she'd had to get away from her father? She'd thought she had been.

And when she'd married Shawn?

Again, she'd been so sure.

The water pounded down.

Listen to your heart.

She was trying. Oh, God, she was trying. What was Fate trying to tell her? When would she know for sure? Would she ever know?

Did she *want* to know?

She stared at the blade hanging within reach.

Listen to your heart.

Sobs racked her body. Taking her breath. Hurting her ribs.

Sinking down to the shower floor, feeling the water beating down upon her, cleansing her, Cara's heart cried out for Simon.

"CARA?" WHEN SHE first heard his voice, she thought she was imagining it.

"Cara!"

The door to the bathroom hit the wall with force, and before she could react—if indeed she could react—the shower curtain was flung open.

"Cara!" Simon reached for her, his head and back blocking the water. She welcomed the respite from the icy cold, shivering.

She was in his arms, snuggled up against the warmth of his chest when she became self-conscious about her nudity. He'd grabbed a towel, lifting a knee to balance her on his thigh as he did so, getting the towel around her shoulders, her back. Then he carried her out to the couch.

He shouldn't put her there. She was wet.

He sat with her on his lap, getting himself wet, using the towel to dry her off.

"Did you slip? What hurts?" he asked.

It was only then that she realized he was a doctor to the rescue again. Feeling incredibly stupid, embarrassed and slightly out of her mind, she sat up. Gathered the towel more tightly around herself, hiding her nudity as best she could.

"I d-didn't s-slip," she said, hiccupping. Leftover evidence of the tears she'd been shedding. She wanted to explain why she'd been huddled on the shower floor letting the icy water pelt her skin, but couldn't.

She didn't know why. Because she hadn't had what it took to get up and turn off the water. To get out and dry herself off.

Afraid to trust herself to stand just yet, she slid off his lap and into the corner of the couch, pulling the blanket off the back of it with her. In the warmer days, he'd put the blanket away with his sheets every morning. Now that the afternoon air was chilled, he left the blanket for her to use while she read.

Her teeth were chattering.

"What's going on?" He leaned over her. Reached into the blanket to find her wrist.

Waiting for him to finish with her pulse, to let go of her, Cara counted the drops falling off her hair and sliding down her back.

Apparently satisfied that she wasn't on her

deathbed, he stayed close. His eyes were wide and filled with concern she didn't deserve and couldn't return, no matter how much of her heart belonged to him.

"I can't do it anymore, Simon." She got the words out without a stutter, but still shivered inside her blanket.

"Do what?"

"Any of this. Staying here. Living with it. Trying to figure it out." She'd given up. And it had gotten her...naked on a couch with a good man wasting his time because of her.

"What is 'it'?" He spoke slowly. Because she'd gone addle brained? Or because he wasn't sure he wanted to hear whatever was coming?

"I...did something. Something bad." She couldn't tell him she'd killed someone. If he knew, he'd be guilty of harboring a criminal.

She'd killed someone.

She'd *killed* someone?

The thought that had just slipped out settled upon her. Clearly. As though it had always been there. She couldn't be sure it hadn't been. Had she known and just been lying to herself?

She'd killed someone. She didn't ask who. Didn't look any deeper into the brutal recesses of her mind at the moment. She just sat with the truth. Accepting what was.

Relief mingled with horror. It was almost as

though she were sitting above herself, looking down. Watching her life from a distance.

She was a *murderer*?

She was a murderer! That was why they'd been on the run.

Shawn had told her so.

It came back to her, as she sat here in the cabin, shivering, with Simon beside her. She remembered hearing Shawn's voice through a haze of pain. She'd been in the van. Their van? She couldn't be sure. But he'd been there, wiping her face with a cool cloth. Giving her something for the pain in her head. She hadn't wanted it, but he'd put it in her mouth, held her jaw shut until she swallowed. Helping her, he'd said. Telling her that he'd always be there for her. That he was getting her to safety and would stand by her. Telling her she'd never be alone.

That was how he'd done it. That was how he'd gotten her to leave her father for him. He'd promised her she'd never be alone again.

The thought rose unbidden. She stared at Simon.

He must have spoken. She hadn't made out the words.

"What did you do?" he asked.

She shook her head. That part was still fuzzy. But she owed it to him to...

Closing her eyes, Cara thought of that last day. Out eating with Joy. The man who held the door.

She thought of her home. The spot on the living room carpet where Joy had dropped a bottle of nail polish remover.

Cara had told Shawn that she'd done it. He'd shrugged it off with a kiss and a statement about them needing new carpet anyway.

Mary had stepped on that spot…

"Cara?"

"I…" Opening her eyes, she looked at him. "I'm trying to remember…"

"You don't remember."

She shook her head. Had a flash of fear—was he going to finally get angry with her?

"I… I've been…ever since I woke up here… I get flashes… I've been getting more and more of them…like my dad…"

"You didn't remember your dad?" He sounded really concerned now. "You've been having memory lapses and you're only just now telling me about them?"

His intense stare, the way his seemed to stop on every inch of her face, zeroing in on one eye and then another, distracted her from the emotions tangling her up inside.

"I remember my dad," she told him. "I remember exactly what I've been remembering for the past ten years. All the things he did that hurt me, all the things that I didn't understand and assigned motivations to that probably weren't accurate. What I didn't remember, I think because

I pushed them too deeply inside, were the good things. And some of the worst things, too…" Like the morning her father had told her that her mom had passed away the night before. He hadn't come to get her at the time, though he'd known she was still awake.

He'd waited until morning.

At the time, she'd found his action to be cruel and insensitive. Had screamed at him that he didn't care about her at all. That he'd wanted to hog her mother for himself. Shame spread through her with the memory. When, looking back, thinking like a mother, wanting to protect a child, she could see that maybe he'd just wanted her to get a good night's sleep. To face the horrible news in daylight, not darkness.

His expression changing from all business to one of a more intimate nature, Simon put a hand on the blanket, cocooning her.

She shivered.

"Shawn has always told me how selfish I am," she said. Simon needed to know. To protect himself. "It was always all about me, he said."

The memories of her father certainly looked that way. He'd just lost a wife. Was left alone with a hormonal, emotional, angry teenaged daughter to raise. It had to have been a daunting task.

Could he have done better at it? Should he have?

Maybe. Probably should have stayed home, at least. Spent some time with her. Let her stay in the home that was filled with memories of love and family. The home that was the only security she'd ever known...

But she had a feeling he'd done his best.

"He's right," she said now. "I have always thought of myself..."

Simon's lips pursed. "So...when you...as a fifteen- to seventeen-year-old kid, gave up everything to look after your mother...that was about you...how?"

"Shawn says I did it for myself, to comfort myself, to cling to my mom, making her tend to me and my emotions even when she was suffering. And that I robbed others of the chance to have their own close minutes with her." How could some memories be so suddenly clear while others were still behind a haze of pain?

"How would he know that? Did he know her?"

"No."

"So...why did you marry him? Knowing he thought that way?"

"I didn't know." His questions threw more confusion into the jumble in her mind.

She was a murderer.

Oh, God. What did she do with that?

"He didn't say things like that to me back then," she said now. "He just always told me how much he loved me. He just always promised that I'd never be alone again..."

A memory surfaced. Shawn making that promise. On the beach in Florida, the night he'd asked her to run away with him to California—telling her that the only way she was going to be free from the pain her father continuously caused her was to get him out of her life. And Shawn making that promise in the back of the van where they'd been staying some weeks ago, too.

He'd promised she'd never be alone, and then, when he thought she was dying, he'd broken that promise. He'd dumped her on the side of the road, thrown her driver's license on top of her and left her there.

CHAPTER TWENTY-TWO

SIMON WASN'T SURE exactly when it hit him that
the moment he'd been waiting for—the one where
Cara was ready to move on—had arrived. Busy
easing his concern that she'd hurt herself, and then
that she was suffering confusion from a possible
brain bleed, he'd been a little late in getting to the
real cause of her distress.

Hearing the water running long after the hot
water would have given out, he'd gone to the
bathroom door. Had knocked. Called out to her.
Eventually, he'd tried the knob and found the door
unlocked.

That was when he heard her sobs.

Hauling her naked out of the shower had wiped
away all professionalism for a moment or two. Not
because of the nudity but because it was Cara.
The second he'd felt the icy water on his back as
he reached for her, he'd known for certain that he
was in love with her.

He'd had to get beyond all that to figure out
what was going on.

She'd reached her breaking point.

"I just… I can't bear being this person who made her mother's last months even harder…"

When tears fell, she wiped them away, impatiently. Angrily, even, as though they didn't deserve to exist.

"As a surgeon who has witnessed, first hand, families going through the long-term loss of a loved one, I would think that having you close was the biggest blessing you could have given to her."

Simon didn't choose his words. They seemed to choose him. "From what you've said about her, being your mother had to have been one of the best parts of her life. You being there with her… It was a continuation of the close relationship she'd built with you since the day you were born."

Mouth open, Cara stared at him, as though assessing every syllable he spoke. He could no more speak the truth of what had transpired the last months of her mother's life than Shawn Amos could. But, in his opinion, his scenario rang with a lot more truth than the one she was harboring.

"I was incredibly selfish when it came to my father," she said, just when he was hoping that she was seeing the truth of his words, after having run them through her memories of those months. "I sure wasn't thinking of him when I cut him off…"

"And perhaps he wasn't thinking enough of you when he buried himself in his work. When he moved you to a new neighborhood and left you there alone so much of the time. I think you were both doing the best you could. You'd lost an incredible woman, the world to both of you…"

What did he know? He'd never been particularly close to his parents. They'd divorced when he was young. He'd been raised primarily by his mother, who'd remarried and had a second family in Tennessee. He and his dad touched base every couple of years. Neither of his parents knew about his current situation. He'd left them both messages that he was taking an extended vacation and would be in touch when he got back.

"I'm weak, Simon," Cara said now. "Shawn's right about that. I ran out on my dad because he wasn't taking care of me. I've relied on Shawn all these years. And now I'm hiding out with you… letting you take care of me."

"As I recall, you didn't want to stay here. I gave you no choice."

There were some things he couldn't know about Cara. He hadn't known her long. Hadn't been in her life to see the things she was talking about. But… "There are two sides to every story, Cara," he told her now. "Instead of listening to Shawn's side of your choices, see if you can find the other one."

She swallowed. Nodded. He felt like he might have just been dismissed. And couldn't just let her go. Not without a better understanding.

He was responsible for keeping her there. He had to be responsible *to* her.

And then he needed her to go. She was getting to him in a way no one else had. Which meant she'd have more power than anyone else to get him to give up his quest to see. She'd be able to convince him not to believe that he would...without ever saying a word.

"Tell me about the memories that have been coming back to you." A shard of fear shot through him again as he recalled her earlier statement that memories were returning. Memory loss could be indicative of more severe brain damage.

She'd never given any indication of memory loss. To the contrary, she'd seemed so lucid. Determinedly so.

"It's just little things..."

"Not that little if you think you've done something bad." He couldn't imagine anything she could have done that would be unfixable. Whatever it might be, she wouldn't have meant intentional harm by it. There wasn't a mean bone in the woman's body.

She shivered again, and Simon stood. "I'm going to take you to your room, let you get some warm clothes on..." He had a wet shirt and damp pants to get out of, too. "And then we'll sit and talk about it." He wasn't asking any more. They'd come too far for that.

Cara must have sensed the change with them,

as well. When he set her down in her room she thanked him and told him she'd be right out.

He hoped she knew he was going to hold her to her word.

HE HAD HOT tea on the table for her. Some saltine crackers in case she was feeling at all nauseous. He'd changed into dry jeans and a different flannel shirt, and had had a firm talk with himself—all in the five minutes it had taken her to dress and join him in the cabin's main room.

The tea was on the table. She picked up her cup and carried it to the couch. He'd thrown another blanket over the back of it.

He was fully prepared to push as hard as he had to get his answers. And then get her someplace where she could get the help she needed to be free of Shawn Amos. To start over.

Without him.

She was a woman who needed security. Her father had failed to give it. She'd lived with an abusive man for ten years because, in his own twisted way, he'd provided it.

It stood to reason that she'd look to Simon, the man who'd insisted on rescuing her and keeping her safe, to provide it next.

He couldn't do that.

It was a disservice to her to let her think, even for a second, that he could.

He loved her too much to disappoint her.

All things he planned to tell her as soon as he knew exactly what they were dealing with. He had to know where to take her.

Simon had it planned. If she'd testify on her own behalf, he'd take her to the police. If she couldn't, he'd take her to a shelter.

Bottom line was, he was taking her.

Their time together was over.

With his own cup of tea in hand, he joined her on the couch. He wasn't sitting in his chair. Wasn't going to read that morning. Their daily routines had ended.

Cara didn't pick up the book on the end table next to her. Holding her cup on her lap, she leaned her head back. Closed her eyes.

Watching the steadiness of that cup, using it as his compass, Simon sipped tea. And waited.

After a minute or so, he thought about taking the cup out of her hand, running his thumb along her fingers. Intensely thankful at the moment that the bastard hadn't broken those bones. Her hands had nursed her dying mother.

Had cooked delicious meals for Simon.

They gestured almost every time she spoke.

"I remember screaming…"

His gaze darted to her face—still slightly swollen on the one side, but Simon was no longer sure that the misshapen cheek was current or from some past injury. The rest of her features had settled into the face of a once-beautiful woman.

A woman who could be beautiful again with enough rest and care. The scars were small, nothing he really even noticed anymore, except for times like now, when he was thinking about all that she'd endured.

She remembered screaming. No more words came forth.

"Who was screaming?" With as neutral a tone as he could manage he tried coaxing. Not wanting her to get lost in the hell in her mind, but rather to take him there with her.

"I'm not sure. It's feminine. I think me. I'm just not sure…"

"Are there words?"

She shook her head. "Just screaming. There's this spot on the floor. Spilled nail polish remover."

"Is it fresh?"

She shook her head again.

"Shawn's sister, Mary, is there. She's standing right by the spot."

Shawn had a sister? "Where is Mary now?" If the woman was there that day, did she know what Shawn had done to his wife? Would she testify?

Why hadn't Cara mentioned the woman before?

Cara's eyes opened. "I don't know where Mary is," she said, looking like she'd seen a ghost.

"So, this is the first you've remembered her?"

"No." She frowned, looking at her lap. "Mary's my best friend. Sometimes I've felt like she's my only friend. She and Shawn are really close. They grew up in foster care and he always looked out for her. She came to California with us when we moved from Florida."

"Does she work at the surfing school, too?"

"No. She works at a gift shop down by the pier."

"So…would she be there? If you tried to call her?"

"I can't do that."

"Why not?"

"I…" She shook her head. "I don't know."

"Cara…" She couldn't shut him out anymore. They had to figure this out. He had to know where he could take her so she'd be safe and get help.

"I thought about her when I was first recovering, thought about her, and… I was picturing her happy now." She looked at him, her brown eyes wide. She'd left her hair down, probably to dry. He liked it that way.

"Happy now?"

"With me gone."

"Why would you being gone make her happy?"

"She…stood up for me against him."

Everything within him stilled. "Did Shawn hit his sister, too?"

"Only when she tried to come between us when he was angry with me. He had no beef with Mary. He loved her…"

"You said he loved you, too."

She nodded. Swallowed again. Brought her tea

to her lips but returned it to her lap without sipping. Both of her hands cradled the cup now.

"So, you think with you gone, he and Mary are close again?"

She gave her head a little shake—something he'd seen her do so often. And began to understand that she did that when she was confused. Couldn't figure something out.

Because she couldn't remember.

If only she'd told him from the beginning…

"I've been trying to picture her happy," she said, her voice soft. "It worked in the beginning… when I was sleeping so much. But now… I don't know. Every time I think of her, standing by that stain, I get…scared."

And she didn't know why. He didn't even have to ask to know that.

She'd said she did something bad. He needed to know what that was.

Had she hurt Shawn? It would have been self-defense. The police could help her…

"What else do you remember?"

"Steps. I remember falling down some cement steps."

"How many of them?"

"I don't know. Not many."

"What else?"

"I remember yelling at Mary."

"Yelling at her."

She nodded.

"You were angry with her?"

She shrugged. "I have no memory of ever being angry at Mary."

She'd taken so many blows to the head over the years...who knew what kind of damage might have been done?

"What about the days before that last day? What do you remember of them?"

She shrugged again. "What do you want to know?" She'd worked. Done laundry. Made meat loaf for dinner. She'd bought a new purse at the pier...

"My purse," she said. "I had my purse in the van. I remember because it had come with this little ID card and I'd filled it out. The pen I'd used, it had black ink and I liked that it matched the purse, but then it ran out of ink and I had to use blue."

Almost smiling in relief at the detailed memories, signs that her brain function was generally normal, Simon fell in love all over again. Wished he'd known Cara all of her life. All of his.

From what he'd put together, she'd been unconscious for a long time before he'd found her. Her hazy memory was a given in those circumstances.

She'd said she'd done something bad.

"What else do you remember about that last day? Or any time in between then and when I found you?"

She talked about the van she and Shawn had been in. About driving for hours when every bump in the road hurt. She talked about the pill he'd put in her mouth, holding her jaw closed and making her swallow.

Bile rose in his throat as he listened to the details of a man treating her like an animal. He wanted to draw her attention to the fact that the treatment was criminal. But as long as she kept talking, he didn't interrupt.

She gave him glimpses into the hell she'd been living in, but nothing that answered his questions.

"You said you'd done something bad," he finally said when she fell silent. He'd long since set his tea on the table. Had his arm along the back of the couch, close to her.

She nodded.

"What did you remember that you aren't telling me?"

"Nothing."

"Then how are you so certain that you did something wrong?"

"Shawn told me I did." She said the words like they were obvious.

"Shawn told you." He repeated her words back to her, maybe in case she could hear them like he did. Mostly so he could think before he said anything else.

She nodded. "When we were in the van. He told me that I'd done something horrible."

"Did he say what?"

Twisting her face, she looked away. "I think he

did. I remember feeling this horrible sense of... life being over. But I think I passed out again. The next time I came to, he was there, drying my tears..."

"Why were you crying?"

"I guess because I was in so much pain."

"I saw you in about as much pain as a human being can take and you never shed a tear..."

Meeting his gaze, she frowned. "Yeah. I don't ever cry when he hits me. It only seems to convince him that he's doing the right thing..." She shook her head. "I don't know why I was crying, but I was, and he kept telling me that everything was going to be okay. That he'd gotten me away before anyone could come get me and that he'd keep me safe. He said it would be just the two of us from then on, just as it had been in the beginning, and that I'd never be alone."

"Until he dumped you on the side of the road."

"Yeah."

He could almost see the thoughts flitting through her mind. Waited for her to put facts together in a way that made sense.

When she sighed, a deep breath that ended on a shudder, he said, "Cara, did it ever occur to you that he was lying?"

Her lips flattened. "Don't you think I've wanted to believe that this whole time, Simon? But I know he's right. When he told me... I can't remember what I'd done, but I have a very clear sense of knowing, deep in my soul, that when he told me, I knew he was right. And that whatever it was, it meant my life was over."

"But you don't remember what it was."

"I started to remember this morning," she said now. "In the shower. It hurt so badly I wanted to die. Then… I don't know, I couldn't help how I reacted." With an embarrassed grin, she added, "And apparently I couldn't help that it happened in front of you."

He ignored that last part.

And had a feeling that, for the first time since he'd found her, Cara hadn't been completely truthful with him.

She knew more than she was saying.

But not enough to fully explain?

Given what she'd told him so far, he actually understood her reluctance to incriminate herself without knowing all of the facts. He didn't like it that she'd lied. But he trusted her, still. Implicitly.

"So…what do you say we give this a little more time?"

Pulling the blanket down, she hugged it to herself.

"Your memories are returning, Cara. In many cases of traumatic amnesia, it just takes time and the mind's ability to relax for the memories to return. You feel safe here. The memories are coming back. It makes sense that, for now, for a while longer, at least, we could continue as we have been and see what happens."

"You need to get on with your life, Simon."

"My sight hasn't recovered nearly enough yet for that," he told her. "Besides, the holiday is coming up. No sense you going to a shelter and being with total strangers over a holiday."

He saw tears in her eyes as she watched him. Had the sense that she wanted what he was offering. A little more time to heal.

He couldn't get her this close and then abandon her.

"To disrupt your process now, to expose you to the stress of a new place, new people, interviews and settling in, could cause you to repress the memories that are returning."

Professionally, he knew his assessment was correct. But suspected that he was also thinking of himself—he just wasn't ready to deliver her out of his life.

He'd tend to his own eye work, be more diligent than ever. He would not quit believing in himself.

He told himself he wanted her somewhere safe, and where she could get the help she needed. For now, his cabin was that place.

Still, when Cara nodded, he knew the palpable relief he felt was not a good thing.

And took note.

CHAPTER TWENTY-THREE

Santa Raquel, California

FOR MORE THAN two weeks now, Edward had been sleeping in her bed. Joy was staying with him—they'd moved a twin bed into the far corner of Lila's sitting room—but many nights the little girl cried for Julie and Hunter before falling asleep.

Shawn Amos's case was in the process of discovery—a time for both prosecution and defense to gather and present their facts to the court—and the man still had not made any known effort to be in touch with his daughter. Or to prevent Edward from having custody of her.

He could just be waiting for the charges against him to be dropped—his attorney had made a motion to that effect that had been denied—or to be cleared of the charges before disrupting his daughter's life, but Lila didn't like the fact that he hadn't even asked after the little girl's welfare.

She saw Edward and Joy every day as they came and went through her office—once in the morning, once in the evening. She'd taken a room in one of the bungalows closest to the main building for those nights when she needed to stay over.

And she was spending more time at her condo in town, too.

She'd made up her mind to have Thanksgiving there alone until she got a text from Brett Ackerman telling her that he needed her at the Stand as he and his wife, who'd mentioned stopping in with their son, were not going to be there after all. They were going to be spending the day with Ella's brother—who'd been Brett's roommate in college—and his family.

While the residents would be just fine with the staff on duty that day, Brett always liked for there to be a family atmosphere with the "head" of the family having a presence at the table.

So, there she was, dressed in her usual brown suit—a skirt instead of pants—her hair in a bun, walking shoes and adding, at the last minute, a fall-colored floral blouse that Sara had given her for Christmas one year...helping the residents who were on kitchen duty put the turkey and dressing on the buffet with all of the other fixings.

She could hear the buzz of conversation as residents filed in and took seats at the tables all set with pilgrim centerpieces, placemats and cloth napkins with turkey napkin rings.

Hunter and Julie had invited Edward and Joy to the Fairbanks mansion for Thanksgiving, and knowing that Edward was not going to be at the

Stand made the day like any other holiday she'd spent with the residents over more than ten years.

Except this year there was a sadness lurking within her that hadn't been there before.

Waiting while everyone got through the line and was seated, Lila called their attention to a short prayer of thanksgiving. She asked each resident to find something to be thankful for. To plant whatever it was in her mind. To think about it in the days ahead. To draw strength from the good in her life—no matter how small that good might seem at times.

And then she went back to the kitchen to get the extra bowl of mashed potatoes. Lila was content with her lot. At peace. Truly happy to be able to be of valuable use to women who had their whole lives ahead of them—and a comfort to those who were facing the last half of their lives alone. Her life had meaning.

She was contributing good to the world.

She was needed.

And this year she was sad.

She'd done the unthinkable and had fallen for one of her families. For Edward. She'd inappropriately crossed boundaries and now was paying the price. Sadness warring with her hard-won peace.

She had it all figured out. And she knew the cure, too.

Time. *It takes time.* Her mantra was repeating in her mind as she came back into the dining room to find a seat among all of the women and children already feasting. A couple of women from different tables waved her over and she was contemplating having dinner at one table and dessert at the other when she saw Edward walk in. His pristine brown suit gave him away, but she'd have known it was him from any distance.

In a pair of jeans with an orange turtleneck and brown sweater, Joy accompanied him, holding his hand.

Her first thought was that there weren't any tables left with three empty seats. And then realized that she had no reason to invite herself to their Thanksgiving table.

He was scanning the room. Hurrying over to tend to him before they drew too much attention to themselves, her heart fluttered.

"Edward!" She'd been about to ask why he wasn't with Julie and Hunter when he sent her a look.

"Hi, Joy, you look pretty today." Lila put an arm around the little girl's shoulders. "Did Grandpa do your hair?"

Joy nodded.

"Have you eaten already?"

She shook her head.

"We're going to eat here," he said. "Julie and Hunter are outside and would like to join us, if that's okay with you."

His gaze had an entirely different message for her. Something was clearly wrong.

Moving with as much speed as she could without raising alarm, Lila efficiently got help putting up another table. Leaving Joy's former housemother to set the table with placemats and napkins, Lila asked another woman to gather dishes, while Darin Bishop, who was a permanent resident at the Stand whose wife and child had mental disabilities, got chairs. In less than five minutes Julie and Hunter were seated with Joy and had plates full of Thanksgiving dinner.

Lila let Edward lead her outside the cafeteria and down to her office where Chantel was waiting.

At the sight of the detective, Lila's heart started to pound.

"Amos slipped out of his bracelet," Chantel said. "Sometime within the last hour. They found it hanging on a surfboard at the school." The judge had ordered the electronic monitoring device as a condition of Shawn Amos's bail.

"Joy can't leave these premises and we're on lockdown as of right now," Lila said, thinking of the women who'd received permission to have family members—adult siblings, parents—share their holiday meal. Unfortunately, every one of them was going to have to leave.

"Julie and Hunter have clearance, so they can stay," Lila said, her mind focused as she picked up a handset that would immediately connect her to every security officer on duty. Issuing lockdown instructions, which included calling off-duty officers, she then looked to Chantel.

"We're already on it," the woman said. "We have extra patrols in the area and someone will be watching the strip of businesses outside the Stand."

Brett Ackerman owned every one of them. He'd be notified.

Chantel wasn't done yet. "A tristate APB has been issued for California, Nevada and Arizona," she said. "They suspect he might be going after his wife. Or to dispose of her body," she said. "Yesterday the prosecutor turned over some evidence found on a set of three cement steps cut into a small hill behind the Amos home and the friend's home where they stole the van." Steps as she described weren't uncommon between yards that weren't on level ground in Santa Raquel.

"What evidence? Why wasn't I told about it?" Edward's tone bordered on sharp without quite getting there.

Lila had to restrain herself from walking to Edward, putting her arm through his. Holding on to him. Holding him up.

"You weren't told because of the sensitivity of this investigation. And it was a fingernail, of all things. It was your daughter's. Shawn's DNA was found on the underside of it. Like she'd been defending herself against him. Since his testimony mentioned steps, we've been scouring all steps in the area…"

"*You've* been scouring, you mean," Lila said, sending the woman a look filled with gratitude. God had sent them an angel when Chantel had joined the high-risk team. She was tireless in her determination to protect victims of domestic violence.

"I've had help," she said.

Lila wanted to keep Chantel talking about nonessential things. To give Edward time to process. Wishing he could trust the police to do their jobs and leave the worrying to them. But knowing that he couldn't. What parent could?

"There could be scars from defensive wounds on Shawn…" he said.

"Yes."

"It would be proof that he hurt her."

Chantel didn't commit to that one. But she didn't argue, either.

"Was there any evidence that Mary had been on those steps? He said Cara lunged after Mary to get Joy away from her. That they fell down the steps together."

"I can't say any more right now, Dr. Mantle. I'm really sorry, but…I wouldn't have told you what I did except that it's information Shawn now has…"

"But you think chances are he's going after

Cara? That if they can find him he might lead them to my daughter?"

"That, or he could be making certain that his disposal of the body is permanent."

"So Joy's probably not at risk…"

"That's not a safe assumption," Chantel told him. "If Cara's alive, he could very well want to use Joy as leverage against her."

Lila's heart hurt for Edward—hurt deeply.

"Okay," she said, looking at the man she wished she'd met thirty years before. She wouldn't ever be a part of his family, but she'd keep his little girl safe or die trying. He was in her world now, and she was good at what she did.

"Let's let Chantel do her job, and you and I do ours." She crossed to stand right in front of Edward, hoping he could feel the support she was trying to give him. Personal support. Straight from her heart to him. Hoping he could trust and take comfort from knowing that she would do her job well. "You have a little girl in there who was about to have her first Thanksgiving dinner with her grandpa. Coming?"

She noticed the way his expression softened slightly, was affected by the small smile that broke on his lips as he nodded.

And tried to ignore the light in his eye that seemed to burn into her.

Leaving Chantel to coordinate the Santa Raquel police coverage, knowing the detective would buzz her cell the second there was any news, Lila allowed herself to spend just one holiday meal feeling part of a real family. To give Edward strength.

And because, until Shawn Amos was found, she was sticking as close to Joy as she could get.

Prospector, Nevada

AT DINNER ON Thanksgiving night, Cara gave silent thanks for borrowed time. For parents who'd loved her.

For Joy.

Her thoughts traveled no farther than that. During her first hours, or maybe even days, at the cabin, Joy hadn't even been present. Since then, her name, her existence had been popping up regularly. But only in terms of nail polish and sweet treats.

Cara knew she'd loved being a mother.

And that she wasn't one anymore. Beyond that…her mind blanked out on her.

She didn't push. Wasn't sure she wanted to know what else was there. And hated herself for the weakness.

"Shawn was right," she said aloud as she and Simon ate the chicken, mashed potatoes and canned green beans she'd prepared.

"How so?"

The blurted-out sentence broke into more than

five minutes of the total silence that had become status quo for them. She found comfort in their silences.

He said it was her time to continue emotional healing.

"I'm weak."

"How so?"

Simon was safe. She could tell him anything. He didn't judge. Or try to talk her into another way of thinking. He just…listened.

The closest thing she'd ever had to her mother's friendship.

With the added complication of finding him excruciatingly attractive. But those minutes when his smile tripped up her insides…they were her relief from the rest of her waking hours.

"It's been two more weeks, and other than little tidbits, I'm no closer to remembering anything significant."

"Little tidbits often pave the path to significance."

"I think I'm not remembering because I'm too weak to handle whatever it is I'm avoiding."

He didn't deny the possibility, taking another bite of potato.

So she kept eating, too.

She'd asked him if he wanted a pie for dessert. He'd said no. Joy hadn't liked pie—of any kind. The memory, which had come to her earlier, returned. An example of the useless pieces she was providing herself.

"What if I never remember?"

He shrugged. Reached to his right for the butter, missed, turned his head and grabbed it. Simon wasn't one to allow defeat into his mindset. Not for himself.

And apparently not for her, either. But after the horrible shower episode she'd given in to his suggestion to allow herself more time. Partially because she'd really believed, in those following days, that she might actually have a breakthrough.

And partially because, now that she knew she'd killed someone, she didn't want to leave the safety of that mountain until she knew what she'd be facing—and had the ability to defend herself.

How did you defend against what you didn't remember?

How did you live with yourself knowing you were a murderer?

It had been bad enough when she'd only sensed that she'd done something horrible. But murder?

Days had begun running into each other. Most of those days the thought of being a killer just seemed surreal. Like she was living inside someone else's head for a while. She had no idea how a murderer felt, but was certain she didn't feel like one.

At night, though, when the darkness closed in,

she couldn't hide from the truth. She didn't deserve to live.

She'd yet to tell Simon what she'd remembered that morning in the shower—that she'd definitely killed someone. She couldn't risk making him guilty of harboring a criminal. There was every chance he wouldn't believe her. Just like he wasn't sure she'd done something bad. Because he didn't seem to believe much of what Shawn told her.

Like the fact that she was weak.

She kept trying to show him. As things came back to her. So far, he seemed unconvinced. Not that she could know for sure. He didn't spend much time trying to convince her of anything.

Mostly, he kept his distance from her. Like they had a professional boundary between them. Other than when she helped him with his eye exercises out in the yard, and the two times a day she put drops in his eyes, they never got closer than sitting next to each other at the table.

Since the morning of the shower, when he'd pulled her naked into his arms, he'd never touched her again.

She thought about that morning more than she should.

Not the reality of what she had remembered—but thoughts of him seeing her completely naked. Knowing what her breasts looked like. Her privates. She imagined him pleased by what he'd seen.

Her thoughts weren't for sharing. Ever. They weren't for real.

She just clung to them as she searched her mind for light in her darkness.

CHAPTER TWENTY-FOUR

THE ONLY REASON Simon went to town the Saturday after Thanksgiving was because he was figuring that he'd blend in better on the famously busy shopping weekend. He hadn't been since picking up Cara's package and didn't want to be recognized as a regular visitor.

He didn't want anyone to feel familiar with him or to feel as though they'd be welcome to stop by his place if they were ever driving up the mountain.

Unfortunately, there was only one place in town that sold fresh vegetables, which was one of the things he was after.

The other was the package of eyedrops he'd had an online pharmacy send to him. He had a year's prescription of them.

The post office happened to be in the back of the same establishment that sold the vegetables. And had the kiosk he'd used to order Cara's things.

As luck would have it—or because he was the only one who worked the register—when Simon pulled into the parking lot he could see the same weathered and slightly overweight silver-bearded gentleman behind the store's counter. A couple of younger employees, one man, one woman, were outside, carrying boxes from a truck to the back door and helping out front with the gas pump. Neither of them were familiar. Simon made a point of avoiding eye contact and conversation with both of them.

Now, more than ever, he valued his complete privacy up at the cabin while he had Cara to protect.

She'd said Shawn owned a surfing school in California, but they'd been up in northern Nevada for a reason. Could be the guy knew someone up there.

Or had purchased a place without his wife knowing about it.

Since Cara only had him to protect her, Simon wasn't taking any chances. At least, not while her memories were trickling in.

A sharp ray of light caught Simon in the eye as he walked through the door. Blinking, he paused and then glanced in the direction from which the light had come.

The hand scanner at the register had been left upside down.

It wasn't until he'd taken a couple of more steps that Simon realized that he was seeing spots in both eyes. Both eyes!

Glancing back toward the register, he closed

his good eye, leaving the injured one open. Sure enough, he could see a red dot.

Hardly believing it at first, he told himself he'd imagined the dot because he knew it was there. He wasn't stupid. He knew Cara was right to be concerned that his right eye hadn't been showing a lot of progress.

Walking down one aisle, he reminded himself of what he was after. Fought butterflies in his stomach as he headed toward the wall of fresh vegetables. Had he imagined the dot? What if Cara was right and he wasn't ever going to see out of both eyes again?

When he got to the register he closed his good eye again. Turned around. And looked for the red light. To prove to himself that he wasn't wrong to believe...

Nothing.

Biting back disappointment, refusing to allow bitterness reign, he moved a little to his right. And then to his left...and...there!

A red dot. He was looking at a red dot!

Opening both eyes, Simon stood there and stared.

Hot damn! He'd seen a red light.

Gathering his vegetables, picking up a few other things, he couldn't finish quickly enough.

He couldn't wait to get home and tell Cara...

He'd seen a red light!

Get home and tell Cara...the thought stopped

him. Not enough to quell his euphoria, but maybe enough to dampen it just a bit. The cabin wasn't home.

And Cara wasn't there for the purpose of sharing his victories. Beyond that, she'd probably think that a red light wasn't proof that he'd regain enough sight to be able to ever perform another surgery. Even if she didn't say it out loud, he'd know she'd be thinking it.

Somewhat sobered, but still with a definite confidence in his step, he approached the counter with his purchases and asked for his package.

"Yeah, it came." The bald man stood from his stool and lumbered slowly toward a cupboard with a US postal sticker on it. Retrieving the bubble-padded package, he carried it back to the counter and set it down by the celery and onions. At which point he proceeded to manually ring in every single one of Simon's purchases, typing them in by number rather than scanning the bar codes.

The same thing he'd done every other time Simon had been in town.

While frustrated with the time it was taking, Simon kind of liked the man's refusal to change something that he was comfortable with just because times had changed. The scanner had been put in by the company that had bought the store, he'd been told. Sometimes a man just had to stick with what a man knew.

Like the fact that he was a surgeon and would see again.

He should have picked up some more wine. Considering whether or not to go for some—Lord knew he had time—he remembered when he and Cara had shared a bottle. And had his answer.

No wine. Period. He couldn't give temptation any chance at all to win him over. Which was why he picked up some liquid soap along with the veggies. He couldn't keep using the same soap in the shower that Cara used.

It was either that or risk making a mistake that would ultimately hurt her. Cara was still married. You'd think that fact would be enough to stop him from lusting after her, since he could no longer convince himself she was just a patient. But Shawn Amos wasn't a man who deserved Cara's loyalty, so Simon had to come up with other deterrents.

Like not touching her at all. Thinking about heart surgery when she put drops in his eyes...

But he'd seen a red dot! Eagerness to give her that proof of his improvement trembled inside of him, coupled with the knowledge that it wouldn't convince her of his eventual ability to see.

"You that guy that bought the old Anderson place up on Butte Mountain?" With Simon's stalk of celery in hand, the old guy stopped pushing buttons to look at him.

Simon shrugged. He hadn't been told the name of the mountain he lived on.

"We was told it sold. The gal that does titles was up to the house for dinner," the older guy continued, seemingly not the least bit put off by Simon's lack of friendliness.

It went against his grain to not immediately put out a hand of greeting, but he still didn't do it. Didn't even nod. He pulled out his wallet, retrieved cash and waited to hear his total.

"Your business is your own," the man said now. "We get lots of folks up this way who want no one's business in their business. It's why we live up here, most of us. I'm just saying, 'cause we had a guy in town this morning talking about some woman who went missing 'bout thirty miles from here. Said he was looking for her. I told him I'd ask around, see if anyone saw anything..."

Thinking that if he suddenly got chatty it might seem suspicious, Simon stood there, shook his head like he couldn't be the least bit concerned by this news. Inside, every nerve in his body urged him to get his ass out to the car and back up the mountain.

Cara knew how to use the .22. But that didn't mean she'd have it close...

Maybe it wasn't Shawn.

The old man pulled out a picture, held it out to him. "This is her. If you see her, hold on to her. Guy says she's his wife and had been suffering from brain trauma from falling down some steps. He's worried sick about her. Broke him up, just talking about it. Said a woman died falling with her. His sister…"

Simon's brief glance at the picture shook him up more than he was sure he could hide. Nodding, he said he hadn't seen or talked to anyone since he'd been up at his place, that he had no-trespassing signs all over his property that he enforced with his gun, and he hoped the guy found his wife.

Acting like he had all the time in the world, he headed out to his SUV, loaded it with groceries, gassed up and then pulled slowly onto the road. It caused him physical pain. Along the back of his neck. The jaw he was clenching.

He took the mountain curves with more speed than was safe, told himself he'd be no good to Cara dead and lightened up on the gas. All the way home he continued to see that picture the old man had shown him.

A younger Cara—without little white scars on her face. There'd been a smile on her lips and a light in those big brown eyes he'd hardly recognized.

She'd been happy once.

And he thought of what else he had to tell her.

Her sister-in-law, Mary, was dead. At least, according to Shawn.

Maybe he should have stopped at the local sheriff's office, had them come get Cara and put her under protection.

His fear that she'd refuse to go had stopped him. Police couldn't force a woman to protect herself against her husband. Or to testify against him, either.

And underneath that fear was another. The memories she was repressing…had she seen Shawn kill his sister? Was that why she'd been so certain, that first day when he'd asked, that "there was no one"?

She believed she'd done something bad. Because Shawn had told her she had. Maybe that belief was her way of avoiding the real truth—that she'd witnessed something horrible.

But then…if Mary Amos was dead by Shawn's hand, he wouldn't be going around telling people she was dead, would he?

His foot was to the metal as he pulled onto his property, leaving a trail of dust behind him.

He scanned the area, looking for Cara…or signs of struggle. Saw neither.

Stopping right by the front door, rather than off to the side as was usual, he'd only gotten as far as opening the car door when he saw the front door of the cabin open.

If…

Cara stood there, in her jeans, one of the black fleece pullovers he'd bought her, the sleeves rolled down to hook over her thumbs as they were made to do, and her hiking boots. She waved. And gave him as much of a smile as she ever did.

A surge of relief made him weak. And then he realized that he was going to have to tell her she wasn't safe here anymore. Not with Shawn as good as sending out search parties for her.

When she'd first come to him, she'd been certain that as long as Shawn thought she was dead, she'd be safe. With all of the weeks that had passed, he'd pretty much taken her safety for granted.

But now, for some reason, the man was back. Where he'd been, why it had taken him so long to start looking, Simon could only guess.

Seeing her stand there, waving like she was glad to see him, cut him to the quick. Because he wanted her there.

And couldn't have her.

He could get her to safety, but he couldn't make her happy. He didn't believe in marriage. He'd grossly disappointed one woman. He couldn't risk doing the same to Cara.

He couldn't afford to be with her, even until Christmas, not with his eye showing signs of healing and his doubting, at first, that he'd seen that light.

Her doubts were getting to him. Just as he'd known they would.

Realizing that if anyone came up his drive she'd be seen standing there, Simon grabbed a bag of vegetables and sprang from the vehicle and up the steps, handing her the groceries and telling her to stay inside where it was warmer.

Chances were, someone would land at his place at some point. Even if it was just the police, trying to help a man find his missing wife. He hoped he'd bought them time, saying he hadn't seen or spoken to anyone, but eventually, when Cara didn't turn up, the search would most likely become official.

He had to get her out of there. One way or another, their time together was ending.

CHAPTER TWENTY-FIVE

CARA KNEW THE second Simon was in the house that something had changed. His movements were precise. Measured. As he pulled the drapes closed over the window—something he'd only started doing the last few nights to keep in the cabin's warmth—he made certain that the edges met completely in the center.

As he helped her put away groceries and lined up the bottles of eyedrops inside the cupboard, he talked about dinner.

He'd brought spinach. Thought they should grill it with eggs and onions and make wraps.

When he passed by her a third time on the way to the refrigerator, without meeting her gaze, she waited for him to turn back toward the remaining bags on the table and then stood directly in front of him. Blocking his path.

"What's going on?"

She appreciated the fact that he didn't try to hide the concern in his eyes when he finally did look at her.

"I was trying to get things put away, first..."

Now he was scaring her. "Simon." She didn't

want to beg. But she would. With her stomach already knotting, she let him sidestep her to get to the table. He looked in the remaining bags. "I think we got everything that needs to be refrigerated," he said.

The words gave her a second's comfort. Must not be too bad if he cared about spoiled milk.

"Come sit with me." Taking her hand—a very strange thing in itself—he led her to the couch.

Before joining her there, he got the gun from the corner by the far end of the table where it usually stood, bringing it to the living area. He sat on the couch and stood it against the table beside him.

"You're scaring me," she said aloud, just to make certain he realized how out of character he was acting.

He nodded.

"You have reason to be scared," he said, all business suddenly. And out of nowhere came the awareness that he'd had to tell people that their child might die.

Her stomach cramped and her heart started to pound. Focusing on Simon's face seemed to be the only thing that kept air flowing through her lungs.

"Shawn's in town. He's showing your picture around."

The way he just put it out there, allowed her to accept what he was telling her, meant she could move to solution.

She had to get out of there. Immediately.

Starting to stand, she fell back to the couch when Simon's hand touched her thigh. She'd imagined his touch so many times these past few weeks.

And now, there it was. Just when she had to leave.

Recognizing the inaneness of the thought, Cara stayed where she was.

"He's telling people that you're suffering from brain trauma due to a fall down some steps," he said. "You said you remembered steps..."

He watched her intently. She was shaking now. Inside and out. Simon pulled the blanket down from the back of the couch. Wrapped her in it.

"I need you to stay with me, Cara. Look me in the eye. Stay here with me."

She nodded. Focused on him. Was scared to death to hear what else Shawn was saying. What he was telling people about her.

What Simon knew. If he knew she'd killed someone. If he knew who. And how. If he knew why.

He hadn't brought the police back with him. That felt like a good thing.

She had to trust him. She *did* trust him. She had to think for herself, too. First and foremost, she had to think for herself.

If she'd gained nothing else out of these two months shut away from life, she'd figured out that much. She couldn't rely on someone else to take care of her. At some point, every adult had to be responsible for themselves. Before they could be any good to anyone else...

A shard of pain shot through her at that thought. She blinked. Looked at Simon.

"I don't remember anything else about the steps," she told him. She'd tried to see. It just wasn't there.

When he took her hand, she braced herself. "He said that his sister fell down the stairs with you, Cara. That she died."

No! Cara pulled her hand away from him, pulling it inside the blanket with the rest of her. Her gaze darted around the room. Landed on the carefully closed curtains. He was shutting Shawn out.

Good. Shawn out.

Shawn out there? In their yard?

Mary. A picture of her sister-in-law's worried face flashed before her eyes. And then what seemed like lightning.

Mary was dead? Mary was dead. She'd been bleeding...

There'd been blood.

She'd screamed.

No, Mary hadn't screamed, Cara had.

"Joy," she said, almost blind to the room, to Simon's features, as flashes of silver went off before her eyes. "Joy."

"Joy?" Simon's voice came from far off. As though he'd left her there on the couch to go into the bedroom. Afraid, shifting, she felt her knee bump up against him and got a good breath.

She tried to get back to that day. Feeling like her heart might beat up into her throat, she didn't want to go back. She had to go. As she reached back, all she could see was Mary. Her best friend. Mary. Alive and…

"I see Mary's face," she said aloud, as if that would bring everything more clearly into focus. "And blood."

"On Mary?"

Looking at Simon, she nodded. "And on me, too."

"Because you fell down the stairs together?"

She tried to see that. To feel it. "I fell down stairs," she said. But she didn't get anything else. Couldn't see Mary there. Or find a sense of her being there.

"Where was she when you saw her? What was she doing?"

She shook her head. Felt it swim. "I don't know. She's concerned."

"About what?"

"Joy, I think." The words barely came out. Her throat was so thick it stung as she tried to draw in air.

"Cara!"

She looked at him.

"Who is Joy?"

"My daughter." She broke. Falling over on her

legs, she shook with sobs. Animalistic sobs came out of her as a grief bigger than she could ever imagine burst forth.

"I...killed...my...daughter."

I KILLED MY DAUGHTER.

Simon had imagined many scenarios that might have contributed to Cara's selective amnesia over the past couple of months. In a million lifetimes, he would not have come up with that one.

"You remembered everything," he said, grasping for a reality too unbelievable to accept. There was no way on God's earth that Cara Amos would have killed any child, let alone her own.

He knew it. Just like he'd known he was going to see again. So it was just a red dot. His optic nerve was alive.

He felt her head move against his chest. For the past hour he'd been holding her.

Letting her know she wasn't alone.

Until she got through the initial heartbreak, there was nothing more he could do.

He'd waited to speak until she'd grown completely silent.

And when she pulled away, trying to sit up, he helped her do so, keeping her wrapped snugly in her blanket. He didn't want her going into shock.

"I remember the van," she said. "It wasn't ours. It belonged to Shawn's friend. I think we were at his house, too. I remember waking up and being on his couch."

"Was he there? This friend?"

"Not that I knew. The way Shawn was talking to me, I feel like it was just the two of us."

The more memories she could bring up, the better.

"So, what about the van?"

He had to know about Joy. Good God, he'd had no idea Cara had given birth. That she was a mother...

His heart ached at the thought. On so many levels. None of which he could deal with at the moment.

Joy. It fit Cara—naming her child Joy. A celebration of the joy a child would bring to her life. The joy that being a mother must have brought her...

"I woke up in it. Really woke up. Like I wasn't as hazy as I'd been. Shawn was crying. And I knew I'd done something horrible, I just couldn't remember what. That's when he told me."

"Told you what?"

"That I'd killed Joy! Mary had her. She was taking her away."

"Where?"

Cara turned her head to the side and then looked back at him. The sight of those swollen eyes, the red, blotchy skin, brought tears to the back of his throat. "I can't remember, but I can guess. Mary and I had a plan. If Shawn ever got really bad in front of Joy, I'd taunt him enough to bring him on me and she'd run with Joy."

For the first time in hours, Simon felt a lightening in his chest. "So maybe she was running with Joy when she fell down the steps…"

His voice fell off. Maybe Cara had run after them. Maybe they'd all three fallen for some reason. But if Mary had Joy, and Mary was dead…

"Shawn said that I was trying to save Joy and I pushed Mary. He said that I pushed them both down the steps and that Joy hit her head and was gone by the time Shawn got to her."

Her gaze was vacant. Simon waited for a minute and then said, "Do you remember that now?"

Blinking, she stared up at him. "I remember Mary's concerned face. I remember blood. Hers and mine. I don't remember Joy." Tears flooded her eyes. "Why can't I remember my own daughter?" A sob erupted. "Oh, God, Simon, I killed my own baby and I can't even remember…"

"Maybe because you didn't kill her." He had no idea if he was doing the right thing, giving her hope. Feeding her the possibility of a memory that might grow into something that seemed real— impeding the return of what she had locked so deeply in her mind. "Maybe Mary's death is a lie, too."

She grew quiet. Watched him. He had no idea what she was thinking.

"All of this…what I heard in town, what you just told me about the steps and the accident…all of it came from Shawn."

"He was there. He saw it happen. And he saved me, Simon. He got me out of there before anyone could take me away, haul me off to jail. He protected me. Took care of me…"

"He left you in the woods to die."

"Only after I faked a brain bleed." Her eyes widened. "I know why I did that now," she said.

"Because he'd told you Joy was dead."

She nodded, staring at him. "I had no reason to stay with him anymore."

"You stayed for Joy's sake."

She nodded again. "Shawn's beatings, they weren't an everyday thing. The rest of the time, he was a good dad. He was teaching Joy how to surf. He was really patient with her. She so badly wanted to please him, so she kept trying…"

"Maybe she was afraid that if she didn't he'd call her clumsy or stupid, like he did you."

Simon was in way over his head. But knew that he was going to be up to whatever challenge lay before him. Until Cara was safe. He had her back. Period.

As tears filled her eyes again, he pulled her against him, prepared to sit there all night if that was what it took.

He had to figure out how to help her without putting her in further danger.

What if Shawn had already gone to the authorities? Told them that Cara was a killer? Who would be able to refute his story? If Mary was dead? And little Joy?

Unless Cara remembered what really happened, she could very well end up in prison for a murder Simon was certain she didn't commit.

CHAPTER TWENTY-SIX

CARA DIDN'T KNOW when darkness fell. She ate a couple of bites of toast with peanut butter when Simon brought it to her. She sipped more water than she wanted. He was concerned about dehydration.

Every once in a while she talked to him. As a memory surfaced. Nothing new or important. Just little things. Like the time she'd tried to call her dad to tell him about Joy's birth and Simon had stopped her—reminding her that, just as he'd had to protect Cara from the pain her father's selfishness caused, so they, together, had to protect their daughter from him.

She'd protected her daughter from the wrong man.

"If you'd like to call him, you can," Simon offered sometime after bringing her the toast. He was on the couch with her again. Staying close. "I have the burner phone."

He'd told her that before. And for a second, she considered hearing her father's voice. Feeling like a little girl again, needing her daddy to come save her.

She shook her head. "I'd be lying if I said I didn't want to," she said softly, her head resting against the back of the couch because it felt too heavy to hold up. "But I have to figure this out, do what I need to do, before I contact him. It's not right, after ten years, to call him up when I'm in trouble…"

"I'm guessing, based on what you described, that's when he'd most want you to call him."

Maybe. But… "I have to take care of myself, Simon. That's the one thing I've known since I got away from Shawn. I have to take responsibility for my choices. I just have to figure out what that means."

She'd been waiting and waiting for answers to become clear. Instead, her heart had fallen for a man at a time when she couldn't have anyone. Falling back on her old desire to be taken care of. Maybe a bit of transference, like she'd thought earlier.

And her mind… It was ditching her. And maybe coming back some, too. Just not quickly enough.

A picture of Joy's little face, the long dark hair mussed around her cheeks, came to mind. It was her wake-up-in-the-morning face. The little girl had always come looking for Cara the moment she'd opened her eyes. From the day she was born, she would set her gaze on Cara and be fine.

Just like Cara had always been with her mom. She'd thought that meant the angel of her mother had been watching over the two of them. That Karma had given her Joy for surviving losing her mother.

Now she just didn't know.

"We can't stay here," Simon said as tears filled her eyes again. Life without Joy... Cara couldn't imagine it. Wasn't sure she had the strength to try. "We're going to have to leave in the morning."

Some part of her had known she couldn't stay. That her time was up. She nodded. "I'll go wherever you want to take me, Simon." She'd had her chance to figure it out. Now it was in Fate's hands.

"I've been thinking..." His gaze was warm, clear, and...strong...as he looked at her. "I'll close the place up—it takes an hour or so. I've got a cooler for the perishables. That'll give us something to eat while we find a place to hole up..."

Cara shook her head. "I'm not going to run again, Simon. It's sweet of you to offer, but...it'd be just like Shawn, you know? I'd be repeating my mistake, and I can't be responsible for anyone else getting hurt..." Her voice trailed off as she started to cry again.

Oh, God. *Joy.*

"I'm not suggesting we run." Simon's comeback surprised her. "Only that we find someplace safe where we can stay long enough to get on the internet and figure out what Shawn has said, what part of that might be true. We might not find much, but we have to know what we're dealing with to know where you'll be safe."

"I belong in jail."

"We don't know that. Nothing on earth will convince me that you knowingly or intentionally hurt anyone…"

She didn't bother arguing the point. The fact that she didn't feel like someone who'd taken another life…that she couldn't remember what it had felt like to cause a death…didn't matter anymore. "Don't you see, even if I didn't…hurt Joy…" she broke off "…I did kill her by not leaving him. I didn't protect her."

"You thought you were providing a good life for her." Simon was getting a little more forceful with his opinions. She wasn't sure if that was good or bad. "You said he made a good living, provided a nice home, health insurance, security…"

"All of the things that I thought were important when all that really mattered was love." Cara closed her eyes on the tears then, and when Simon suggested that they retire, she didn't argue.

Dreading the night ahead, she went into her room and sat on the bed. A second later she realized that Simon was there with her, the .22 resting against the trunk at the end of the bed.

"I'm not leaving you alone tonight," he said. And then, before she could thank him, tearfully, of course, he continued. "I want us together until we get out of here. Chances of Shawn finding this cabin, or having any reason to visit, especially after dark, are slim, but I'm not risking it. I'll sleep with my clothes on. On top of the covers. But I'm not leaving you alone."

Cara hadn't been about to ask him to. And she was too distraught to keep herself from asking for what she did want.

"Will you hold me?"

Simon never answered her question. At least, not with words. Moving the gun up to lean against the nightstand, he turned on a nightlight, stretched out on the bed and opened his arms.

SIMON HADN'T EXPECTED to sleep. Two months ago he'd been a guy with emotions to deal with and an eye that needed to heal. Now he was lying with a gun by his head with a very real possibility that he might need it to fend off a bad guy.

Who'd have thought that doing a good deed, protecting a woman in an emergency in the middle of nowhere, would change his life so drastically?

Cara had never discussed Karma or Fate with him, but she mentioned both terms in regular conversation enough that they were on his mind as he lay next to her looking for a logical explanation for what his life had become.

Certainly something stronger than logical science had led this woman to the doorstep of a cabin he'd just purchased at a time when he'd been struggling more than any other time in his life.

Whatever it was that had brought her here, he'd been given a chance to make a difference in her life and he was up for that challenge.

What came later...he didn't know. Whether or not they kept in touch...stayed friends who called now and then...depended on where her life led her.

He wasn't going to marry again, but he could be a damned good lifetime friend. Once he had his sight back and didn't need to worry about her making him doubt himself.

Aware that there were aspects of the situation he wasn't seeing as he lay in the darkness, listening to her breath, feeling the warmth of her weight against his side, he knew better than to make a concrete plan where she was concerned.

Moans... Someone was... Simon hadn't known he'd drifted off until the sounds woke him. Lying still, he first noted the agonized rise and fall of Cara's back against his hand, which rested there.

"Cara." He didn't think. He just called to her. Stroked her back with one hand, moved the hair away from her face with the other. "Cara," he said again, as her ragged breathing continued.

He had no idea what time it was. How long he'd been asleep. Her head, which had been resting on his shoulder, was on his chest now. Her thigh resting between his. He'd woken up hard, but as another moan came from deep within her, his penis settled and his mind took over.

"Cara." Speaking softly, he gently touched her face, trying to wake her without scaring her. No one should have to live in her hell. No one. Most particularly not a woman as giving and gentle, as willing to open her mind and consider others, as she was. Even when she talked about Shawn's mental and emotional abuse, she'd found good things to say about him.

And Simon… She'd somehow known that he needed help believing that he'd see again and, other than suggesting that he have a plan B, had pretty much left him to it. Even encouraged him by helping him exercise his eye. Because she'd known that was what he needed, and in spite of what she might personally think, she'd been able to give it to him.

Her breathing had settled some and he lay still. Listening.

He hadn't told her about the red dot yet. Hadn't thought of it himself much in the past few hours.

"Noooooo!" Pushing against his chest, she sat straight up, their legs still entangled. Her hair over her face, she remained upright. He wasn't sure if she was awake or asleep until she shuddered and her head fell down toward her stomach.

"Hey, come here," he said, pulling her back down to him as she started to cry. He could only imagine the amount of grief the woman had been containing inside her small frame.

Years of it, to be sure.

Before she could heal, she had to get it out. She cried for a while, not huge racking sobs now, but more of a steady outpouring that tore at him just as much. He handed her tissues. And held on. Until she quieted. Reaching for a bottle of water on the nightstand, he uncapped it and handed it to her. All those tears, she'd get dehydrated…

Cara drank, handed him back the bottle and settled back down against him. Wanting her to sleep if she could, he remained still, listening to her breathe. She moved her hand. Adjusted her arm. Her foot.

"I'm awake if you want to talk," he offered.

Not sure if she needed silence or help, Simon focused on her breathing. And brushed a hand across the hair lying on the side of her face. Ran his fingers through it. Hoped he was calming her.

His strength of purpose grew. He committed to meeting the challenge head-on. Successfully.

At first light he was getting her out of there. He'd stop in town to alert the shopkeeper that he'd been called back to his practice, so his departure didn't draw curiosity. Cara would have to lie down on the back seat. The clothes bar he put up with all of his clothes hanging on it would cover her from view. He'd be quick about it. Because he didn't ever want Cara to have to hide again.

Most particularly from the demons in her own mind.

Hard to believe that she was still so strong. Still trying so hard to figure it all out. Get it right. Still looking for the good. Striving for it. While he'd fallen apart and run away because his eye was damaged...

"I don't think I can do it," she was saying softly.

"Do what?" Go to the police? A shelter? Testify against Shawn? Hide in the back of his car for a moment while he ran into the store...?

"Live without..." Her voice broke. "I loved her so much..."

Joy. His tongue stuck in his mouth.

"She was the light in my life...truly..." She sniffed, rubbed her nose with the tissue in her hand, then settled her hand back against the side of her face at his chest. He felt her every movement.

"Just to be in the same room with her...or know that she was...somewhere...anywhere...to know that she was smiling..."

He swallowed. It didn't happen easily.

"In the worst times...she'd be asleep, or at school or with Mary..." Another pause. Her sniffles were coming more rapidly. "I'd think of her... with every blast of pain... I'd hang on for her... knowing that when we got through it, things would be fine again. She'd never know the difference and her happy life would go on…"

She'd taken beatings to give her daughter what she remembered having…a secure and seemingly happy home.

"I just can't… How do I fight without her to fight for? How do I breathe without…"

Cara's shudder had gained force over the last one. He had to help her. Had to find a way to share her burden so that she wasn't carrying it all alone. So that she didn't give up right when help had arrived…

"It's always darkest before dawn." The words sounded stale to him. As a first go, it was all he had. A couple of other trite phrases occurred to him. True. But so overused they weren't going to have the power…

Truth. His truth.

"I know how you do it," he said. And he did. He got it right then. Right there. He just didn't know how he reached inside himself and offered his guts to her. He'd never been that in-the-muck guy. He was the one who was supposed to maintain boundaries. Offer all of the compassion in his heart from a professional distance. Offer facts, realistic solutions, perform to the best of his ability in the operating room, maintain his skill and his focus, and…move on.

He'd overstepped once. He'd let things get too personal. And he'd lost the sight in one eye—

possibly the ability to help any other children needing heart repair—because of it...

Cara's breathing had evened out. Her body against his stilled. As though she was waiting.

As though she was open to his telling her how she was going to get up in the morning, get up every morning after that and continue on.

She was giving him the chance to help her hang on.

To do that, he had to get personal.

CHAPTER TWENTY-SEVEN

"YOU GO ON without her by living every single day of your life in her honor." Simon's words came out slowly, as though he was choosing each one separately before he spoke it. "Everything you do, you do it to make her proud. You do things with the idea that, where she is, you're making her smile. You do it because you know she somehow knows." In the end, the words came in a rush.

Chills spread over Cara's body in her stillness. And she remembered…that first day, or the first few days…she'd had the feeling he had a death on his conscience. The boundaries between them had been so clear for so much of their time together— for both their sakes. She'd had no business in his conscience. Had been too busy trying to find out what was in her own head so she could quit being a burden to him…

"Who was she?" she asked, her head still on his chest, counting his heartbeats. They were strong. Sure. Steady.

"Her name was Opus." Even expecting the confirmation, it came as a surprise. *Opus*. A body of art, of beauty. A musical composition. A great work. She loved the name. Wanted to know about the child.

But…with HIPAA, the laws governing patient confidentiality, he could lose his license to practice medicine for even telling her the name.

"Is she…the only patient…you've lost?" Thoracic surgery came with high stakes. As tragic as it was, she thought him incredibly lucky—and talented, too—if he'd managed to save every other child.

"No," he said. "Though, to date, I've only lost two. Opus…wasn't…a patient."

"Who was she?" A sister? A cousin?

"She was my daughter."

Hand on his chest, Cara pushed herself up. Stared at him. "Oh, my God, Simon. You had a daughter?" Her eyes filled with tears when she realized what that meant. "You lost her… You already know what I… I'm so sorry." She reached for his face. Running her hand along his jaw. "All night I've been going on like this, and you… The feelings I must have brought back…"

He pulled her back down to lie against his chest. "Technically, Opus was my stepdaughter," he said. "I just… From the moment I met her, she wrapped herself around my heart. Took ownership…"

Cara wanted to hear every detail. Needed to know his little Opus. "How old was she?"

"Six," he said. "Her mother had had her as a single woman through artificial insemination. As far as Opus ever knew, though, I was her biological father."

"Your ex-wife, Emily. Opus was hers?" He could have been married more than once. Their personal lives had been wrapped up in boundaries.

"Yeah." His chest rose beneath her cheek as he sighed. "Opus started out as my patient. She had a degenerative heart disorder. Emily wanted her to have a transplant and she wanted me to do it."

"Did you?"

"No. She wasn't a transplant candidate. I referred her to a colleague of mine and, at Emily's request coupled with my own desire, I was with them every step of the way. There were some things he could do, a trial she could be a part of..."

When he broke off, she was right there. "But it didn't work."

"The trial worked," he said. "Opus's heart responded and there was every chance that, as she grew, her condition would fade to, perhaps, more treatment when she reached adulthood. Worst case scenario was that she stopped responding, but would, by then, be strong enough to withstand a transplant. Opus was three by then, and her mother and I got married."

They'd started with the tragic ending. Cara fidgeted with the button on his shirt, waiting for whatever he chose to tell her between that and the part where they thought they were going to live happily ever after. She shivered in spite of her jeans and fleece pullover. Simon pulled the blanket up around her shoulders, and she snuggled into his body warmth.

"She was six when her heart stopped responding to the drugs. As expected, she was so much more healthy all-around, her heart was so much stronger, that she was a candidate for a transplant…"

Surely he hadn't…she knew firsthand…doctor code strongly urged physicians not to attend their own family members, except in cases of emergency…

"Emily insisted that I do the surgery."

She wanted so badly for him to have said no. A parent…cutting into his own child…

"And I insisted that I couldn't." He sounded incredibly regretful.

"You couldn't, Simon. A parent, operating on his own child's heart…"

"I was the best qualified."

"She was your daughter."

"Not biologically."

"Biology has nothing to do with the reason why doctors aren't supposed to be involved in the care of their family members. It's the emotional bond that makes it impossible to remain neutral, unbiased, to see every aspect…"

She stopped. Had a flash of her father's worried face as he stood over her mother's bed one night, shortly after she'd been diagnosed. She'd thought he'd been crying…

That was why he'd called in so many other doctors. Because he'd known he was unable to make the best decisions. To see his wife as a sick body, which was what he'd have had to have done to be able to see all the facts.

"That's what I told myself." Simon's words were a long time coming. And sounded weary. As though he'd been telling himself over and over. For a lot longer than that conversation.

"She didn't make it through surgery," he said now. "Emily blamed me…"

"It wasn't your fault."

He said nothing.

"Where's Emily now?" she asked, wondering what the woman thought of his long sabbatical. If she knew about it. Wondering if they were still in touch, even as she knew it was none of her business.

That night, in that room, in that life, it felt like her business.

"In jail."

Cara sat up again. "In jail?"

Where she might very well find herself? Was he kidding? Was this Fate's cruel last way of turning on her?

He nodded, his gaze holding hers.

"What for?"

He blinked. "For this," he said, pointing to his right eye.

She couldn't believe it. And yet…as coincidence seemed to flood down upon them…she started to believe.

He told her about Emily coming to his office on what would have been Opus's seventh birthday. How he'd agreed to see her because he'd been grieving, too, because he'd understood. She'd been hysterical. He'd gone into his private bathroom to get a wet cloth for her face, and she'd followed him in with an ice pick in her hand.

She'd stabbed him, catching him in the corner of his eye socket, doing little damage, considering. She'd only stabbed once. And then she'd panicked. She'd locked them in the bathroom and put the ice pick to her throat. If he tried to leave, if he so much as moved, she was going to kill herself.

He'd determined, at that point, that his wound was superficial and had spent the next four-and-a-half hours trying to talk her down. In the end, he'd succeeded. She'd agreed to wait while he called someone to get her some help.

He'd called the police, because he'd known that only a court order would make her submit to getting the help she needed.

By that time, his eye had swollen shut. He'd expected as much. What he hadn't expected was that when he got down to emergency and they opened it, he wouldn't be able see. The cornea hadn't been damaged, but the pressure on his optic nerve, due to the swelling, had reached the critical point...

Still sitting, her hand on his chest, Cara listened as the horrific story played itself out until she felt almost numb. And then, without warning, an avalanche hit and she teared up.

"It's wrong, Simon. So absolutely, completely wrong. All you did, even there at the end, even after she blamed you, was continue to try to help..."

His shrug made it seem like he wanted her to think he had it all under control, but she didn't believe that. Could feel his pain.

"It occurs to me now that maybe I've been so determined to see again, to be able to do surgery again, to prove to myself that I'm not somehow to blame..."

She'd played those same games with herself.

Every time she'd heard Joy laugh had been proof that she'd made the right choices in her life. She was giving a little girl the same happiness she'd known as a child...

"Crazy, the two of us...stumbling upon each other..." Simon's lips tilted as though he was trying to smile.

She didn't think it was crazy.

Fate could do this...bring two people together who'd both been injured by their spouses, two people who'd just lost little girls, give them those similarities so that one could help the other.

Cara's life had been spared…she'd collapsed near Simon's cabin because she was meant to help him. She, with her doctor father, she who'd judged Edward Mantle so harshly, was there to show Simon that Opus's death was not his fault. That, in not operating on her, he'd made the right choice.

Just by sharing her story with him and letting him see her journey, she could help him.

Just like Mom had said. Until you drew your last breath, your life served a purpose.

Her breath caught on a latent sob. Cara's pain was as acute as ever, and yet, she felt…better. As though she'd gained just a glimpse of that for which she'd been searching.

This wasn't about her. Her life wasn't about her. It was about making Joy smile.

It was about helping others. No matter what it took.

She'd go with Simon the next day. And when the time was right, she'd let him go. For his sake.

Their gazes met and she made the silent promise, from her eyes to his. And then she leaned toward him. She'd let him go, but could she have just one breath of his air to take with her?

Her lips meeting his seemed to be outside of her doing. Touching. Gently at first. And then with an all-consuming heat that shocked her. His mouth opened and hers did, too. His tongue found hers and every part of her body came to life, her breasts, farther below… She needed him, not just sexually, but in an animalistic way.

She was a married woman.

A murderer.

She couldn't bring him down with her.

Breaking away from that kiss hurt Cara in a completely different way than anything had before. And yet, she knew it was the right thing to do.

She should have left the bed, spent the rest of the night on the couch, but she just wasn't that strong.

Lying back down beside Simon, careful not to touch him in a way that would weaken their resolve, she laid her head on his chest, felt his arm settle on her and his hand curl against her side, and closed her eyes.

What had seemed like it was going to be an unending night had just become far too short.

CHAPTER TWENTY-EIGHT

THE FIRST TIME Simon had shed tears in his adult life had been the night Opus died. The second time was the morning that he drove away from his cabin in Nevada with Cara lying in the back seat covered by his hanging clothes.

Her few possessions were in a bag in the back, beneath his underthings and toiletries.

Their time together was over. It had to end. He'd known all along, just as he knew that his patients, as much as he cared about each one of them, as much of his heart as he put into every single incision he made, would go on without him. Some wouldn't even remember his name.

In spite of the tension gripping him, they made it into town and out to the highway with no problem at all. The old shopkeeper had been the only person in town Simon had ever exchanged words with, so his goodbyes were quick and he was out of there.

Ten miles down the deserted highway leading back toward California, he pulled over long enough for Cara to move up front with him and buckle in, and then he was moving as fast and as far as he could away from the godforsaken area where Shawn Amos had almost killed his wife.

Miles of endless desert sped by. Ten and then twenty. A sign indicated another twenty until the next town…a burg he remembered from his trip to the cabin. Two gas stations, a couple of small eateries and a few houses along the side of the road—a highway pit stop. Not a place he'd want to stop with Cara.

And then it hit him. They'd head to Vegas. Among the tourists there, they should have enough anonymity to be able to get a room and a tablet, and get on the internet…

"What's next for you?" She'd been silent for miles and now, breaking into his thoughts, it was almost as though she was reading his mind.

He told her about Vegas. "We need enough time to find out what we can and then determine where you'll be safest…"

She looked like she was about to argue. Instead, she said, "I mean after me…what'll you do? Go back to the cabin?"

No way could he stand being there without her. "No," he said. And told her about seeing the red dot.

Her excitement, the way she squealed, the full-bodied smile that broke across her face— the first one he'd seen on her—fueled his excitement all over again. "I need to get back to my eye doctor. See where we're at. If the prognosis has changed any."

And come up with Plan B if he could no longer be a surgeon. Her lack of faith in his ability to see again had gotten to him more than anyone else's.

"You know doctors can practice medicine with vision in only one eye, right?"

It was as though she'd read his mind again. He considered the idea that all of those mostly silent weeks together had done some kind of telepathic melding of their minds. And gave himself an inner shake for his ridiculousness.

He did know doctors could practice with partial vision. Just hadn't wanted to open the door to that possibility in case it sucked him in.

"Just in case the next six months doesn't bring enough of your sight back," she added.

He nodded. And drove.

Another ten miles passed. He spent them wondering what she was thinking. If being out on the road was reminding her of anything. He thought she wiped tears once or twice and he wanted to share every second in there with her. And knew how wrong that was.

Five more miles passed. The burg was nearing. "Were you dating anyone...you know...before everything happened?"

He got hard just knowing that she was thinking about him in that sense. And calmed himself immediately.

"No." And because he wanted so much to sleep with her, most particularly after the kiss they'd shared the night before, the one he'd sworn he would not think about ever again, he added, "Most of the women I know are the type who want to settle down. You know, the whole get married, have a family thing."

Like her. Not that he had any reason to say so.

He could feel her gaze on him. Watched the road. The Vegas turnoff would be a little two-lane road within about the next thirty miles. A truck went by in the opposite direction.

"After the way things happened with Emily… There's… I was partially responsible for one ex-wife being in jail. I'm not doing that again."

"She had mental issues, Simon. She needed help."

"I know. But before that…when Opus got sick again…we both knew we weren't in love anymore. She drew comfort from us being together. I tolerated her, felt sorry for her. And with her health insurance having been transferred to mine, with our finances joined and the money it would cost both of us to fight it out in court…"

"If you had to do it again, would you?"

Hadn't she heard what he'd just said? "Do what?" He glanced at her. He wasn't getting married again…

She couldn't open that door. Not tempt him.

He couldn't imagine going through a relationship demise with her as he had with Emily.

"Be Opus's father."

"In a heartbeat." The response took no thought at all. It was a certainty.

Which meant...he'd marry Emily again if he had it to do over.

Cara nodded. "Because loving her for a while is better than never loving at all..." Her voice broke on those last words.

It was like she'd hit him across the forehead. She'd probably been referring to herself, to her marriage to Shawn—who'd given her Joy.

And yet...he had some more thinking to do as he got back to his own life. How did his refusing to open himself up to family, to being a father again, honor Opus?

Glancing over at Cara, he wondered if she knew what she'd just done to him. He could almost hear her whisper. *Physician, heal thyself.*

SHE HADN'T AGREED to go to Vegas. But she hadn't argued, either. It didn't much matter to her where Simon felt comfortable dropping her off. She'd have hopped out at the first gas station and let him get on his way to California, except that he didn't stop at one.

As for his insistence that they go on the internet to find out what they could, if anything, before she just showed up after having been missing for two months—she had to admit that she'd like a heads-up on what kind of trouble she was in.

Surely the authorities would be looking for her. She'd disappeared with a...dead child in her wake. If Shawn had returned to Ventura, he'd have told them she killed Joy. And...if Mary was gone...as Simon had reported from town the day before... was she being blamed for that, too? Could she possibly have harmed both of them?

Out on the desert and mountain roads, she didn't see any police cars, but as they neared town, she started to watch for them.

And felt like a fish in a bowl each time one got close.

Maybe they weren't looking for her. Maybe Simon had told them she killed herself.

Wait! The thought froze her. Closing her eyes, she could hear his voice. So clearly. She replayed it twice more, and then said aloud, "He told me... that day he dropped me on the ground and left me there...that he'd tell them I committed suicide..."

Simon looked over at her. Grabbed her hand and squeezed it. "The man's a bastard, Cara," he said. And then swerved to miss a car that had turned in front of him.

All those weeks in the cabin...she'd been considering it—killing herself. Over and over, she'd thought that was what she should do.

Because Shawn had planted the thought?

Nauseous, light-headed, she sat there...watching as Simon maneuvered through traffic…waited in the car as he pulled into one of many electronics shops on the Strip and came out with a tablet… and waited again when he pulled into the check-in lane at an upscale resort just down the street from there.

She saw two cops while she sat there. Figured either of them could come haul her out of the car and slap cuffs on her wrists. The thought didn't scare her at all.

Living without Joy did that.

And the thought of the time in the very near future when she'd also be saying goodbye to Simon—that scared her, too.

HE DIDN'T LOOK at the bed. He looked at the desk. Was intent on getting the tablet charged and on-line.

"You really should distance yourself from me, Simon," Cara said, standing in the entryway of the hotel room he'd rented, watching him. She'd yet to come fully into the room. Even to go into the bathroom after all their time in the car.

"I'm going to get you to safety and then be on my way," he assured her. He was not leaving her alone. Period.

"I'm sure I'm wanted by the cops. You need to seriously consider what that's going to mean for you when they find us together."

For the second time that day, Simon responded automatically, no need for thought. Getting the tablet plugged in, he said, "In the first place, I'm a renowned surgeon in California and can prove that I treated you for severe head wounds after finding you collapsed on my property. You had amnesia."

"But you didn't call anyone and report me."

Tablet now charging, he held the On button. "You were an adult, capable of making the call yourself. You chose not to do so."

"But if they determine I was out of my mind, they could try to hold you responsible..."

The screen lit up. He looked for the wireless setting...impatient to get signed on. "If it came to that, I'd rather face the charges than leave you alone to figure this out..."

As he said the words, a rock hit his gut. He'd rather have lost Opus, been stabbed by her mother, than not have been her father...

Because love was worth whatever it cost.

With an uncharacteristically unsteady hand, he moved his finger along the tablet, tapping where needed, typing where needed, until he was online with the browser open.

Cara had come into the room. Was sitting on the edge of one of the two beds, not far behind him.

She was watching. He didn't have to turn

around to know. He typed in her name and Ventura, California. Hit Enter.

And heard her gasp when the headlines popped up.

Woman Missing and Endangered. He scrolled. Took in basic facts with record speed.

She couldn't possibly see the small print, and didn't lean in any closer.

"You're listed as having been abducted. There's a van model. A license plate number."

He turned around.

She was staring at him, white as a sheet.

Simon forgot all about the tablet. Taking her hand, he walked her into the bathroom. Used a cloth to put cold water on her face. Remembered telling her that he'd done so for Emily.

And was glad to be doing so again. For the woman he loved.

"Cara?"

"I can't remember, Simon." She coughed. Was shaking. "I just remember being more scared than I've ever been in my life. I knew someone was going to die…"

"Okay…this is good." He tried to infuse calm into himself, so she could find some, too. "We need to get you to the police," he said, and felt her shudder. "I'll be right there with you, Cara. You aren't getting rid of me yet. Not until you're safe. I promised."

He wasn't a psychologist, but he was a damned good doctor who knew how to deal with shock.

At the rate she was shaking, he considered the very real possibility that her knees might give out on her. Wet cloth in hand, he guided her back to the chair at the desk. Sat down and took her on his lap, wrapping his arms loosely around her.

"Are you okay to look for more?" Whether it was selfish or not, he couldn't know, but he wanted to be with Cara when she faced whatever news was to come. Wanted to make certain that if she needed to be held, there was someone there to do it.

She nodded.

Arms still around her, he reached for the tablet and typed in Shawn Amos's name. Wasn't surprised when it immediately popped up. But...

"Oh, my God..." Cara said the words, staring wide-eyed. "He's... That's a mug shot..."

"There's an APB out on him," Simon said, in case she couldn't see that through the tears that were now falling steadily from her eyes. "He was arrested a few days after I found you. Three hours south of where he dropped you. That's why they weren't looking for you up by me. They had no evidence that he'd taken you that far."

Cara was crying steadily, shaking in his arms. He had to get her through this quickly. Holding on to her, he continued reading.

"He was charged with first-degree murder in the death of his sister."

Cara let out a wail, falling over his arm, and then righting herself. "Oh, God. She's really gone…"

He kept reading. They had to know. She needed him to find out.

"He was out on bail and cut off his electronic bracelet Thanksgiving Day," he said.

The man had jumped bail and come straight for Cara.

Thank God Simon had gotten them the hell out of there.

He scrolled a little bit more. There were several articles, from various sources, about the arrest of a surfing school owner. Including one that gave an account of his release on bail. The man was claiming that his missing wife had killed his sister…

"I need to call a friend of mine," he said to Cara, praying that she hadn't read that last bit.

She nodded and started to get up. Because he had to get answers immediately, he led her to the bed. "I want you to lie down, just for a few minutes," he told her. As a doctor he'd have suggested the same.

Cara didn't argue. She also didn't reach for him. Turning over, she hugged a pillow to herself, leaving him with a view of her shaking back as she dealt with her grief alone.

CARA'S HEAD WAS stuffed up. It hurt, but after about an hour she'd cried herself out. Now, sitting in an armchair in the room with Simon, she looked up at him, prepared to hear that her daughter was dead.

"I've been on the phone with a colleague…getting medical records." His words confirmed what she expected to hear. Pediatric medical records would state time and cause of death.

"Mary died from blunt force trauma to the head." A new wave of pain came as Cara thought of her sweet sister-in-law. She breathed her way through it, knowing from losing her mother that it would be with her forever. "Records show that she was brought in by ambulance, which was called to a house at 1104 Amber Street…"

Sharp pain hit her head. A flash of light. "Eleven-oh-four," she said, as if from a distance. Trying to think. To focus on Simon.

"That's what it says."

"Eleven-oh-four…" Amber was her street, but…

Hit by a physical pain in her head so intense she cried out, she forced herself to hang on. Thought of her mother. Of Joy.

And…

"My whole head hurts," she said, feeling like a zombie. Her lips were thick, her face stiff. "There's a sharp pain in my scalp, not inside, from my neck to the top of my head…"

"Here?" Simon's touch made the pain go away.

"No…" she said, looking up at him, confused and yet…not. "I mean, yes, but not now. Then. That day. It was like he was tearing my hair out…"

Flashes of memory played in her mind, warring with her attempt to focus on Simon's steady features.

"I'd told Mary to take Joy and run. He tried to keep her from getting to Joy. He backhanded her again and again…"

She stopped. Swallowed bile. Waited for a second and continued. "One time the diamond in his wedding ring hit her cheekbone so hard it split and blood flew… It hit me. I launched myself on him…"

She tried to remember Mary after that but drew a complete blank. "He threw me off his back and kept backhanding me." She looked at Simon. "I told Mary to enact the plan. She was supposed to take Joy to the neighbors. She knew them from down at the pier. If that's where the ambulance picked her up, then…what happened to Joy?"

Simon looked as though he was about to say something, and she just wasn't ready. Couldn't bear to hear his words yet.

"He dragged me out of the house," she said. "I must have passed out. I remember him shaking me. Telling me to stand up. And then he pulled me out of the house by my hair." She was shaking, and yet felt…stronger, too. She'd gone after a monster to save her child.

She knew that woman. Felt like her.

She looked at Simon. "When I passed out, that must be when he hurt Joy."

Simon took her hand, pulled her back into his lap.

"I can't find anything on Joy, Cara. No medical records. No mention of her in the news. Nothing. It's like…she wasn't there that day."

"Shawn wasn't charged with killing her?" She'd kind of thought Simon had spared her that part.

"If he was, it's not anywhere public."

"Because she's a juvenile?"

He shook his head. "I have no idea. Usually, when children are…gone…they're named. There should at least be medical records. And maybe there are, but I haven't been able to find them. My colleague and I checked every hospital in Ventura. There's no mention of her."

She couldn't stand it. Her baby. What had happened?

"We have to go to the police. Now." She stood on shaky knees but wasn't going to let them stop her.

She'd come this far.

She still wasn't positive she hadn't done something awful that day, during those minutes she couldn't remember, but she wasn't going to let that stop her, either.

She had to know what had happened to Joy.

CHAPTER TWENTY-NINE

SIMON WOULD REMEMBER that day for the rest of his life. He'd insisted on walking with Cara into the police station. Sat with her in the small private room a uniformed employee at the front desk had shown her to immediately after she'd given her name and they'd recognized it from the news. They'd been sitting together on a couch in front of a scarred table filled with old magazines. He'd stood when two detectives walked in, one man and one woman.

He backed her up when she refused immediate medical treatment. He saw the panic in her eyes when they mentioned calling an ambulance.

"I'm a doctor," he told them. Showed them the badge from his bag. His driver's license. He'd expected to have to show both out front. "She's had memory lapses due to traumatic brain injury and just an hour ago regained critical pieces of memory that led us here."

It was up to Cara what she wanted to reveal and when. But he was going to make damned sure that she got a fair shake.

"It was an obviously emotional moment," he continued as the female detective studied her intently.

Cara looked at all three of them.

"I just remembered part of the morning that my husband put these most recent scars on my face," she said. "There are still blank pieces over the couple of days after that, but I remember him dumping me on a mountain and leaving me to die. I wandered until I couldn't go any farther and passed out. That's when Simon found me."

She looked at him. "I'll give whatever statements you need me to give," she said. "But...I need to know about my daughter..."

"Your daughter?"

"She was with us in the house...with my husband's sister, Mary, who we just found out is dead."

Simon felt a shaft of alarm. "I'm sorry." He put a hand on Cara's shoulder and looked at the two detectives. "Her husband, Shawn Amos..."

"There's an APB on him, we know." The male detective, whose name tag read Sanchez, spoke then. "We found it when we looked Mrs. Amos up in the system." He nodded toward Cara.

Simon told them about the old shopkeeper, about the man showing Cara's picture around the Prospector area the day before, saying she was his wife. Sanchez left to make calls.

"Now, what about your daughter?" the female detective, Diamond, asked, sitting on the other side of Cara.

"I need to know... We couldn't find anything..."

"I bought a tablet when we arrived." Simon told the detective about getting Cara off that mountain once he'd heard Shawn was in town, about trying to fill in pieces of her memory by reading the news once they got to Vegas. About the address being the catalyst that had brought her this far.

"I need to know what happened to my daughter." Cara had a one-track mind. Simon didn't blame her. "Please, anything you can tell us..."

The detective, after another couple of questions and concerned glances, looked up as the door opened and Sanchez peered in. He glanced at Diamond, nodded toward Simon, and then nodded at Diamond again. He had a feeling he'd just passed a very quick background check.

"If you'll excuse me for just a few minutes, I'll see what I can find out for you," she said to Cara.

They were a long few minutes, though probably not more than five. Simon watched Cara. She mostly watched her feet.

"Thank you for staying..."

"I told you. I've got you until you're safe." And then, considering where they were, added, "And we know what's going on."

She nodded. Glanced toward the door. He thought about the many parents who'd waited for hours for him to appear to tell them that their child had survived surgery.

Reminded himself that the human spirit was resilient. And that Cara's seemed even more so than most.

The door opened and one look at the detective's face—the smile there—had Simon on his feet. Ready to catch Cara who'd also shot up.

"She's fine," the detective said, completely unaware that until that moment Joy's mother had thought she'd killed her own child.

"She's fine." Cara stood still, as though on the brink of running.

"Absolutely fine. In Santa Raquel, about five and a half hours from here. Your father is there, too, and would like to speak with you…"

"Daddy?" Cara's eyes filled with tears as the cell phone in the detective's hand rang.

She looked at Cara, who nodded back on the third ring.

"Detective Diamond." The woman was walking toward Cara as she spoke. "Yes, sir. Here she is."

She handed Cara the phone.

Simon didn't have a plan. He just moved to Cara, supporting her weight with his body and putting a hand over hers as she raised a trembling arm toward her ear.

"Daddy?"

"Oh, my God, baby girl, it's you. My Cara…"

Simon was so close he could just make out the man's booming voice.

"I love you, Daddy. I'm so sorry. Joy… Is she really there?"

"In the next room, with a friend…" he said. Cara held the phone out a little, looking at Simon, and he leaned in closer so he could hear it all. "She's… They tell me it's best that she sees you in person, not just hears your voice on the phone. It's been so hard for her… It reminds me of you and your mom…"

"But…she's really okay? He didn't hurt her?"

"Not physically. She saw him drag you off… saw her aunt in bad shape. She's had some struggles, but she's been talking more and…once she sees you she'll be fine soon enough. I'm sure of that one."

"I'm so sorry, Daddy. I'm just so…"

"Sssshh. Don't you dare feel like any of this was your fault, baby girl."

"Ten years…and before…with Mom…"

"We have a whole lifetime ahead of us now. That's all that matters…"

"I love you, Daddy."

"I love you, too, baby girl. Now, please, get back to us…"

Simon knew he would never, ever forget the moment that told him, irrevocably, that love, family, was worth absolutely whatever they cost.

And knew, too, that Cara had someone else at her back now.

His time to back away had come.

Santa Raquel, California

THOUGH HE'D BEEN to Santa Barbara, a little bit south, Simon had never been to Santa Raquel. And most certainly he'd never been to the nondescript shopping mall where the police escort from Vegas had led him.

They'd offered to take Cara off his hands.

She was the one who'd asked him to drive her himself. Because it was on the way to LA anyway, she'd said.

He didn't care if it was in Timbuktu, he'd have taken her.

"This is it?" she asked, looking around at the strip mall shops—a used clothing store and a computer repair shop among others.

He shrugged, yearning, for just a second, to be back at his cabin with her all to himself. He was elated for her. She hadn't lost her daughter, after all. Nor had she done anything bad. To the contrary, she'd sacrificed herself to save others.

They'd already had a call from local Ventura detectives to say that Cara's account of Shawn's ring hitting Mary's face coincided with an ME's report and pictures taken at the hospital when she'd been brought in of a cut just below Mary's right cheekbone—the blow that was determined to have caused the brain bleed that had ultimately taken her life.

Other than that, the drive from Vegas to Santa Raquel, their last time alone together, had been spent with Cara talking about Joy, interspersed with Cara saying about a hundred times, "She's alive." Simon learned so much about the little girl, he felt like he knew her.

The police car that had been in front of them the entire way pulled over and parked.

The one behind him was still there, waiting for him to follow.

Pulling in, Simon felt like he should be saying something. Telling her how much the past two months had meant to him. How she'd helped saved him from a self-induced lonely life. But the words sounded so…uneventful…considering what had to be on her mind.

He'd been important during her time out of time.

He was pretty certain he'd be someone she'd always remember and…

She opened her door before he had the SUV in Park. Ran out into the middle of the parking lot, toward the door right in front of them. A single glass door with only a number on it.

Partially there, she stopped, looked back at him. He expected a wave. Had empty arms longing for one last hug.

"Come on, Simon!" she said, instead.

He didn't belong there. He knew that. Knew that as soon as she was back with her family, the real healing would begin.

And she had a little girl who'd also need special care and Cara's close attention. But because she asked, because he loved her, he was by her side before she reached the door, his body touching hers enough to let her know she wasn't alone, but not enough to hold her back.

Or hold her at all.

There were always boundaries. He understood.

They walked in together behind a uniformed Las Vegas police officer and the detective who'd met them at the door. Through a small entryway and into a small vestibule with linoleum floors...

"Mommy!" The scream that rent the room took Simon's attention from anything, anyone else. He saw the long dark hair—just like Cara's—as the tiny, jeans-clad body hurled herself at the woman Simon had been protecting. "Mommy!"

Cara swung that body up off the ground and into her arms, laughing and crying. "Joy...oh, my baby, Joy." The two heads were a tangle of dark hair and tears, until a distinguished-looking suited gentleman stepped up right behind the little girl, tears on his face as he hugged them both tight.

Cara didn't look for Simon. Probably didn't even remember he was there.

Which was at it should be.

With one last look, he took his leave.

THAT FIRST DAY she was back, Cara was never more than a foot or two from Joy. As she met Lila and Julie, Sara and even the nurse, Lynn, she was present in the moments, but her focus was entirely on her daughter.

And Daddy was there. His presence was a huge comfort to her—and carried a lot of pain, too. Every time she looked at him, heard his voice, she filled up with more tears than she could shed. Late that afternoon, Daddy left to move back to his hotel room. Cara was admitted to the Stand, and she and Joy were given their own little bungalow, where she made peanut butter sandwiches for them to share for dinner. Because Joy wanted them. She went to bed early, the same time Joy did, and slept all night, cuddled up to her little girl.

And dreamed about Simon.

The following few days were a blur. Because so many insisted on it—and with Simon's voice in the back of her mind—she agreed to a battery of tests at the local hospital, all of which confirmed that she was physically healthy. She had sessions with Sara—alone, with Joy and with her father.

Shawn was back in custody, held without bail, and Cara would be called upon to testify against him about Mary's death. The prosecutor expected him to make a plea, with the hope of getting life with the possibility of parole instead of the death penalty. Either way, he was gone from their lives.

Mostly, during those first days, she spent time with her daughter. Cooked for her. Pretty much memorized the Amy books that had saved Joy when Cara had been gone, slept long hours at night and missed Simon.

She had no idea where he was—hoped he was back in LA with friends who loved him. And yet…wanted to picture him at the cabin, too. *Their* cabin.

It had been two months out of time. A different life. And yet…they'd touched her forever.

Had they touched him, too?

He'd said he had no interest in marrying again. He didn't want to be trapped when the bad times came—which they always did.

He'd already loved and lost a little girl.

He had months yet to get through before he'd have to accept the fact that his sight had been permanently damaged. Before he'd know the extent of the damage, know if enough sight would return to allow him to resume his practice.

But…did he think of her now and then? Miss her?

Could they…maybe…someday be friends? Who called each other now and then just to check up? Maybe met for Sunday brunch a couple of times a year?

The idea was a pipe dream; she knew it, and

yet…thinking about it helped her get through the confusing array of emotions that were her constant companions those first days. They ranged from utter joy to complete despair, regret, anger and bone-deep gratitude. Grief. And…calm, too.

She'd been stripped bare up on that mountain—had found herself there.

There was no talk of the future during those first days. Just a lot of talking. About the past. Sorting through years of trauma—both in Florida and since her marriage to Shawn. Looking for clarity in the confusion.

She met Julie Fairbanks and invited the woman to join her and Joy at the bungalow for dinner one night. They had a lot in common, including a deep and abiding love for Joy. And they'd both lost their mothers to illness at seventeen, followed by abuse from men they'd thought they loved—men they'd thought had loved them.

They'd both met other men, too. Ones who made their hearts race. But while Julie was in a relationship with hers…Cara was only hoping to hear from hers again someday.

Cara didn't question the similarities. She accepted them as Karma's gift. With…maybe…a bit of nudging from a particular angel in heaven…

Regardless of the whys and hows, Cara would be grateful forever to the other woman for the love and care she'd given Joy. From what she'd been told, Julie had pretty much saved Joy, bringing her out of mental and emotional shutdown. The way Julie told it, Joy had saved *her*.

Either way, the woman had become a part of their small family. She wasn't Mary—but in less than a week, she'd become a sister, just the same.

And then there was Lila…

The morning of the fifth day she was back, after dropping Joy at her temporary school classroom on the premises, Cara found herself knocking on the director's door. She'd spent time with Lila—in counseling, over a couple of meals with her father, walking the grounds. This was the first time they'd be alone together, and while Cara liked the shelter director, she wasn't quite sure what to make of her and was feeling oddly nervous.

"Cara, come on in." Lila greeted her with that kind of half smile she had, showing Cara back to the private suite behind her office. She'd heard of the place, of course. Her father and Joy had spent a couple of weeks there together after Shawn's release.

In another gray pantsuit—from what she could tell the older woman only owned brown and gray—with her hair in a bun at her nape, Lila was a complete mystery to Cara. Her features were beautiful, much younger than her appearance would have one believe, and yet…her eyes seemed ancient.

Iced tea was waiting for them, glasses on the

side table between two floral armchairs that invited cozy chats.

In new black leggings and a black-and-white belted sweater that hung past her thighs, Cara felt like a new person. And somewhat lost, as well, sitting there.

Cara and Julie had gone shopping—Julie's suggestion—as Cara hadn't wanted to wear any of the clothes that were still in the house in Ventura. She wanted no reminders of that life, and her father had already arranged to put the place on the market.

She'd go down sometime in the next weeks, choose the personal things—both hers and Joy's—that she wanted to keep, and then she'd never have to step back into that life again.

"What can I do for you?" Lila asked, her usual serene expression inviting requests for help.

"I… You…all of you… I couldn't ask for anything more," Cara said. "I'm still pinching myself, struggling to believe that this is all real. That you all loved my baby girl…welcomed me… I had no idea places like this even existed. When I think…" She shook her head.

Her feelings could be dealt with in counseling. She was there to get to know Lila better. Because she'd seen the way her father looked at the other woman. Daddy hadn't said anything to Cara, she supposed out of respect for Cara's feelings for her mother, but Cara wasn't blind.

And had no desire to see her father spend the rest of his life alone, either.

They weren't yet at the point where she felt comfortable telling him so, but she could let Lila know…

"When you think…what?" Lila asked, her gaze fully focused on Cara. She sat there, soaking up that look for a moment, needing it, like a child, suddenly…

She stopped. Lila hardly knew her…and yet… Lila took on all of the residents as though they were her family. You didn't have to be there for more than a day to see that much. Her residents were her grown children—even the ones who were older than her. They were at the Stand in need of nurturing while they healed, and Lila had an unending well of it to give.

"I should have left him," Cara said now. "I stayed there, exposing my daughter to…" She shook her head. It wasn't what she'd come to talk about.

"You did the best you could with what you had, Cara." Lila's voice, calm and sure, fell over her like a warm blanket. "And in the end, you offered your life for hers. Put yourself in his path, taking him on, so that Mary could get Joy to safety."

She *had* done that. In one sentence Lila had shown her a self Cara had been struggling to see. One who'd made a right choice, instead of a series of bad ones.

There were other good things. She knew that. Sara was helping her to find them. Like the fact that Joy was, overall, happy, secure and well loved.

It would take time, they'd all told her.

Like the time she'd spent with Simon on the mountain...she'd started her healing there.

At his gifted hand.

"And when you thought you'd done wrong, a heinous wrong, when you had the chance to get away, you chose instead to turn yourself in, to face the rest of your life in prison in order to bring honor to your daughter. You take accountability, Cara, and that's the hardest, and in my book, one of the most decent things a person can do. That's what defines you."

Tears sprang to her eyes. She'd expected the meeting to go very differently.

They talked a little more. And then Cara sat up. "I just... I came here this morning to let you know I've noticed the way you and my father look at each other sometimes, and yet... I can't help but see the distance you keep. And if it's because of me... I just want you to know it's not necessary.

"I struggle with how my dad is, some... You know the way he just quietly goes about doing what he thinks is right, taking care of those he loves, without actually checking in with them to make sure he's got it right? But I love him far more than I ever realized, and I want him happy.

If that's with you… I just want you to know that I would welcome you with open arms."

Lila's entire countenance changed. Withdrew. It was like she had left the room and an identical woman took her place. There was no rudeness about her. Or even unkindness. But the welcome sign was clearly gone.

"I appreciate the sentiment," Lila said, her lips tilted like she might think she was smiling. She looked…pained. "But I'm afraid you're mistaken. There's no…"

Her voice stopped…just stopped, and Cara had the thought that Lila had been unable to say there was nothing. Because there was?

More than just Cara's deceased mother had to be standing in the way. Something from Lila's past? Something Cara's father had said or done?

But…

What did she really know about either one of them?

She should leave it alone. And she didn't want to.

Before she could come up with what to do next, Lila glanced over at her.

"If I were ever going to have a… I would be honored for it to be your father. And you and Joy…but that's not my life," she said. Her sadness gripped Cara. "This is my life." Lila spread her hand to encompass the room, but Cara knew she meant The Lemonade Stand. "These people are my family."

"But…"

Lila shook her head. "I've had my family, Cara…"

"What happened to them?"

She wanted to know, needed to know, but Lila just shook her head. And Cara couldn't let it go… maybe didn't know Lila well enough to know that her best course would be to let it go.

"How long ago?" From what she'd heard, Lila had been at the Stand since its inception several years before.

"Almost fifteen years."

Longer than she and Daddy had been apart, and that seemed like a lifetime. But the pain of losing him, and finding him again, the regrets, were still debilitating.

Far, far, far longer than she'd known Simon and yet…missing him was a constant pain in the confusion of her current days.

"So…the pain doesn't ever go away?"

Lila's smile seemed more real this time. "It lessens," she said. "I don't live with it day in and day out. I'm truly happy here, Cara. I found my course, as you will find yours."

Lila's course… The woman emanated peace. Was that what Cara needed, then? To focus on finding peace?

"You seem peaceful," she said now. "But you're sure…you're happy?"

Her father clearly had feelings for the woman.

"I just spent two months hiding out in a cabin in the mountains," Cara started, knowing what she had to say now. "Hiding gives you a chance to think. To remember things. To let everything flow over you. You hear the small voices. It gives you a chance to find your inside self, if you care to look. And when you find that self, you find peace."

There were many things she had yet to learn, to figure out. To work through. But this one thing, she knew.

"It's what my mother taught me," she said. "To listen to your heart—really listen. To seek out the inner you and listen. I watched her do it again and again during those months she was sick. After every disappointment. When the pain was almost more than she could bear. Each time, she'd find that inner place and be at peace."

Lila was nodding. "She gave you the best gift and the best life tool she could have given you."

Yes. This was right.

"But she was dying," Cara said. "Peace was the end of her journey. She wanted me to use it for the beginning of mine."

Just like that, it was all so clear. She leaned forward, wished she knew Lila well enough to touch her. "Don't you see? For those of us who are alive, this peace that you've found, that I've found, it's not meant to be the destination. It's meant to guide us as we reach for more. The peace… It's not happiness…it's only the door through which happiness waits."

It had to be that way. Or what was the point of any of it? The struggle. The pain? The lessons and accountability—they all led to the glory, right?

The happiness and joy?

She didn't know what it all meant in terms of her immediate future. Or Lila's or her father's or Simon's or Julie's or anyone's. But the concept…

Lila had tears in her eyes. She stood, and just like that, their meeting was apparently at an end. Not sure what she'd just done…if she'd totally messed up again, Cara followed her to the door, was ready to walk through it when Lila reached out, pulling Cara to her.

"You are a fine woman, Cara," she said softly by her ear. "I will think about what you said." Then she pulled back. Cara opened the door.

"Cara?" She turned around, and Lila was stoic again, back in the room, there by the tea neither of them had touched. "About your father and I? It can't happen," she said. "I just need to make sure you understand that."

She wasn't sure she did. At all.

But she nodded anyway.

The Lemonade Stand, Christmas Eve

LILA WRAPPED THE last present and put it with the others on the kitchen counter. She had half an hour or so before she'd need to carry them in to put them under the tree in the cafeteria.

Any resident who was safe to go home had done so, to return the next day. But the rest, the majority of them, would be gathering for a church service and then meeting for punch and cookies and a gift exchange.

It had been tradition, since day one, that each bungalow—or cul-de-sac of bungalows, depending on the population—put up a donated tree of their own and decorated it with provided ornaments. Those residents also had gifts for each other under their trees to be opened Christmas morning.

The gifts could be purchased with monies saved out of what was given to the residents for their care, or they could be homemade in any of the craft buildings and classes on premises. Their purpose was to give each resident the chance to give. And to receive. To embody the spirit of Christmas. The hope of Christmas. To bring alive the hope that children feel at the thought that Santa might bring them something they wouldn't ordinarily get.

The residents at the Stand, most of them, had long ago lost that hope. The idea was to bring that back to them. That sense that anything was possible. That if we did good for others, good would abound with happiness available as a result.

Lila believed in Christmas with all her heart.

For the night's gift exchange, they drew names. But Lila always had something under the tree for every single resident in her care. Something that she chose with them in mind. Giving those gifts was her happiest moment every year.

Sara and the other counselors would all be there. Lynn Bishop and her family would bring life to the party. The shelter had four kids that year—including little Joy.

Selfishly, Lila was glad that the little girl who'd captivated Lila's heart was with them for the holiday. And she also knew that it was time for her and her mother to leave them. Any help Cara needed at this point could be provided with regular counseling. Her ex-husband was behind bars. And her father was ready and financially able to give her a fresh start.

A happy ending. One of the best.

Cara had found her peace and through it was finding happiness. She was a wise one, that girl. A woman who'd put thoughts in Lila's head that had never been there before.

Entering the silent cafeteria after she knew everyone else would be gathered for the service, Lila took the gifts off the cart she'd used to bring them from her suite and placed each one under the brightly lit tree.

It had been a good year.

For each one that passed with more women being given new lives, she was thankful. At peace.

When she was done with the presents, she took the last thing on the cart—an angel ornament, this one made out of sea shells—and, giving it a kiss, hung it on the tree—a tree covered in angel ornaments, all of them different, all of them handmade by Lila. Every one of them to honor her little girl and the work they still did together.

"Here's another one, Mom. Ella and I made it together." She froze. Sure that she'd imagined that voice.

He wouldn't. He *couldn't*.

Frightened, needing to reassure herself that everything was fine, that she was just particularly emotional that year, she swung around and saw them. Ella and Brett and that precious baby boy, standing there holding out a raffia-and-lace angel with the word Livia written in gold on its dress.

She'd only told one person about the angels on the Stand Christmas tree.

Edward. In a moment of conversation between friends.

So, how had Brett known?

He didn't come toward her. She couldn't move. He looked...so good. Soooo good. He'd been a young man heading off to college the last time she'd seen him in person.

And now...the broad-shouldered man before her, in a suit and tie—with a beautiful woman attached to one elbow and a waving baby in his arms...

Her son.

Lila's heart pounded. It broke.

He'd become everything she'd known he could be.

Everything she'd known he'd become.

Soaking in the sight of him, promising herself that that was all she needed, just that Christmas glance, she hated the tears that sprang to her eyes, obstructing that view.

"So...here's the thing..." Brett's voice reached her ears, though he continued to respect her need for space between them.

"You have a right to your choices, to live your life as you see fit. Just as we...your family, have the right to love you. And sometimes loving someone means believing in what they can't see. Knowing them when their own mind convinces them that they are something else."

She shook her head. He was using rhetoric that she taught every day. It wouldn't work on her. She wasn't one of them.

She was one of the...

"I can't do it anymore, Mom." Brett's voice

broke. "I can't watch you waste the rest of our years together."

Her son…her firstborn baby boy…the grown man he'd become, had tears in his voice…on his face. He was hurting…

"We're coming to you, Mom. For as long as it takes. As of tonight, Ella and I have moved into The Lemonade Stand." He named a bungalow she knew to have been vacated the day before. "I own the place. I have the right to live here. You go ahead and go home to your condo every night if you need to. You stay in your suite. You do what you must. But every day, we will be here. We will see you. Eat at a table with you. For as long as it takes for you to see the you that the rest of us see. To forgive yourself…"

The sound of movement caught her attention before she saw more people move forward. Julie. Hunter. Cara and Joy. And…Edward.

"I met your son a while back through Hunter," Edward said, not keeping his distance. "When Hunter told me that Brett was the founder of The Lemonade Stand I had to tell him how much the woman he had managing the place for him impressed me. To the point that I'd found myself having fallen in love with her."

Lila shook her head. "You can't love me…" she whispered. And was filled with shock when she heard herself—sounding just like one of her victims.

Openmouthed, she stared at him. He kissed her. Quickly, chastely, and yet… Lila felt exposed.

And…

"You're going back to Florida," she had to point out. To bring some sense to whatever was going on. Either she was losing her mind or the rest of the world was.

She searched desperately inside herself for the peace that kept her safe.

And safe for others.

Edward shook his head. Took her hand. Knelt down. "I'm going into practice here in Santa Raquel," he said from down on one knee. Which made no sense to her at all. Why didn't he stand up? "I've already applied for and received my license to practice in California, have my space picked out and doctors who are ready to send referrals. Joy needs a lot of family around her, not just one of us or two of us, and with Hunter and Julie here, Cara and I decided that it was best that we stay."

He was just babbling now. Ridiculously. In front of other people.

Things were happening inside her. Intense things. They made peace harder to find. But she needed it. Had to cling to it…

He squeezed her hand. "Cara's going to start college in January, by the way," he said. "She wants to be a nurse…"

Lila had expected that might happen. Glanced

at Cara and nodded her approval of a very special resident.

She looked at Joy, who was watching her with serious eyes. Eyes that saw far too much for such a young soul.

Much like Livia had…

"So…when Brett heard that you'd told me about your son, he told me that he was that son. I can tell you, I was pretty much floored with that one, but when I thought about it, it all made sense… The two of you working together in the way you could, to bring help to all of the victims, who, like both of you, couldn't find their own way out…"

She'd tried to find a way. Tried so hard. She'd found peace.

Lila looked at Brett, lips trembling. He still had tears in his eyes as he smiled at her, and his sweet baby boy stuck a finger in the corner of his eye. Ella reached for little Jerimiah's hand and gently pulled it back. Brett didn't even blink.

He'd take a finger in the eye without a flinch. Just as he'd taken her fists…

"Brett, interestingly enough, has a different version of that day." Edward was talking again, from down on the floor. He really needed to stand up. "He said your blows didn't leave a single bruise, Lila. Did you ever think to ask, my love? Did you ever see this damage you thought you inflicted?"

"I…" She hadn't been able to bear the sight. The fact shamed her. And yet…

She looked at Brett. "I lost control of myself," she said. "The emotions…they took over and I lost control…"

She had to find her peace. Her calm. Couldn't let…

"And even then, while you lashed out with pain and grief, your blows landed on my chest, Mom, not on my face, not my ribs or bones or organs. And there was no strength behind him. They left no mark. Whether you knew it or not, even out of control, you weren't trying to hurt me."

"But I did. I saw the look on your face…"

"I was shocked to see you striking out, yes, but only because it was so out of character. I was scared to death you were losing your mind right before my eyes. I've tried to tell you this…so many times…"

She'd scared herself to death.

The truth crashed down around her with so much force she thought for a second that everyone in the room could hear it.

In those few brief moments she'd seen a self she didn't recognize and she'd been frightened beyond her ability to cope. So much so that she'd gone into emotional hiding. Her gaze sought Cara's. The younger woman's look was intense, her eyes moist. She knew.

Through years of counseling, of seeking her inner truth, Lila had found her peace. And had been hiding behind it ever since. She was dying. Not living.

"So...I'll wait for as long as it takes," Edward was talking again. "And I'll be repeating my question as many times as it takes, but here's the first go round. Lila McDaniels...will you marry me?"

Everyone was staring at her. Most of them crying. The pressure closed in. She'd... For so long... There'd only been...

She looked at Brett—whom she hadn't hurt. Even in her grief, her out-of-control burst of emotion, she hadn't inflicted pain? He nodded.

Then at Ella, who also nodded.

Cara and Joy, both nodding. Even Julie and Hunter.

"We've all got your back, Mom," Brett said. "Just give yourself the same chance at happiness you give to everyone else."

Julie coughed, drawing Lila's attention. She remembered saying something similar to the younger woman about giving herself a chance to be happy.

"Excuse me a minute," she said to Edward. She pulled her hand away and, like an automaton, moved toward her son. She didn't stop until she ran into him, wrapped her arms around him and took a long breath. "You're completely sure?" she asked, looking him in the eye.

She and Brett and Livia—they'd been a real family. Brett would tell her if...

He nodded. "I trust my family with you, Mom." Almost as if he understood what was going on, her grandson leaned forward, grabbing at Lila's bun. Smelling his baby scent, she started to tremble. She kissed his chubby cheek. Kissed her son's cheek. Hugged his wife—a woman she'd met, professionally, through The Lemonade Stand. Hugged and didn't want to let go.

"Our family needs you," Ella whispered.

Cara was next, when Lila could move on. Lila didn't have any words for her. Couldn't begin to explain how, after years of counseling victims, it had taken one special one to show her the victim inside herself...

"Welcome home," Cara said, smiling through tears.

The exact words Lila had said to the young woman when she'd met her the month before.

Lila felt Edward behind her. Her entire being yearned for him. She was afraid to face him.

"It's okay." His voice came from just behind her. "I said I'd wait for as long as it took..."

Lila shook her head. "You've waited far too long to have love back in your life," she told him, and turning, reached up and kissed him. In front of everyone. Not at all chastely.

She was still afraid. Knew that the road ahead would have bumps. But she'd opened the door peace had shown her to—it was time to move forward to happiness.

CARA HAD JUST kissed Joy good night, leaving the door to the bedroom she currently shared with her daughter open as she made her way back to the living room. Her father had been staying at his hotel, but that night there'd been a quick change of plans. He'd be staying with Lila, who needed him more.

He needed her, too.

This past month with him, seeing him every day, in counseling with him at The Lemonade Stand, had, in some ways, been the best in her life. They were very different—the way they handled things—and still had work to do to help each other, but they'd reached an understanding they'd never had before.

With daily counseling and his help reframing much of what had taken place during her last year in Florida, she'd fought her way out of Shawn's voice in her head. It might always be there, popping in from time to time, but from what Sara had told her, what everyone in the group said and what Lila and her father had told her, she'd already taken herself back from him before she'd arrived at the Stand.

Her mom had had a lot to do with that. A mom's voice stayed forever in a daughter's head for a reason.

And Simon...

She hadn't heard from him.

She didn't blame him. Their time together had

been…completely unreal. She'd been anything but someone he could rely on. Her feelings… How could anything real and lasting have grown within her during their two months up on that mountain?

She had no explanation, but knew, as she sat there alone that Christmas Eve, that she was in love with him.

There were no doubts. And there was no panicked need to have him take care of her, either. She'd rather he be in his world, happy and successful, than taking care of her. She just missed him.

Like hell.

The knock on her door came as no surprise. Her father had told her that he and Lila would be by for a sip of brandy before she went to bed—a tradition he and her mother had shared every Christmas Eve after Cara had gone to bed.

A tradition she'd only heard about that evening.

He and Lila had gone out to get the brandy.

Lila McDaniels, a woman she'd grown to love and respect over the past month, was going to be her stepmother. They were going to live in Hunter's place, which her father was buying, since her new cousin by marriage was moving into Julie's wing in the Fairbanks family mansion.

Cara had grown closer than she could have imagined to Julie. More than just life circumstances, they shared secrets. And fears. And doubts.

Cara and Joy were welcome to stay with Edward and Lila—Hunter's house had plenty of room and a pool, too—once Cara was ready to leave the Stand. She hadn't thought that far ahead yet. With the sale of her house and the money from Shawn's business, she could afford a small place of their own.

At the door now, she pulled it open, smiling. And stopped. Edward was there. Lila, too. But they weren't alone.

Her entire body lit on fire. It was like the sun rose right then, at close to midnight.

"That's it," Simon said to Edward. Opening the door, he pulled Cara into his arms and kissed her like…well, way too personally in front of her father. And future stepmother.

She tried to care.

But didn't. She kissed him back. Every bit as hungrily.

He was trembling as much as she was. Her doctor. The professional who was so certain that he didn't want to be trapped when times got bad…

"When your father called, inviting me here for Christmas, I…"

"He didn't think he should come," Edward interrupted, coming inside with Lila right beside him.

"He thought you needed more time. That he should wait until you invited him," Lila said.

She wouldn't have.

Cara looked at Lila…and she knew. As she'd

been a part of helping Lila find her way home, Lila was now giving Cara the same. They got it for each other.

And neither of them had been able to…

"I agreed to come. There was no keeping me away, really…"

"He's been calling me every night to see how you were doing," Edward said.

Cara stared at him. "You have?"

Simon's shrug caught her heart. "You know me. Conscientious doctor and all…"

He'd given her his heart. She saw that now. In so many ways…

"I just didn't want you to know I was coming," he said now. "I didn't want you welcoming me for me… I needed to know it was what you really wanted."

"Of course I…"

He smiled at her. "The look in your eyes when you opened the door was all it took, Cara. I lived with those eyes as my only real communication with you for weeks. I knew as soon as I saw your expression…"

"I've missed you more than I would have thought possible," she told him, not caring about their audience.

"You needed this time with your family…"

She thought of Joy. "We'll need to be careful with Joy…she's been through so much…she'll need…"

"Grandpa and Hunter already told me." A little voice came from the bedroom door. "Grandpa said to be really quiet and wait, and I'd get to see the good man who chased the monster away…"

The monster. The name she'd used to describe what Shawn became when he was angry. Joy had to hide from the monster. But not from her daddy.

Cara had failed her little girl so miserably…

In her nightgown and bare feet, Joy walked out into the living room, coming to stop in front of Simon, looking up at him with wide-eyed inspection. "Are you the good man?"

Kneeling down, Simon met her eye to eye. "What do you think?" he asked her. "Do I look like a good man to you?"

"You made Mommy smile."

He nodded.

"I like it when Mommy smiles."

"I do, too. You know what else?"

"What?"

"I had a little girl like you once. You want to see her picture?"

When Joy nodded, he pulled a wallet out of his pocket, flipped it open to the first picture and handed it to Joy. "She's pretty," the little girl said. "Is she here, too?"

"No." Simon put his wallet back in his pocket, still kneeling. "Things were broken inside of her when she was born, and she got to go be with God early, to help him with special jobs…"

Cara should have been surprised at Simon's ease with such a tough subject, but she wasn't. He'd dedicated his life to dealing with traumatized children and parents.

"Like Amy's friend Michael," Joy said. And because she'd read the entire series of Amy books again and again over the past month, Cara fully understood.

"Yes, just like that," she interjected, knowing Simon would have no way of knowing that Joy was talking about a series of children's books that Julie had written and Joy had clung to.

"Well, the thing is," Simon continued, "she's happy now, where she is, but I'm sad, because I have a place for a little girl in my life and it's empty right now. I was kind of wondering… If it's okay with your mommy, if maybe you and I could be friends…"

Joy looked at Cara, who, with tears in her eyes, grinning like an idiot, nodded.

Joy reached up, her fingers fiddling with Simon's collar. "But only if you don't ever hit. And Mommy's your friend, too, and you don't ever hit her, either."

His expression completely serious, Simon took her hand, held it. "You have my solemn promise on that," he said. "Because hitting is wrong."

She nodded. "Grandpa told me that when Mommy was gone because she was hurt, that you were the doctor who helped her get better. Is that really you?"

"Yes, it is," Simon said. "And can I tell you a little secret?"

Joy nodded, leaning in as she turned her ear toward him.

"When I was helping your mommy get better, she helped me, too."

"Mommy always makes people better." Joy's words were so matter-of-fact, they changed Cara's self-concept again. Added a little more depth. Another little piece of gold on the inner scale of her life.

"So...is it okay with you if I hang around here, then? And make you and Mommy smile a lot?" Simon was asking Joy.

Joy looked at Edward. And Cara and Lila exchanged a heartfelt glance. For so long the little girl had held herself apart from the grandfather who'd been afraid to open up to her because his true self had failed his daughter.

"He's the good man," Edward said.

"Then, yes, you can stay," Joy said. "But I have to go to bed now so that Santa can come." She looked back at Edward, at Cara and then toward Simon. "Santa *is* still coming, isn't he?"

Laughing out loud, Cara assured her he was. Joy still believed in Santa Claus. She'd done something right.

And would get better and better at being her mother every day.

After she'd tucked Joy in for the second time that night, Cara and Simon and Edward and Lila had a toast of brandy. They honored Beth. And Livia. And Opus. And all the others who'd died too young.

Her father and Lila left, and as Simon grabbed her up and headed to the second bedroom in the bungalow, Cara gave Fate a silent thank-you.

She'd expected Simon to—maybe—rip her clothes off, but he set her down inside the closed bedroom door and just looked at her. Studied her. Like he'd done so much during their time together.

"I need to see that you're okay," he said, running a finger down the cheek that would probably never be what it had once been. "You look incredible." His voice was soft. Almost reverent.

"So do you." She touched his cheek, too, looking into his right eye. Wondering if it saw her back.

"It's getting better every day," he told her. "But I'm not going back to my old practice."

It was a testament to how blown away she'd been by his presence that she'd given no thought to his life in LA—only an hour away, but...

"Your father asked me to go into practice with him. To cover pediatrics..."

"But...your surgery...your patients..."

"I'm probably never going to see as well as I

did," he said. "There will always be clouds. And for now… I want to work hours that will allow me to be home with you. And Joy. She's going to need a lot of time with us if we're going to make that monster in her nightmares little more than a distant memory…"

Cara nodded. Having him close, in her life every day…it was more than she'd dared dream.

"I'm probably going to be moving in with my father, and now Lila, when I leave here," she told him. "Just until I find my own place."

"I was kind of hoping, and I think maybe your dad is, too, that you'd be moving in with me. I put an offer in on a house on the beach this morning."

He'd been planning to move to Santa Raquel even before he'd known that she was ready for him. Or would ever be ready for him.

Because they were that connected.

"I am so, so thankful that Fate didn't let me kill myself," she said now, thinking about how close she'd come.

Simon, looking her straight in the eye, actually smiled. And shook his head. "If you were going to die, you'd never have made it to my place. Why do you think you didn't just stay and let Shawn kill you?" he asked. "Why pretend to have a brain bleed, the one thing you knew would scare him into dumping you?"

She shook her head. He made it sound like

she'd had some grand plan, when really, she'd just been…

"Because, deep down, you already had control of your own mind, Cara. He tried to steal you away from yourself, from the woman your parents had raised you to be, but even after ten years, using Joy against you, beating you down, you were still here…still fighting for what you believed…"

She looked at him. Taking in his words. Into her mind, but also into her heart. And she listened. To her heart. Just like her mother had taught her.

"I love you, Simon. For the rest of my life. You don't have to ask me to live with you. I'm just thankful to have you here. To be able to walk into your arms and know I'll be held. To hear your thoughts and cook food for you. To make you smile…"

"Wait." He pulled back. "I'm not just asking you to live with me, Cara. I'm expecting you to marry me. Your father said your divorce from Shawn is final already, partially because it was uncontested. I'm ready for you to be my wife tonight. But am prepared to wait until you're ready…"

She might not have been able to take his words at face value. To really believe him. But when she looked into his eyes, she knew that he needed her as badly as she needed him. That he was as ready for her as she was ready for him.

"I'm ready tonight, too," she told him. "But

we should probably wait until tomorrow, or the next day—" since tomorrow was Christmas "—because I can't have a real wedding without my father there to walk me down the aisle."

Simon kissed her then, and there was no more need for words. Not for a long time. They were a couple who'd learned to listen more to what wasn't being said, to listen with their hearts, while their minds had taken time to heal.

Their time at the cabin—it hadn't been time out of time.

It had been the beginning of time.

* * * * *

Be sure to check out the
other recent books in the
WHERE SECRETS ARE SAFE *miniseries,*

FOR JOY'S SAKE
THE FIREMAN'S SON
HER SECRET LIFE

All available now from
Harlequin Superromance.

And look for the next book in
WHERE SECRETS ARE SAFE,
coming soon!

Get 2 Free Books,
Plus 2 Free Gifts—
just for trying the Reader Service!

Get 2 Free Books,
Plus 2 Free Gifts—

HARLEQUIN *Presents*

just for trying the
Reader Service!

Get 2 Free Books,

Plus 2 Free Gifts—
just for trying the
Reader Service!

◆HARLEQUIN®

SPECIAL EDITION

YES! Please send me 2 FREE Harlequin® Special Edition novels and my 2 FREE gifts (gifts are worth about $10 retail). After receiving them, if I don't wish to receive any more books, I can return the shipping statement marked "cancel." If I don't cancel, I will receive 6 brand-new novels every month and be billed just $4.99 per book in the U.S. or $5.74 per book in Canada. That's a savings of at least 12% off the cover price! It's quite a bargain! Shipping and handling is just 50¢ per book in the U.S. and 75¢ per book in Canada.* I understand that accepting the 2 free books and gifts places me under no obligation to buy anything. I can always return a shipment and cancel at any time. The free books and gifts are mine to keep no matter what I decide.

235/335 HDN GLWR

Name   (PLEASE PRINT)

Address   Apt. #

City   State/Province   Zip/Postal Code

Signature (if under 18, a parent or guardian must sign)

Mail to the **Reader Service:**
IN U.S.A.: P.O. Box 1341, Buffalo, NY 14240-8531
IN CANADA: P.O. Box 603, Fort Erie, Ontario L2A 5X3

Want to try two free books from another line?
Call 1-800-873-8635 or visit www.ReaderService.com.

*Terms and prices subject to change without notice. Prices do not include applicable taxes. Sales tax applicable in N.Y. Canadian residents will be charged applicable taxes. Offer not valid in Quebec. This offer is limited to one order per household. Books received may not be as shown. Not valid for current subscribers to Harlequin Special Edition books. All orders subject to approval. Credit or debit balances in a customer's account(s) may be offset by any other outstanding balance owed by or to the customer. Please allow 4 to 6 weeks for delivery. Offer available while quantities last.

Your Privacy—The Reader Service is committed to protecting your privacy. Our Privacy Policy is available online at www.ReaderService.com or upon request from the Reader Service.

We make a portion of our mailing list available to reputable third parties that offer products we believe may interest you. If you prefer that we not exchange your name with third parties, or if you wish to clarify or modify your communication preferences, please visit us at www.ReaderService.com/consumerschoice or write to us at Reader Service Preference Service, P.O. Box 9062, Buffalo, NY 14240-9062. Include your complete name and address.

HSE17R2